IRON
CURTAIN

1987

[A THRILLER]

RAF BEUY

Identifiers

Hardcover ISBN: 9783982406404
Paperback ISBN: 9783982406411
Ebook ISBN: 9783982406428

Cover design by Christophe Bugetti

For my father.

AUTHOR'S NOTE

Language can be brutal. It decides whether you are in or out as it tells us if you come from the area or from somewhere else—and thus whether you can be trusted or better not. Anyone familiar with the Uckermark and its inhabitants knows that such a language is spoken here. The locals' directness can seem clumsy. Unaffected warmth is often masked by brusqueness. A particular tone of voice prevails in the area, with a select vocabulary that is hard to translate into English. Out of respect for the speakers, I didn't even try. Furthermore, it would have been doomed to fail miserably from the start. The dialect is most comparable to the language of the white working class in cities like Pittsburgh or Boston. It helps to be aware of this while reading.

Also, those familiar with the locale will notice that I have taken extensive liberties in describing the topographical and geographical features. That was quite intentional. Both serve as a projection screen for the German Democratic Republic of the late eighties and have been altered where the story or my intuition required it. They should therefore be considered entirely fictional.

"Where there is power, there is resistance."
—Michel Foucault

This story takes place in a time when two systems relentlessly opposed each other. Good and evil were separated by insurmountable walls and defended with nuclear weapons. It didn't take long until either camp had so much dirt on them that they no longer knew whether they were still good. It was a time when friends became enemies and relatives became strangers. That time lies only a few years back and is far from being history.

Dull light fell into the children's room. The boy was lying in his bed reading a book when his father came in.

"So, little one, it's time to study," he said, sitting down at the boy's desk.

The son jumped up from his bed and stood next to his father.

"How many pencils, Dad?" he asked, looking at the pencils stored in a tin can.

"Sixteen, son."

The boy took one pencil after another from the can and counted quietly. When he reached the desired number, he divided the pencils on the table into two equal amounts, leaving a handsbreadth of space between them.

"Good, then let's begin. Have you been practicing hard?"

The boy nodded and took eight pencils in his left hand and eight in his right. Then he went to the center of the room and placed the pencils neatly side by side on the floor. Again he left a hand's width of space between the rows of pencils. He turned his back to his father and stood up straight.

"Let's get started," the man said.

The boy took off his pants, folded them, put them on the bed, and knelt on the two levels of pencils. His kneecaps gave way under the pressure of the wood. After a few seconds, he no longer felt the pain—only gentle pressure. The father opened the book. Stapled inside were dozens of notes peeking out from the pages.

"The source, my boy?"

"Goethe, Faust, Part I, Dad."

"What issue?"

"Reclam, Stuttgart 1950."

"Then we can begin. Page fourteen, line fourteen, position two?"

The son nodded. He said the number combination slowly to himself. Fourteen, fourteen, two. Fourteen, fourteen, two. Fourteen, fourteen, two. Then he was silent for a moment and turned his head slightly to the left.

"*U*, Dad."

"Fine, but please look ahead."

The boy turned his gaze forward again and did not make a face. The father opened another page and looked into the book.

"Eighty-five, thirteen, twenty-one?" he asked.

The boy recited the combination of numbers to himself again. Eighty-five, thirteen, twenty-one. Eighty-five, thirteen, twenty-one. Then he paused and took one of the pencils out from under each of his knees. He left the two pencils to the left and right of his knees.

"Page eighty-five, line thirteen, position twenty-one?" the father repeated.

"I don't know, Dad."

"Eight-five, thirteen, twenty-one. It's just as easy as any other combination. You just have to study hard. Of course, that's an *N*."

The boy nodded. The father opened another page in the book.

"Two hundred, ten, five?"

The boy did not have to think long.

"That's a *D*, Dad."

"Fine, then one, one, five and one hundred fifty-three, nineteen, twenty-four?"

Again, the boy did not think twice.

"That's a blank, Dad."

"Fine, then what?"

"*A W*, Dad."

"Good."

The boy felt the pencils digging into his knees. He could not yet deduce what the complete sentence was. He had to recall each combination of numbers from his memory and visualize the matching letter until he knew. He concentrated on his task and pushed the pain aside.

"Two, two, fourteen?" said the father.

The boy knew and immediately answered.

"*I*, Dad."

"Good. One hundred thirteen, twelve, thirteen?"

The boy was sure what the answer was.

"*P*, Dad."

When he said it, he realized it wasn't right.

"No, it's an *R*."

"You know what you have to do, son."

The boy nodded. He slowly pulled a pencil from under his left knee and one from under his right knee and left them there.

"One, one, five and one, twenty-five, one?"

"Space and a *Z*, Dad."

"Good. One hundred fifty-three, nineteen, twenty-four?"

The boy repeated the number combination quietly to himself. One hundred fifty-three, nineteen, twenty-four. One hundred fifty-three, nineteen, twenty-four. One hundred fifty-three, nineteen, twenty-four. One hundred fifty-three, nineteen, twenty-four. The father counted down from three. That was the clue for the boy that he had already deciphered that letter once that day. Two. He felt hot. One.

"*D*, Dad."

"Two pencils!"

The boy pulled two pencils out from under each of his knees. One more pencil and the row would be so narrow that it would cut right into the boneless part of the body between the kneecap and the shinbone.

"So one more time. One hundred fifty-three, nineteen, twenty-four?"

The boy smiled. He remembered.

"*W*, Dad."

The father turned to another page in the book.

"All right, two, two, fourteen and fourteen, fourteen, two?"

"*I* and ..."

The boy thought about it. His knees felt numb. The first beads of sweat formed on his forehead. His father counted down from three again. Three ... two ...

"*I* and *N*, Dad."

"Good."

This time, the boy did not let his joy and pain show on his face. He looked straight ahead with a serious face.

"Five, fifteen, twenty-eight?" the father asked.

The boy thought about it. Five, fifteen, twenty-eight. He didn't know. The father counted down.

"Three ..."

"That's a *V*, Dad."

"Did you guess, son?"

"No, Dad."

"One pencil!"

The boy swallowed. He pulled a pencil from under each knee and placed them beside himself. Firm wood bit into soft skin. Fluid gathered in his eyes. He clenched his baby teeth.

"Five, fifteen, twenty-eight?"

"That's a *P*, Dad."

"Did you guess?"

"No, Dad."

"The first time, I let you get away with it. The class enemy will know no mercy. You know that. So two pencils."

"But, Dad ..."

The boy pulled two pencils out from under his left knee. He barely dared to put weight on that knee to pull two pencils out from under his other knee. He took a deep breath. The father counted down again. Three. Two. The boy shifted his weight to his left knee, now also pulling two pencils out from under his right knee. A sharp pain shot through him, starting from his left knee, and jerked like lightning through his slender body. He put weight on both knees at the same time and was relieved for a moment. But immediately, the thin pencils stabbed his knees simultaneously. Tears welled up in his eyes. On his forehead, cold sweat was building up. Hot shivers ran through him from his back to behind his ears. A drop of the tear fluid slapped the floor. The boy raised his head in the air so that the next drop would land on his shirt and not on the floor.

"What's the phrase, son?" the father asked.

The boy tried to push the pain out of his head. He moaned softly. "Und wir …," meaning *and we*, he said, breaking off the answer in pain. He started to speak again.

"*Und wir zwing …*" *And we force …*

"Good, do you understand that sentence, son?"

"No, Dad."

"And why don't you understand that sentence?"

"Because it's not complete, Dad."

"And what is it in full?"

"I don't know, Dad."

"Yes, you do, son."

The boy noticed how the pain took complete possession of him. Blood came out from under his knees. Tears flowed in rivulets down his cheeks and landed on his shirt. He kept repeating the sentence softly to himself. And

we force ... And we force ... And we force ... And we force ...
And we force ...

"Son!" said the father.

The boy changed the rhythm of the sentence.

"And. We. Force. And we. Force. And. We force."

He knew the phrase.

"And we force it together, Daddy," he said, then clenched his teeth. A tremor came over him.

"Good. And now from the beginning," said the father.

The boy took a deep breath and pressed the words through his rows of teeth.

"And we force them united."

"No. Everything. All of it from the beginning. The whole verse."

The boy sobbed and lost his posture.

"Son!"

He straightened up again, drawing the oxygen-deprived air of the room into his lungs.

"Risen from the ruins
and facing the future,
let us serve you for the good,
Germany, united fatherland.
It is necessary to force old adversity,
and we force it together,
because we must succeed in getting
the sun to shine over
Germany like never before."

The man got up and left his son's room. The boy toppled to the side and curled up on the cold floor, crying. That day he had deciphered and recited the first verse of the national anthem of the German Democratic Republic. The next day, another lesson would be waiting for him.

Book I

Chapter 1: STEEL MONSTER

November 6, 1987
Angermünde
District Frankfurt/Oder
German Democratic Republic

Today is the day.

He propped his arms on the shovel and blew air out of his lungs. A cloud of steam formed in front of his face. It was bitterly cold.

Today is the day when the have-nots win against the *Bonzen*, the party bigwigs. The day when the executioners stand before their executioner. The day when justice prevails.

A smirk flitted across his face. He was not used to so much pathos. At least not since the socialist dream had been shattered for him. And that had been some time ago. He envied people without ideals. All those who had never believed in them or who had lost their faith after a short time and fled. More than two hundred thousand Germans had left the socialist East of the country for the capitalist

West since the Wall had been built on August 13, 1961. It wasn't that he wanted to trade places with them, only that he would have liked to have had their indifference to the great cause much earlier. Then he would have been spared a lot.

He took a deep breath and picked up the shovel again. He jabbed the work implement with the weather-beaten wooden handle and the sooty metal blade into the pile of brown coal. Then he heaved the heavy mass of coal into the lorry. It was already sitting heavily loaded on four steel rollers perched on railroad tracks set into the concrete floor of the factory yard. He threw the shovel into the mountain of coal and braced himself with all his power against the steel monster until it finally moved.

Once it rolls, it rolls.

Every move had been perfected. The procedures had been etched into the subconscious down to the smallest detail over months. He no longer had to think about what to do next.

Push, push, push. With all your power. One hundred twenty-four steps to the factory floor. A few more, a few less. Form of the day. Braking the movement just before the gate to the factory. Bracing yourself against the acceleration with your whole body weight until the rollers come to a standstill. Taking the steps to the enormous gate, tearing it open, feeling the heat of the hall. Immediately setting the monster in motion again. Pressing your shoulder into the cold steel with full force. Up to the coal furnace in which an 850-degree fire blazes. Getting rid of the sweaty quilted jacket. Pulling the hot air into your lungs and wiping your face dry with your soot-smeared undershirt. Opening the hatch to the coal feed with numb hands. Letting the heat whip into your face. Again using a shovel to force the steel monster to vomit out the coal and throwing it into blazing embers. Driving the fire. Never letting the embers go out. Pulling the quilted jacket back over your blackened skin. Setting the lorry in motion again. Back to the coal yard on the crooked rails.

Over and over again. Seventeen times in one working day. That was a work unit. And his way of counting, so that the working day had a structure. An order that could be grasped. A goal that was attainable. Seventeen times slogging in the cold. And seventeen times in the heat. A cold that ate into his bones. And a warmth that he didn't even know from his homeland at the height of summer.

Everything went by itself. His head could wander while his body slaved away. He was the master of coal hauling. Not that it meant anything to him. Maybe that was why he was perfect for the job. He didn't care. Crushing it between his fingers like a mayfly. It was not his pay, not the fulfillment of duty to the collective, and certainly not the praise of the factory manager that drove him. His reward would come when his work was finally over. And the harder he worked, the faster the time passed.

Today is the day.

He didn't yet have a clear idea of exactly how he wanted to do it. He could block the man's carotid artery. Death by strangulation had been a popular execution method used on deserters by the British Army in the eighteenth century. He would be following a time-honored tradition. But he wasn't interested in that. The advantage of this killing method, however, was that it required little force. Not even two pounds to a square inch were necessary to stop blood flow to the brain, so that brain death occurred. A toddler could do it. If the victim held still. But that was not to be expected.

He could stab him, shoot him, or beat him to death. But the method did not matter. He realized that he could not think the deed through to completion. His own fate was too connected with the man. Too firmly was his history interwoven with that of the man. Too little could he imagine how his life would continue after the man's death. Just as you cannot dream your own death, he could not imagine the man's end. But he didn't have to. All he knew was that he would do it. How was not crucial. That would come to pass. That was what he was trained to do. His subconscious, muscle memory, would decide for him. He didn't have to agonize over the details. He knew it wasn't hard to end a human life. It happened almost a thousand times every day. In a year, that was as many deaths as Luxembourg had inhabitants. The population of an entire country was murdered in one year. Unimaginable.

He didn't know how many of these people had simply been in the wrong place at the wrong time, had met their deaths by accident or out of an emotional act. But he knew that this one murder had to be committed. Because all other means had been exhausted. It was not about revenge. It was about justice. It was not a wish. It was his duty. He owed it to himself. For a short moment, he thought about whether he owed it to humankind. But he realized that he expected nothing from humankind anymore and therefore didn't owe anything to it at all.

It was easy to extinguish human life. It was more challenging to get to this human being without notice. The element of surprise was crucial for the execution. But this wasn't up to him. That was why he didn't have to think about it any further. The plan was not allowed to lead to dead ends if a prediction did not come true. And his plan was as simple as it was risky.

He had only a tiny window of opportunity, and he had to use it. The man was in this place of vulnerability for only seventy-two hours, possibly less. He had received the information from a source he didn't know was safe. It could just as easily be a trap. But that was a risk he was willing to take. As long as the man was at the location as bait for him, he had the opportunity to fulfill his self-imposed mission. He just had to get to the man faster than the trap could snap shut. Otherwise, it was a simple undertaking. Ride his bike under the cover of darkness to the target, find the man and kill him.

Until then, he still had two units ahead of him, which dragged on in an unprecedented manner. And yet, they never went off with the same ease as on this day.

He pushed the lorry the last few yards to the coal mountain that towered in front of him. Behind it stood the tall factory wall made of red brick. Above it, only the dull gray of this November day. Crows flew in the distance. He wiped the cold sweat from his forehead and picked up the shovel again. Just as he was about to start the penultimate unit of the day, he heard a man's voice calling his name several times. "Hedman."

The voice came closer. He turned around.

It was another worker running toward him. "Finish your shift for today and then stay here. You'd best just come to the meeting hall."

He owed his name equally to his parents. His father had chosen his first name, Adam. The first man, the new beginning of the family history. From his mother, he had received the surname Hedman. That the mother gave her name to the whole family had been done on purpose. It was to seal the end of his father's Jewish name and bury the past once and for all.

The worker waited for his answer.

"Is it something important?" he asked.

"Just be there, Hedman. You'll see."

The man grinned, turned, and went back to the factory floor from where he had come. Adam got to work again. Of all days, it had to be this one, he thought. It was probably just a speech, a little ode to the collective. But no matter what it was, he had no choice but to show up at the assembly hall after he finished his shift. So he put the shovel into the coal pile and heaved the mass into the lorry. The same routine as always. The excited anticipation of the end of work gave way to the annoyance of having to stay in the VEB, the so-called people-owned enterprise, after work.

After completing the last two units of the day, he made his way to the locker room.

He hung his jacket on a hook just behind the locker room door. It was stuffy and hot and smelled of sweet sweat. A group of workers came in whose job it was to coat metal vessels with a layer of enamel on the heated factory floor. His was to shovel coal. They were inside. He was outside. They were upstairs. He was at the bottom. So far down that he couldn't go any lower. Whoever was down there could only be imbecilic, which was expressed at least by the lack of a high school diploma, or antisocial, for which a stay in prison was sufficient. Opinions in the VEB differed as to which of the two groups he belonged to.

"Hey, Hedman, what's the weather like out there?" one of the workers asked.

"Like a vacation on the Baltic Sea," Adam said.

The men laughed.

"How many runs did you make today, Hedman?" asked another.

"Seventeen," Adam said.

Every day they asked him this question, and every day his answer was the same.

"Seventeen. Not bad. Seventeen isn't bad at all, is it? It was nice and hot today, the fire, really nice and hot," said the worker, wiping his sweaty face with his undershirt.

Adam got rid of his coal-smeared workwear. He stuffed everything into the narrow metal locker and took out his civilian clothes. They were spotless. Without a single coal stain. He slipped on his pants and shirt, stepped into his shoes, and was no longer recognizable as a coal shoveler except for a bit of soot behind his ears. And as the signs of the day fell away from him, so did the men and turned back to their conversations. The topics were all too familiar to him. Soccer, booze, and complaining about the wives at home. But new events had joined them. For weeks they had been the topic of conversation in general in the small Uckermark town, which was nestled in a terminal moraine landscape dating back from the Ice Age that had left behind two large bodies of water, the Mündesee near the town center and the Wolletzsee further out. Here, in the fertile nowhere halfway between Berlin and the Baltic Sea, densely packed on the Polish border, people told each other horror stories of unprecedented proportions. Depending on who you heard talking, there was once a girl who had disappeared and was then found drowned. Or was it a young woman who had been strangled and then dumped in Wolletzsee? What everyone agreed on, however, was that the girl's death was accompanied by barn fires, ignitions and cows, sheep, and pigs killed in pastures and stables. The people of Angermünde did not disclose the name of the girl. The workmates in the locker room wanted to know for sure that it was murder and that the man—they were also confident that it was a man—was one who happened to roam their homeland as a vagabond or drifter. One who was not from the area. Because one from there wouldn't do such a thing. It could only be one who had set foot on Uckermark soil recently. And this ground should burn under his soles if the men had their way.

The foreman of the work crew called his name. He was a stocky man with a mighty paunch and parted ash-blond hair over a weather-beaten face. So, now Adam was part of their conversation again.

"What is it?"

"You'll join us when we find the guy who's been killing everything around here, right?"

No way, he thought. "When?" he asked.

"Tomorrow we'll head out. And if we have to, we'll search all weekend."

"What about the police? Wouldn't that be a matter for the authorities?"

The men shook their heads and laughed contemptuously. Next thing would have been to spit on the floor in disdain.

"Yes, the ... so far nothing has come out of it. We'll have to do it ourselves if we want to see results. Our town, our job. You know?"

Adam nodded and thought about how to free himself from this obligation. The foreman came over to Adam and planted himself in front of him, which seemed as pally as it was intimidating.

"Hedman, you're not exactly from around here. But we from Angermünde tend to note very carefully who joins in and who bails on us. You see, what kind of a man is it who doesn't help to find the man who slaughters our animals and our women?" the worker asked him, putting one of his rough hands on his shoulder. He had the authority of a man whose twenty years of sweaty work hadn't gotten him down but had only made him tougher. The hand felt as heavy as if all the men in the locker room had laid their hands on his shoulder. And that was not surprising, for the man spoke for all men.

The worker squeezed Adam's shoulder firmly and then released him. "We'll come to get you, then."

A threat, not a promise.

"When exactly?"

"When it's on, it's on."

The foreman did not allow any further questions and went back to his locker.

The hall was filled with about two hundred workers. Apparently, the entire workforce had gathered. Adam leaned against the wall right next to the entrance and waited for the beginning. Shortly after that, Lothar Kletzsch, the factory manager, took the podium. He was an athletic man in his midforties with thinning blond hair. Kletzsch didn't have a family, but he devoted his life entirely to the works. Behind him hung the red flags of the VEB Gustav Bruhn and the *Betriebskampfgruppe*, the factory's brigade group.

He stepped up to the lectern and bent down slightly to the microphone. "Dear workers, dear party comrades, without going too much into a hymn of praise now, I would like to inform you that our VEB Gustav Bruhn was able to exceed the planned target for the third time in a row."

The staff clapped. Adam felt tiredness come over him. Fewer and fewer words reached his conscious mind.

"... Let's toast to that ... beer ... champagne for the ladies ..."

Adam just wanted to do his work and, after that, be left alone. But a good socialist worker had to master many disciplines. He had not only to do his job in such a way that he exceeded the five-year plan, he also had to know when to duck away and when to show up to strengthen the collective. And the same was true for female workers. Because under socialism, equality reigned. Ordered from above.

Adam looked around. Words pelted him. Snatches of those words reached him.

"... deserving employee of the collective ... birthday ... finally of age ... Anna Sievers ..."

The workforce was expressionless. They were masters of all disciplines.

And then a woman came on stage. It was not Anna Sievers but a woman he had never seen before. She wore a smock apron and presented a tray of thin apple pie. What was going on here? The women in front of him were whispering something.

"You hear that? Sievers, a deserving employee? Don't make me laugh."

"With Kletzsch, she earned that with this and that, didn't she?"

She pointed at her chest and butt.

"But I have to say, there's quite a lot to be jealous about. She looks like a real star. You know, like the one girl from *Three Angels for Charlie*, only with red hair."

Indeed, there were similarities. The toothpaste grin, the slim figure, the high cheekbones, the wild hair. She was the red Farah Fawcett. A socialist worker's dream come true.

"I wouldn't be surprised if we see her on TV sometime. Anna is somehow bigger than all this," she added.

Adam could not say whether that was true or not. But she was in any case larger than Angermünde. Perhaps than the entire GDR. But what good would that do her? She was without any chance to see the big wide world or to make a career beyond the Wall. Whatever that would be.

He continued to listen to the conversation of the women.

The other one nodded.

"Right you are. But it's not really fair. She's just eighteen, and she's supposed to have already earned all that hoopla?"

The speech was not over yet. But the factory manager paused for effect. He spread his arms. The woman in the smock apron next to him showed a broad grin. In front of the stage, the birthday girl was persuaded by colleagues to comply with the boss's request. Her friends clapped after Kletzsch had already started to do so shortly before. Gradually, the rest of the workforce joined in.

As the workingwoman had climbed the three steps onto the stage, the man spread his arms again.

"Anna! Here she is, at last, our birthday Anna."

She remained at the edge of the stage. He took a few steps towards her with his arms stretched out and pressed the girl tightly against his chest. Then he gave her a kiss on the cheek, left, right, left.

He escorted her to the lectern and spoke exuberantly into the microphone. "Frau Sievers, our Anna, deserves a little birthday serenade. Let's sing in her honor."

Adam did not feel like singing. He felt like screaming.

Kletzsch grinned with pride at Anna and then sang into the microphone. "Happy birthday ..."

There was a loud beep, a feedback noise. And laughter among the workers.

Kletzsch stepped to the front of the stage, raised his arms in the air, and made rhythmic movements. "And now, one more time. One and two and three and ... Happy birthday to you ..."

Gradually, the workers joined in. "Happy birthday to you, happy birthday to you ..."

And then, apparently, people in the workforce were not so sure how to proceed. Some sang "Dear Anna," others "Frau Sievers," and a few, like himself, did not sing at all. When the pitiful singing had come to an end, the VEB boss applauded and once again embraced the workingwoman tightly. The workforce applauded cautiously.

Kletzsch stood behind the lectern again.

"Let's go, cake and beer in the canteen."

The woman who had presented the cake walked off the stage. The VEB boss and his female worker followed. This was Adam's chance to slip away undetected. He had already lost enough time. The workers streamed past the stage left into the factory canteen. He pushed off from his leaning position and left the meeting hall.

Adam had already covered a few yards on the factory floor when someone called after him. It was Peter Heyer. One of the few who forced him to chat. A tall, skinny man who walked bent over and was always friendly. At least to him. That could only be because he was grateful to him. Because when Adam had joined the works, Heyer had risen from coal shoveler to metal cleaner.

"Wait a minute, Hedman."

Adam stopped. The man reared up directly in front of him.

"Well, Hedman. You're not just going to run away like that, are you? No, no, my friend, that's not possible. Let's have a drink first. We've earned it. We overachieved. We can be proud of that. We should even drink to that. Come on, Hedman."

Heyer grabbed Adam by the arm. Today was the day, but he wondered how much time he could lose without getting in trouble. It was still early. He could undoubtedly pinch a few minutes, so he didn't want to oppose the proud metal cleaner and went along. They were the last to enter the canteen.

Adam glanced over the well-filled rows of chairs. "Too bad, there's nothing free at all."

"Oh, I'm sure we'll find something."

Heyer pointed to a table in the corner. "Look, there are some open seats in the back."

Heyer walked straight toward one of the aft tables, where two seats were still free. Adam followed him at some distance.

One beer. He just had to have a beer with Heyer, and then he could go, no doubt about it. That was all the time he had for the collective. This afternoon was not going according to plan for him. He saw Heyer sitting down at the table and immediately opening a bottle. The man seemed engrossed in the drink. Maybe he should turn on his heel and get out of the factory into the cold. Adam couldn't even finish the thought when he felt a hand on his shoulder leading him in another direction. He turned around and looked into the eyes of Evelyn Sievers. The birthday girl's older sister had another plan for him.

"Hey, Adam, weren't there any chairs left for you? You can join us. It'll be fun, I promise."

"I was actually going to join Heyer. He's sitting in the back."

"Well, no one *wants* to go join Heyer, am I right?"

She pulled him along with her.

"Come on, don't resist."

It was the birthday table. Besides Anna's boyfriend, Sebastian Koslowski, VEB manager Lothar Kletzsch, her sister Evelyn and the workingwomen Anita, Susanne, and Maria were also seated at the table. From Heyer, he could have gotten away more quickly, Adam thought.

He was assigned the seat next to Evelyn. Kletzsch looked around and stopped at him.

"Oh, you brought us Hedman. Good man. Gets something done."

Before Adam had even taken his seat, Sebastian shoved a beer into his hand. The birthday girl came to the table with a glass of champagne in her hand. Kletzsch examined her from top to bottom. In the process, he smiled at all the body parts one by one. Shamelessly. He didn't do that with her sister, who was twelve years older. Her gaunt figure, thin brown hair, and pale skin were apparently unsuitable for ogling.

"Hedman, tell us. How many loads did you do today?" asked Kletzsch.

"Seventeen."

"Seventeen, that's something. Heyer made thirteen in his best days. Not once more than that. Thirteen was probably his lucky number. That's why he never made more. But seventeen, that's something. So let's drink to the overfulfillment of the plan. Comrade Council Chairman is proud of us."

He raised his beer to toast.

"Here's to plan overachievement!"

The others toasted each other. The VEB boss whispered something in the birthday girl's ear. She laughed and playfully slapped his hand. Sebastian watched the two of them and took a deep sip of his beer.

"Lothar, tell us again about old Hepper," Evelyn said, laughing.

"Not today. You all know the story anyway."

"Oh, come on. Please!"

"All right, persuaded."

He set his beer aside.

"Well, you all know old Hepper. A real daredevil, our party comrade, I can tell you that much. And what did Hepper do for his birthday? He invites them all ... the State Council, the party presidency, his people from the Ministry of State Security. It's a big deal for him. Thirty people for sure, if not forty. With their entourage. So all the women were there too. Well, how could it have been different, you know? Except Hepper's wife wasn't there. And that's where it starts to get interesting."

He looked at the women in the circle, raising his eyebrows suggestively.

"She must have been on a beauty treatment in Crimea, I hear."

The women laughed. When Adam thought of the Crimean Peninsula, the first things that came to mind were not beauty, champagne, or caviar but death and destruction. A mass murderer had been active in the area for years and had already killed several dozen women. The Soviet authorities tried everything not to let the world know about it, but it was an open secret. These were only his thoughts. He didn't let it show and smiled.

Sebastian didn't follow his boss's lead. "Yes, we already know the story. And what happened to Hepper afterward?" he asked.

Kletzsch had not yet taken off his put-on smile and looked at Sebastian.

"Easy there, what's all the fuss about? It's a perfectly normal matter of job transfer. Hepper is now taking care of matters in Saxony. And comrade Stahl, who succeeded him, is and remains in Berlin. But he now lives here with us in the beautiful Schorfheide."

"Saxony? That's where Bautzen is, right?" Sebastian said, letting his words hang in the air, alluding to the prison for political prisoners.

"You know what they say about Stahl. And why he's here with us now."

Everyone was silent. Sebastian did not speak further. It became quiet at the table. The VEB boss became friendlier by the minute.

"That's right, Sebastian. But that has nothing to do with Hepper. In any case, we are pleased that party comrade

Stahl is with us now. I'll say hello to him from you, Sebastian, when I pay him my next visit."

Dismayed expressions at the table. They looked past Kletzsch and Koslowski or took a sip of their drinks.

"Where was I?" asked the VEB boss, and everyone laughed again.

"That virtually everyone was at Hepper's hunting estate."

"Thank you, Maria. Look at that, she's quiet all the time, but she does an excellent job of paying attention. So they were all gathered at the hunting lodge, the Schalck-Golodkowskis, the Stophs, the Honeckers. And they have a big dinner in the evening with the game they've shot. And at first, everything is still good. They eat, they drink, they talk animatedly. But Hepper drinks one too many, and the good man gets a little cocky."

Everyone at the table waited eagerly for the punch line. Anna looked at the VEB boss and giggled. She obviously could hardly wait. Only Adam didn't know the story yet.

"Anyway, at some point, he has to carry his beer away, and as he's going to the bathroom, he meets the wife of the comrade Chairman of the Council of State, and they chat a little. No big deal. *Hello, how are you? Yes, I'm fine. Thank you for asking.* And so on. But Hepper is dead drunk already. And then, out of the blue, Hepper is like, *Well, how's it going with Erich as far as marital duties are concerned? Wouldn't it be nice to hear whether everything is going according to socialist principles?* And Hepper looks at her in all earnestness. Because he really wants to know. And Margot is not at all shocked, as one would think, but she even giggles like a young pioneer girl and then apologizes. And when the Chairwoman of the Council of State is about to leave, and he feels challenged by her schoolgirlish manner, he—"

"It's burning, it's burning."

One of the foremen came running into the hall, shouting repeatedly and as loudly as he could. The crowd went silent.

"It's burning, it's burning."

Adam didn't even know what had happened when everyone was already making their way out. Reluctantly, he went along. Like a startled flock of sheep, everyone ran agitated into the factory yard and from there into the street. Those who didn't know any better might have thought that a spontaneous protest march was rolling through Angermünde.

He walked alongside Evelyn. "Where are we running to?"

"There's a fire in the city."

"Isn't that a task for the fire department?"

She laughed. He didn't know what was so funny. Every time he drew attention to the responsibilities of the authorities, nobody took him seriously anymore.

"Nah, really, why are we running there?"

"The monastery church is burning. By the time the fire department shows up, the whole building will be gone. We've seen that before. It was the same thing with the old town hall. The bigwigs don't give a damn about old masonry. So everyone has to lend a helping hand."

Adam nodded and mimed understanding. But he still could not fathom it. So far, he had not met any religious people. The people in this atheistic fire brigade probably considered themselves rebels against the state and its mandated God-aversion rather than feeling genuine affection for the church building. No matter from which angle he looked at it, he didn't care. But he did not want to destroy their enthusiasm and left it at that.

"How did the story end?" Adam asked.

"Well, the town hall burned to the ground. Nothing was left. There's this ugly new box now."

"Nah, I don't mean that. The story Kletzsch told."

"Ah, I see ... well, Hepper slapped Margot on the ass."

He nodded. "I see."

He thought about it for a moment and saw that more and more people were joining the procession. Some had buckets with them.

"Yes, and where is Hepper now?"

"You heard Kletzsch. He's been transferred. Besides, that's just one of Kletzsch's stories. You don't have to take it so seriously. What do I know about Hepper? A funny story is a funny story. Nothing more, nothing less."

That was one way to look at it, he thought. It was just a little story for amusement. Whether Hepper was punitively transferred or imprisoned didn't make much difference for the punch line.

He raised his hand in farewell and moved away from Evelyn.

"Where do you think you're going?"

"Home."

"Nah, my friend, you will help us."

She grabbed him by the shoulder, as she had done in the canteen. He wanted to tear himself away, but that would have been an exaggerated gesture. Adam knew that he could afford to waste some time. Besides, it was an excellent alibi.

They came to a square. People had fallen silent. The sight was infernal. The enormous Gothic nave of the Franciscan Monastery Church of Peter and Paul was on fire. The flames crackled and hissed. The wind kept fanning it. Then they ran to the helpers, who had already formed chains and passed buckets filled with water from the extinguishing pond to the church. Firefighting work like from a century long gone, he thought. Where were there still fire ponds? Apparently in Angermünde. He lined up and let one heavy bucket after another slide through his hands. The monotony was comparable to that of his work at the VEB. The only difference was that the people around him were almost frenetically motivated. After what felt like an eternity, he heard sirens. The fire department arrived with a fire engine. Many of the helpers shook their heads, some cursed. By now, the fire had reached the wooden roof truss. The arrival of the official firefighters only fueled the efforts of these ordinary people. Adam took advantage of the excitement to get away unrecognized.

Back in the factory yard, he was all alone for the first time since his shift. He stood there for a moment, soaking up the cold night air and enjoying the silence. Then he went to the place where he had parked his bike. But he couldn't find it. Had it been stolen? He hadn't locked it. That had never been necessary before. However, he had never left his bike in the factory yard at night either. Adam had devoted almost four hours of his precious time to the collective. And the self-imposed task, from which he would not let anything in the world stop him, he could not carry out without his means of transportation. He searched the yard for another bicycle and found none. He ran out into the street. But there were no bikes parked there either. He cursed.

At this time of the day, there were no more trains or buses. So his last option was a car. One he didn't own. So he had to organize one. But that made his venture infinitely riskier. After all, it was unlikely to steal a vehicle and return it later without being caught or at least seen.

Adam strolled through the streets. The cars were parked in plain uniformity at the roadside. Trabants and here and there a Wartburg. All equipped with loud bleating two-stroke engines and therefore unsuitable for his purposes. Directly in front of the houses, he would not get away with theft. But there was nothing else to be found. The few Western cars like Volvos were almost all owned by state officials, and they didn't live in the factory's neighborhood. So it had to be a Trabant. Adam found one parked a little way off in a parking lot. So far away from the buildings that the owner wouldn't notice when the car's engine howled.

Adam approached the vehicle. At least they were easy to steal, he reckoned and started looking around for some wire. A bit out of the way on a patch of wasteland, he found a piece that should suffice for his needs. Adam formed a small loop from it and stuck the wire between the door rubber and the window frame. Then he pulled on it, and the lock came open. With a few more hand movements, he had started the two-stroke engine. He couldn't remember if he'd driven a car in this decade. Adam looked at the fuel gauge. Almost empty. But if he moved economically, it should be enough. And it had to be enough because not a single gas station was open at night. So he drove thoughtfully out of the parking lot. On the country road, he moved fast enough not to be noticed and slow enough not to use too much gas. Stars stood out in the black sky. The plastic of the dashboard was thin and rattled with every pothole.

Adam clawed his way along the narrow road through the dense forest and realized much too late that he had taken the wrong turn. In the dim headlights, he had overlooked the signs. Or there weren't any. He turned around, drove mile after mile, and finally found the turnoff. After a short drive, bright lights appeared on the road ahead of him. He slowed down and turned off his headlights. Then he recognized the outlines of two cars parked on the street. He drove toward a roadblock. One of the police cars shone its light directly into the highway. If they were waiting for him, intending to annoy him, they were successful. Adam slowed his pace further to only drive at walking speed. He couldn't let them see him. There was a forest road off to his right. Slowly, he turned into the boggy path, drove a few meters, and turned the headlights back on. A path wound up a hill through the dense forest ahead of him. The weak engine struggled uphill. Adam bumped along the rough terrain.

When the road was no longer visible in the rearview mirror, Adam stopped, got out, and listened into the night. All he could hear was the wind sweeping through the trees.

He thought about how he would be able to reach his destination that very night. The only access road had been blocked for him by the Volkspolizei, which meant as much as People's Police. So he had to leave the car and walk. After that, he could pick it up again.

Suddenly, the sound of engines mingled with the rush of the wind. Adam fixed his gaze in the direction of the road. The roar of the engine grew louder. He continued to look straight ahead, spellbound, waiting for the engine roar to pass him by. Then he saw the light cones of the car shoot through the trunks of the trees. Immediately he sat back in the car and fiddled with the ignition. The light was getting closer, his hands were shaking, the car wouldn't start. He looked in the rearview mirror. It was a Lada Niva of the Volkspolizei. Bad luck. His twenty-six-horsepower wouldn't do much against their seventy-six. He didn't have much time before the four-by-four would catch up to him. Adam closed his eyes and took a deep breath. With the next try, the engine started up again. He stepped on the gas pedal. Groaning, the car settled into gear. His pursuers turned on their blue lights. The forest was bathed in a ghostly glow. The vehicle came closer and closer. The forest road narrowed. A fork opened up in front of him.

His pursuers turned on their fog lights and shouted something through the car's speakers that he couldn't hear over the roar of the engines. At least Adam didn't have to worry about them being able to read his license plate. It wasn't his car, not his license plate, and thus not his identity that would be revealed.

He took the narrower of the two paths and rumbled across the ground littered with puddles, branches, and leaves. Suddenly the Lada behind him was gone. He saw the cone of light in the rearview mirror disappear to the side. Had they had enough of the chase? What game were they playing with him?

Adam slammed on the brakes. Too late. A steep slope opened up in front of him. He stepped on the brake—no deceleration. He clutched the steering wheel so tightly he could feel the bones of his hands on the hard plastic. The cones of his headlights danced in the trees. He could no longer see the dirt road ahead of him, could no longer make out where it ended. There was nothing more he could do. So he loosened his grip and took his foot off the brake. He just kept the car loosely in the lane. Adam was shaken through the small passenger compartment. He rolled and rolled. Then the car drove as if on glue and finally stopped. The engine was still running. He put it in first gear and hit the gas. Nothing happened. The tires spun. He got out and sank ankle-deep in mud. In the distance, he saw the blue lights of the Lada coming toward him.

Adam quickly bent down into the passenger compartment and wiped off everything he had touched. Then he walked around the car and pulled a soot-smeared piece of cloth out of his overall pocket, with which he had already wiped one or two drops of sweat from his forehead during this workday. He opened the gas tank, stuffed a scrap of cloth inside, and lit it with his lighter. The Lada came closer and closer. Adam ran through the forest, as he didn't have the time to find a real path. In his back, he heard the fire taking possession of the car. Then a loud bang. He stopped and turned around. The Lada had stopped in front of the burning Trabant. The Vopos, policemen of the Volkspolizei, had gotten out and were backing away from the explosion. Adam, like the Vopos, had not expected the tank to explode. There was hardly any fuel left in the tank after all. Maybe it was a gas explosion. He had been running on fumes anyway. Adam kept running and did not look back.

An inhabitant of Angermünde had been robbed of his vehicle forever. A loss difficult to replace, with a delivery time of up to twenty years. Quite ironic that it was destroyed in a matter of seconds. Not his intent, but he felt sorry.

Adam was almost back home. He had tried, had fought back against all odds. But they had won against him in the first move. He could no longer put his plan into action. At least not that night. But what was one lost night against years he had endured? The man had to wait a little longer for his death.

Chapter 2: MANHUNT

November 7–8, 1987
Schorfheide
District Frankfurt/Oder
German Democratic Republic

Outside, black slowly turned to gray. He walked through the cold parlor, stopped for a moment, and looked at his feet. The blue Adidas with the three white stripes on the sides were the only thing that didn't want to fit into the image of the coal shoveler Adam Hedman. His colleagues thought of him as a poor sod who didn't even have Western relatives who could send him ground coffee. Yet he had running shoes from the West. No one knew how he got them, and when they asked him, he just smiled and said it was his little secret. They did not envy him this treasure because he had nothing else. He saw their pity and was ashamed of it. The profile was long run-down, the seams were opening at the sides, and the stripes were worn almost beyond recognition on the left and right sides.

It's amazing what value material things attain when you can't afford them, he thought and decided to discard the shoes after this run and replace them with a GDR make.

He no longer wanted anything in his life that meant anything to him. It was the last measure to disappear entirely into the masses. Of course, this only applied in the event that he should return from his mission. And that was not certain. He estimated his chances at about seventy to thirty. Against him.

Due to the previous night's occurrences, Adam had to change his plan. He had no bike and he definitely didn't want to borrow another car. He would have to run, or rather jog the approximately twelve miles to the target object. It was the logical consequence for him to go on foot. In daylight, it was the most inconspicuous thing to do. At night, you looked like you were running from something. Not the best disguise. And if it weren't so damn far to where the man was, he would walk because that would be even more inconspicuous than jogging. Other than that, nothing had changed in his plan. Search and destroy. The only difference was that the plan would work out that day in broad daylight.

No doubt.

Taking the way back into account, Adam would run a marathon that day. Nothing he was afraid of. Because ever since he had started boxing as a teenager, he had been going running. It was as much a part of the sport as sparring. He hadn't been in the ring for a long time, but the running had stayed. And he wasn't going to let that be taken away from him. Not by the weather. Not by a church fire. And certainly not by the general crappiness of life.

After his father had told him about their Jewish roots, Max Baer had become his role model. The greatest boxer of all time. A strong, invincible Jew. He wanted to be like that, too. Nature meant well for him. He grew into a tree of a guy. Standing at nearly six feet three inches, paws like a grizzly, reach like an albatross, litheness like a feline predator. Coupled with his mother's heirlooms of blond hair and blue eyes, he was a Max Schmeling if Adolf Hitler had painted him according to his ideas of the Aryan race. That physique had brought him titles in his school district and championships in the military. It had brought him a fighting spirit and had given him mental strength. The strength he needed now. He had fought his way to this point. It was going to be his last fight. The final round was coming up. He was surrounded by the weight of someone who had long since been defeated. He could hardly lift his fists. The invincibility had long since been forgotten, washed down with his family history. Within him slumbered the indifferent courage of one fighting a losing battle. All he had to do was stand up one more time. One last time to use the break between the rounds to regain his strength. To then attack the monster in the other corner of the ring with everything he still had at his disposal. He had to learn to remain patient, not to overheat, to land a lucky punch at the decisive moment. That was his only chance. To wreck him, whatever it took. Even if it was his own life.

Putting everything on the line for the last fight, the last round, the last moments before the final bell.

But before Adam could start the fight, he first had to get to the man.

On his running routes, he knew every pothole and curb. And this was one of those routes. Every day he reeled off his miles. And no matter how strenuous his work at the VEB, the day began with a run. For him, there was nothing better than to suck fresh air into his lungs and run. And run. And run.

He took the first steps through the old town of Angermünde. No people as far as the eye could see. The city was asleep. Only a few houses were still inhabited, mostly by pensioners. Those who worked were allotted an apartment in a prefab building with central heating on the outskirts of town. At least, all those whose résumés showed the required degree of loyalty to the line.

Adam ran through Clara-Zetkin-Straße, rounding the potholes and trying to find his running rhythm. He ran faster. He was focused and hadn't noticed that he had turned into the church square. In front of him, he saw the still-smoldering ruin of the monastery church. So the inhabitants of Angermünde had not been able to save the building after all. A sight of disturbing beauty. He left behind the broken charm of the small town along with the burned-out church walls and picked up speed again. He breathed in. He breathed out. One of the best feelings in the world.

As he crossed the street, a Trabant came shooting out of a side street. Adam was startled. The car braked. He looked into the faces of two women with wide-open eyes. At the wheel was Evelyn, her friend Maria in the passenger seat.

Evelyn rolled down the car window. She had a lit cigarette in her hand.

"What are you doing up so early, Adam?"

He walked around to the driver's side of the car, which stood in the street with its engine bubbling, blowing its toxic cloud of exhaust into the cityscape.

"Early-morning exercise, a little bit of running. And you?"

"Busy. We're going to Anna's. She didn't show up yesterday."

"Really? Wasn't she still with you at the church? And afterwards you wanted to go to Susanne's ..."

Evelyn shook her head and ashed out of the car. "Haven't seen her since yesterday. She was only at the church for a short time." She thought for a moment. "Even shorter than you. Have you seen it? It's all burned down. We were all there until late, but ..." She took a drag on her cigarette. "Well, there was nothing to be done, I guess. Let's see what they put there for us."

"Maybe it will be rebuilt."

Maria and Evelyn looked at him pityingly. They knew better.

"Anna will certainly be with Sebastian," he said.

"She's not there. We've already been there."

"I see. Well, it will be all right."

Evelyn became impatient with him. "But you've heard what's going on here, right?" she said, punctuating her words by poking the smoldering cigarette in the air. "You know, with the girl who was found dead in the lake. I'm sure the parents or the sister or whoever thought everything was fine, too."

Evelyn was right about that, he thought, and just shrugged.

Cranking the window back up, she remembered something else. "Can you keep your eyes open? If you see anything, I mean."

Adam nodded and raised his hand in farewell. Evelyn drove off without looking back again. Maria waved goodbye to him.

He walked on. Soon he left the dilapidated uninhabited and the dilapidated inhabited houses behind and reached the city's outskirts. Along the country road, he headed dead straight west. He felt the hardness of the asphalt through the soles of his shoes. He wanted to shift up a gear, get the motor running. So he increased the cadence. But the brakes were on. It was too exhausting. So he shifted down a gear again and reduced his speed. Still, he did not see the forest ahead of him. As only then would the run begin. His run. At this speed, it would take him forever to cover the distance. Again he tried to step on the gas to heat the engine. He concentrated. One foot in front of the next. And so on. It was so easy. But it was in vain. He dragged himself around. What was broken? Had he not refueled his energy? It was too early for hypoglycemia. Did he not have enough water in his system? But his fluids were balanced. Had he not maintained his running apparatus well? His tendons and muscles were stretched to the best of their ability. He could not explain his body's refusal. It had never let him down before.

At last, he saw the first trees of the forest. He sucked cooling air into a machine that had not yet really run hot and trotted on. He could not come to terms with his slowness. Angermünde, with its cranky inhabitants, seemed to creep slowly under his skin. Not even on the most crucial path of his new life did they leave him alone. But he was sure that his engine would warm up soon enough. Everything else was a triviality that he would not remember tomorrow. He knew that his body would not betray him again.

In his back, he heard the sound of engines. He stopped and turned around. One, two, three, four four-by-fours drove past him. In the Ladas were men with *ushankas* on their heads. They seemed to take no notice of him. Sublime ignorance. The column headed for the forest. Adam diligently worked his way further across the road and, after a few minutes, reached the edge of the woods. As soon as he had left the first trees behind him, it should go faster. Forest ground was his preferred surface for running. At a forest intersection ahead, he saw a vehicle parked in the middle of the road. At a slow but acceptable speed, he wanted to run past the obstacle. It was a *Kübelwagen* of the Nationale Volksarmee, mostly abbreviated to *NVA*, the National People's Army. Two soldiers were lined up in front of the vehicle, machine guns at the ready.

"Pull over!" one of them said.

He stopped.

"This is as far as you can go."

"Well, this is new. I always jog around here."

"Not today, restricted area."

He looked questioningly at the two soldiers.

"Just run back. Come back tomorrow."

"I see, thank you."

Adam turned around and did as he was told. The next question would have been about his papers. And he didn't have them on him. He had nothing with him. Just the clothes and the shoes he wore on his body. The morning was not going as he had imagined. So far, it was not his day. And when he thought about it, it wasn't even his decade. But he could still fight it. With all his power, make fate compliant. The thought exhilarated him. Seven agonizing years and yet he was still there, still going on. Why, in fact? He noticed how he shrugged his shoulders as he walked. The involuntary movement loosened him up and simultaneously robbed him of concentration, of the unconditional focus on his goal.

When Adam regained his composure, he saw a path leading into the forest. He hesitated briefly and then turned from the country road onto the forest path. The cardinal direction was still correct. It would only be a short detour, and he would end up back on his former track.

The ground was frozen. It was slippery. He walked slower until he reached a walking pace. As he marched through the forest, only a little light fell on the ground. The conifers stood close together here. The path wound through the trees. Snowflakes found their way through the treetops. The snowfall became heavier. He went deeper into the forest. Carefully, his low-profile soles felt their way over the ground. In front of him, the rows of trees now opened up, and he entered a clearing. At the edge of the open space of the primeval coniferous forest, he saw a doe and stopped. He did not want to startle it. It was foraging on the frozen ground. Its cold snout gently poked at mosses and withered grasses. There was a crackle in the woods. The doe looked up. It did not move. It looked directly in his direction. He looked back. The animal turned back to the ground. He watched it scan the floor of the clearing in careful movements. How it scratched the hard sandy soil with its front hooves. How it found something, perhaps a root, and chewed quickly.

A breeze passed over the clearing. He looked up at the sky. It had stopped snowing. The sun broke milky out of the clouds for a brief moment. There was another crackling sound. He heard heavy breathing. A stag entered the clearing. The reddish fur shone in the light. Its hooves made a snapping sound whenever they hit the hard forest floor. It was a majestic sight. The doe stopped in her tracks and looked first at the other animal and then into the forest. The stag had spotted Adam. He held his breath. His blood pulsed calmly. The stag's forelegs slumped, and it fell headfirst onto the forest floor. Only then did Adam hear the whip of the gunshot. The doe disappeared into the thicket. The stag writhed in its death throes. A few moments later, its eyes stared lifelessly out of their sockets. Adam was transfixed. Then something grabbed him by the shoulder. Adam immediately grabbed it, clutching the unknown hand tightly and twisting it with a jerky motion. The man gave a sharp cry, and Adam released him from his grip. He looked into the pain-distorted face of a man about sixty years old. At second glance, he might have been older.

"Too fast. Way too fast. Too fast. Too fast," the old man said hastily.

Adam did not know what the man wanted from him.

"Too fast. Too fast. They're coming. They're coming," he kept saying.

"What?"

The man did not answer and instead pulled Adam from the clearing into the forest.

"There you see, you see. Way too fast. Way too fast. They come. Too dangerous. Way too dangerous. Got to get out of here. Got to get out of here."

Adam followed the man, who again held him by the shoulder and trudged with him in quick steps down the forest path.

"I've seen you before. Seen you before. But today is not a good day. Not a good day."

He talked fast, mumbled incomprehensibly, and seemed rushed. And not only that, his whole figure seemed to be driven by an invisible hand. The gray mop of hair ruffled in all directions on his crooked head, which sat on an emaciated body. The man made Adam nervous just by looking at him.

"Way too fast today. Way too fast. Hunting is today. Hunting. Way too fast. Did you see it? Did you see it? The beautiful stag. There he was, the beautiful stag. Did you see?"

Adam had already figured he was in the middle of a hunt. The man finally let go of him. Then he stopped and put a finger over his mouth.

"What is it?" Adam asked.

Then the man put a hand on Adam's mouth. Adam wiped the hand away. The man hissed.

"Quietly. Very, very quietly," the man said in a whisper.

The man looked into the forest. He seemed to hear something and pulled Adam further.

"Fast. Way too fast. They're coming. They're coming."

"Who's coming?"

"The hunters. The hunters. They're coming."

Adam stopped. The man wanted to pull him on. But he freed himself from him.

"You have to go. Gotta go."

"They're hunting animals, aren't they? Not us."

"Fast. Way too fast."

The man grabbed Adam again. He let himself be pulled along. They went deeper into the forest. The sun had disappeared. It was snowing again, and it just wouldn't get any brighter again that day. The man dragged him from the forest path onto a narrow path.

"Where are we going?"

"Fast. Much too fast. It's safe here. It's safe here."

The man went ahead. He pulled Adam behind him by the sleeve. Like a child with its playmate on the playground. After a short walk, the man stopped and let go of Adam. He went into the forest and soon Adam did not see him anymore. He followed the direction of the man's walk. The musty leaves were frozen and crunched under his shoes. His clothes could not be more inappropriate for a forest walk. Adam was getting cold. He reached a mighty beech tree that stood in the middle of the trail. He circled the tree and turned around. The beech tree was hollow. There he saw the old man crouching in the belly of the tree, which offered him shelter from the weather.

"There you are. There you are. It's safe here. It's safe here."

"Don't you think you worry a little much about the hunters?"

"They're the same hunters. The same hunters."

"As what?"

"The same. The same ones from the girl. From the girl."

"Which one?"

"The beautiful girl ... beautiful girl."

"Anna? Anna Sievers?"

The man shook his head. "The beautiful girl ... beautiful girl."

"I don't know what you're talking about. I'm leaving now," Adam said and turned around.

The man jumped up and grabbed Adam by the arm again. He said nothing but just looked at him with wide-open eyes. Again Adam tore himself away and went back to the path. He hoped he would find the forest path again quickly. Adam had to hurry. He had already lost too much time. This damned country. First Evelyn, then the soldiers, and finally that old forest fogy. You couldn't even jog in peace. And as soon as you strayed from the path, you were shot at. Only weirdos here, Adam thought and ran faster through the forest. Soon he again reached the trail from which he had come. He forced himself to run faster. He fired up the machine and got to the clearing again. There was nothing left of the stag, only a pool of blood on the churned ground. Adam walked quickly across the clearing.

Then he heard another crack. As if someone had stepped on a branch. Adam looked in the direction of the sound. For a brief moment, he thought he saw a person some distance away. Then he looked in the other direction. There was a young man, almost a child. He had a rifle at the ready. And pulled the trigger.

Adam opened his eyes. Absolute darkness.

He stretched out his arms. Nothing.

Is this death? Is this what it feels like to have died? The immortal consciousness surrounded by all-swallowing emptiness?

His tongue stuck to his gums. A pain hammered in his head. Gradually, his eyes became accustomed to the darkness. He perceived dim outlines. He tried to stand up. A sharp pain flashed through his body. He was alive, and it hurt. He remembered again that he had been shot. The left side of his rib cage felt as if a dagger were stuck in it. He felt up his body. His torso was wrapped thickly with a bandage. Must be a gunshot wound from buckshot ammunition. Only a few grains of the shot had hit him. But he undoubtedly had broken a rib or two. He sat up and exhaled. But he couldn't take a deep breath. If he moved thoughtfully, the pain was bearable. Carefully, he stood up and felt his way around the room.

He had to get out of here as quickly as possible. His goal was still attainable. Never give up.

He reached a curtain and pulled it open. It was night. Only a little light shone into the room. Adam had to be on one of the upper floors of the house. From there, he looked out over a lake that lay black and still before him some distance away. He went back to the bed and turned on the bedside lamp. A warm light spread through the room. Amidst antique furniture, he searched for his clothes as he was naked except for his underpants. After he could not find them, he went to the room door, which was locked. He looked through the brass keyhole. The key was in from the outside. That shouldn't be a problem. He found a hanger in the closet whose hook could be bent into a makeshift door opener. The key fell to the parquet floor in front of the room door. He pulled it with the hanger through the gap between the door and the parquet floor. It was a trick he had once seen in a teenage movie. A few moments later, he had freed himself. He was amazed that it had worked. It was dark in the hallway, too. He left the door to the room open and oriented himself. On the other side of the wood-paneled hallway were three doors, just like on his side. He wanted to find his clothes and then get out as fast as he could. Behind one door, he found a spartan study with a desk and bookshelves. No clothes. In the next were a bed, a desk, a bookshelf. Just as spartan. There was a closet, though. He tore it open and pulled out a pair of pants and a sweater. Too small for him. He threw everything back into the closet, closed the door, and set off for the next room. In the corridor, someone had turned on the light. A woman was coming toward him. She had seen him. He could not hide. She wore a gray dress, was middle-aged, and had an austere air. Perhaps she had once been a teacher in her former life. Or a prison guard.

"Good afternoon," she said, stopping a few feet away from him.

"Howdy."

"Good, you're awake. Are you feeling better?"

"I think."

"I'll get you something to wear. It's best if you wait in the room," she said, pointing with her hand to the door, which was supposed to be locked.

She was not interested in how he had gotten out of the room.

"Where am I?"

"Kienhorst country estate. In the middle of the Schorfheide."

"Then that's Werbellinsee out there?"

She nodded. Then he was almost at his target object. Werbellinsee was even a little farther away from Angermünde than his running destination. The target was at Grimnitzsee, just a few minutes away. It was dark outside. He had lost a few hours, but there was still time. The plan was still running. No change necessary.

"How did I get here?"

"Everything will be explained to you in a moment. Now you'd best go back to your room," she said and headed for the door.

She stretched out an arm and showed him the way into the room. He went in, and she closed the door behind him. He had left the key stuck on the inside. At least now, he could not be locked in again. However, he could not possibly escape dressed only in his underpants. If he was caught, they would immediately put him in the loony bin.

The woman didn't seem particularly friendly, but not hostile either. He was going to take his chances. Once he had clothes, he could still think about escaping. But why would anyone want to hurt a poor coal shoveler? The thought reassured him. But did they even know he was a coal shoveler?

There was a knock at the door, and he could not finish his thought. A young man entered. He wore a black suit that fit him like a glove. It was hard to guess his age. But he was certainly not older than twenty.

"May I come in?" he asked, looking down at the floor.

"Sure, can I get something to wear now?"

"Yes, my father says to give you some of my clothes."

"Fine, but why not my own stuff?"

"Well, I guess it's all wasted. All that blood," he said, tilting his head with the blond mop of hair.

"That's right. I got caught pretty good."

"That was an oversight."

"You did this."

The boy looked at him sheepishly.

"Great. What time is it anyway?" asked Adam.

"It's after eight already. Sorry about that, by the way. That was a foolish accident."

"It's all right. But it looks like you didn't take me to a doctor. No one at the VEB would believe that I woke up shot in some house somewhere."

"I guess that's going to be okay. We called a doctor. He said you didn't lose as much blood as it looked like you did, and it's going to be all right. He then gave you something to help you sleep. I think my father will take care of everything. There's no work today anyway, is there?"

"Yes, there is."

"On a Sunday?"

Adam winced inwardly. He had been asleep for almost two days. There was no more chance to confront the man who had robbed him of everything his heart was attached to. And he didn't know if he still had the strength to track him down one more time, to make the next plan that would only fail again. If he had just been able to stay on his feet until just now—but he had now been sent to the boards for good. Technical knockout in the last round. It was over.

"Then I was knocked out for two days."

"That's right. It's been quite a while. I kept checking on you, though, so we knew you were still alive."

"That's comforting."

Adam wondered what the doctor had given him. Perhaps it was the local veterinarian who had injected him with a horse tranquilizer.

He noticed that his survival mode kicked in. He did not yet want to let despair take complete possession of him. He tried to hammer into his head that it was merely the momentary shock that was dragging him down. He had to sleep on it once, and then he would see if he could continue or if it was all over for him. As hard as it was, he had to put his mind above his dark feelings.

"Who is your father?"

The boy left and didn't seem to hear him anymore.

"I still need the clothes ..."

In the hallway, the boy turned around. "Of course. Let's pick out something for you to wear. Then we can go downstairs, and I'll introduce you to my father," he said, leading the way.

Adam followed him. The boy went into the room he would have searched next for clothes for himself. Stupid coincidence that he had started looking in the wrong room, he thought.

"What's your name?" asked Adam.

"Immanuel," the boy said, opening the door to his room.

"Ah, like Kant."

The boy pulled up one corner of his mouth. He could not interpret whether it was a tired smile or recognition of his knowledge. The room looked exactly like the other one. Solely furnished with the bare necessities.

"We're about the same size, I think," Immanuel said.

"Stand up straight."

The boy followed his instruction. Adam stood in front of Immanuel. So close that the tips of their noses almost touched. He looked into his eyes. Blue with a tinge of gray. The boy took a step back and opened the closet door.

"I would say I'm a bit taller. But that shouldn't be a problem. What do you have for me?" asked Adam.

"Well, actually, I don't have that many suits."

"Better give me something comfier."

"A suit would be better for the occasion. We'll eat together."

"I was actually about to leave."

"My father will insist."

Adam raised his eyebrows.

"Well, let's see what we've got. Can't remember the last time I wore a suit to dinner."

The boy pulled out one black suit after another. They all looked alike. Nothing flamboyant—fine fabrics, though.

"You had those made, am I right?"

"My father says that clothes make the man. The top one here is almost as new as the one I'm wearing. It should fit."

Adam took the suit from him.

"By the way, do you know an old man wandering around here in the woods?"

"An old man?"

Adam nodded.

"Bit of a drifter. Wood gnome, tramp ..."

Immanuel looked away and shrugged his shoulders.

"Doesn't really matter," Adam said.

Immanuel turned back to the closet.

"It's all right, boy. I'll take this one," Adam said.

"Good."

Immanuel winced. Someone had just called his name. Adam looked at the boy questioningly.

"It's just my little brother. I think we're supposed to come down."

Immanuel pressed another shirt and shoes into Adam's hand.

"So, I'd better ... when you're dressed, just come down. We're sitting in the dining room. You can't miss it. See you in a minute."

Adam nodded and slipped the shirt on. The boy left the room. The suit fit. The shoes pinched a little. Adam made his way to the ground level. He hoped they would at least give him back his worn-out Adidas for the walk home. At the end of the hallway was a wooden partition that led to the entry of the stairway. He walked through the door and stood in a spacious vestibule. Murmurs of voices and music drifted to him. The wing they had placed him in seemed hermetically sealed from the rest of the house. Adam walked down the carpeted wooden staircase. He followed the sounds. At the bottom of the stairs, he came right up to the front door. His chance to leave.

Adam dismissed the thought again and went right around the stairs into a brightly lit parlor. He looked out at a group of men. They were seated at an enormous dining table set with a white tablecloth and the most delicate china. At least, that was how it appeared from a distance. They had not yet noticed him. He looked over the rows of men at the table.

What had he gotten himself into? Were these the hunting friends of the shooter's father?

A spooky circle of old men. He knew every single one of the men. Not personally, but he had seen their faces before, heard their names, and knew their functions in the state. It was ironic that he had met this group the very day when the have-nots were supposed to win against the bigwigs. The score was one to zero. To their advantage.

He took a deep breath and walked toward the table. The woman in the gray dress came out of nowhere and assigned him a seat. She didn't have to, as the seat in the center of two men was the only one that was still unoccupied. He counted nine chairs in all, three on the left of the table, four on the right, and one at each end of the table. But there was enough room for twelve or sixteen chairs at the table. Across from him sat Immanuel, who was also framed by two men. The only one who did not fit in beside him was a child. A boy sitting at one end of the table across from another man. Maybe in his midforties. Robust with a round face. Blond hair parted loosely to one side. Alert blue eyes. Someone who one would trust with secrets. Whether one wanted to or not.

"Ah, there he is, our mystery guest of honor."

The conversations fell silent.

"He made it to us without any papers at all," said the man from the end of the table. Laughter from the group.

"Why don't you sit down? What do you want to drink? A beer?"

Adam nodded to the crowd. Then he confirmed with a nod to the host that it should be a beer for him. He sat down, and already a beer was poured for him by a younger woman in a gray dress. The man at the end of the table raised his glass.

"Well, let's have a toast together that my son didn't send for the ferryman waiting at the banks of the Hades."

Styx, Adam thought. The men laughed and raised their glasses. Wineglasses. He was the only one who held a beer tumbler in his hands.

"Can you imagine, we don't even know who we're dealing with yet?" the man said.

"Hedman is my name. Adam Hedman."

"Go on. What do you do, Herr Hedman?"

"I work at the VEB Gustav Bruhn."

"That's a noble task, isn't it? And it even corresponds to the truth. I wouldn't be who I am if I hadn't already gotten this information myself."

Polyphonic laughter at the table. Adam smiled, looking at the empty plate in front of him. Then he looked up at the host again.

"A beautiful name you have there, Herr Hedman. Father German, name from the mother, a Swede. Unusual."

"Yes," Adam said, not letting any further explanation follow. His host was content with that.

"I am Friedrich Stahl. And these are my friends. We're having a little something for dinner, as you can see."

The men laughed again. Adam glanced over the table. A little something was immoderately understated. Potatoes, green beans, gravy, bread, and butter were on the table heaped in large bowls. But he saw no meat. That explained itself a few moments later when the two servants pushed in two small carts. On one, a roasted boar was displayed. On the other, a stag. The men applauded as they laid eyes on their prey, prepared ready for consumption.

"Ephraim, introduce our guests to Herr Hedman. We are not barbarians. Before you sink your tusks into the meat, you want to know who you're dealing with. Don't you, Herr Hedman?"

The child got up from his chair at the end of the table.

"Good, Father."

"There's really no need for that, comrade. The food is getting cold," said the man to Adam's left.

"Then Ephraim will just have to hurry up. A little decency must be maintained. Well, then, Ephraim!"

The boy nodded. "So this is Herr Schabowski," the boy said, looking at the man sitting to Stahl's right.

"Pleasure," the man said.

"Next is Herr Rogalla," the boy said, looking at the man to Stahl's left.

"Pleasure."

"Right before Herr Schabowski, we have Herr Grossmann."

"Pleasure."

"On my left is Herr Döring, and on my right is Herr Meyer."

"Pleasure."

"Pleasure."

"And my brother Immanuel Stahl you already know," the boy said, looking at his older brother to the left in the center of the table.

Ephraim nodded and sat down again. Immanuel nodded as well.

"Well, now we can get started," said Schabowski.

In a blink of an eye, after he said that, the two women started moving with the carts. They heaped meat from the hunt onto the plates.

"Friends, enjoy. It was indeed a successful hunting weekend," Stahl said after all the guests were seating in front of lavishly filled plates.

Schabowski leaned over to Adam.

"What's that VEB doing you're working for?"

"Enamel."

"Something like that still exists? Amazing. And what are you doing there?"

"Shoveling coal."

"Don't you have electricity there?"

"We do, but the furnaces run on coal. It's scorching."

"I see. Quite amazing. It's always nice to talk to some ordinary folks."

"What are you doing?"

"I'm a member of the Politbüro."

"Oh, I see, a politician."

"You could say that. Something like that, anyway. Disappointed?"

"No, why?"

"Sounded a little like it."

"Nope."

"Don't you know anyone at this table?"

"Immanuel, who shot me. And Herr Stahl by hearsay. I already met his wife upstairs very briefly ..."

Friedrich Stahl laughed out loud. He must have been listening to the conversation between the two.

"No, that's not my wife, if you mean Frau Wehner. No, no. That's an employee of the house."

"I didn't know that."

"You couldn't. Don't blame yourself."

"Isn't your wife here?"

Silence fell around the table. Schabowski wanted to take the floor.

Friedrich Stahl looked at him. "Let it go, Günter."

Then he turned to Adam. "Unfortunately, my wife cannot be here today because she is no longer with us."

"My condolences!"

"Thank you very much! Where were we? Oh yes, that's right, you only know me and my son here at the table. And only from this weekend and from hearsay ..."

"Quite amazing again. Don't you have a TV?" asked Schabowski.

"Nah," Adam lied.

"That'll be why."

"Think so."

He decided to keep the mask of the clueless worker on, even though he knew every single one of the officials at the table. The chief of the Felix Dzerzhinsky Guards Regiment even personally. Adam was lucky that the encounter had been years ago, and the man apparently did not recognize him.

"Well, let me enlighten you. Because you've gotten yourself into an outstanding bunch."

Günter Schabowski beckoned him closer. Adam inclined his head toward him. Schabowski spoke more quietly. As if he were divulging secrets.

"Listen closely. The coal shoveler from the Volkseigener Betrieb is dining together the head of the HVA, our foreign intelligence service, that's Herr Grossmann. Then we have Major General Manfred Döring, commander of the Wachregiment Feliks E. Dzierżyński, good man. And Colonel Jürgen Rogalla, who is responsible in the HVA Abteilung XI for everything the Yank does in West Germany. Good contacts in the West, I can tell you that. Then, and you should actually know him, comrade Hans-Joachim Meyer, who is the chairman of your city council. You're from Angermünde, aren't you?"

Adam nodded. It was close enough to the truth.

"And not to forget Herr Stahl with his two sons."

"What does he do?" asked Adam.

He knew the answer, but he still wanted to hear the exact term again from the man's mouth.

"This is the head of the MfS responsible for your district."

"The Ministry of State Security?"

"Don't be shy. You can say Stasi. Haven't heard anybody calling our beloved Ministry by its full name in a long time. Well, you know your way around a bit, don't you?"

Adam tried to move his mouth into a smile. But the horizontal line stayed. None of his work colleagues would ever believe him that he had dined with the top brass of the GDR security apparatus. And the men at the table would not believe what secrets this worker had.

"Or am I not right?" asked Schabowski, nudging Adam.

"What?"

The men at the table laughed.

"A bit dreamy, eh? I meant that food is a fine thing, but doing the dishes afterwards is the worst thing there is. Am I not right?"

Adam nodded. The men laughed again.

"How do you do it at home?" asked Schabowski.

"Well, by hand."

Again the men laughed.

"See, and that's just about the worst thing you can imagine. No woman to do the dishes for you?" asked Schabowski.

"Nah, nah, never mind. No woman."

Laughter. But this time not at him, but in total agreement. The guys sitting here thought they didn't need women. At most to do the dishes.

"Maybe you have a man?" said Rogalla.

The laughter increased.

"Give it a rest, men. You'd better dig in. Our dear Hedman is already blushing," said Stahl.

That was not true. But Adam was glad that Friedrich Stahl drew his attention away from him.

"In my case, a Miele does the trick," said Schabowski.

"What do you mean? Don't you have a dishwasher from one of our VEBs?" asked Döring seriously. Then he snorted.

And all the men with him.

Schabowski looked at Adam. "Why aren't you laughing?"

"I don't think I got the joke."

Laughter again.

"Ever seen a GDR-made dishwasher?"

"Nah."

Laughter.

"See!"

The mood was boisterous. The men piled their plates full of meat over and over again. They talked about the merits of their West German–made household appliances, antique hunting weapons, and Western Allied military equipment. In the meantime, the two sons were sent off to their rooms and the circle was moved to the smoking room. Stahl approached Adam and put an arm and his shoulder.

"Oh, Herr Hedman. That was a nice evening altogether. Did you enjoy it?"

"Yes, thank you."

"Still tastes best when hunted yourself, am I right?"

Adam nodded. The men hadn't noticed that he had only eaten the side dishes. In the GDR, it had become a habit for him to leave out all foods that seemed to him to be of especially poor quality or that simply did not taste good. He avoided processed meat, eggs, and dairy products. Even if this meat was unadulterated, he had noticed that not eating these products had made him healthier. That was why he didn't touch it at all anymore. He felt fitter than in his best boxing days. The hard work at the VEB and his morning runs had sweated every ounce of fat off his body. He consisted only of muscles and tendons that stretched over his bones.

"And don't worry about work. That's already been cleared up," Stahl said.

"Thank you."

The evening in the circle of GDR officials was apparently over for him at this point.

"It goes without saying. After all, you were shot by my son. That's the least I can do for you. And the medical officer in Angermünde has been notified. If there are complications ..."

"That won't be necessary."

"Tough, very good. That's the way I like it. If I could say that about my sons, I'd be happy. Wait a minute. I have another little something for you."

"Anyway, I was just about to ask where the bus ..."

"Now, don't be silly. You're being driven. No question about it. Wait here."

Adam nodded. Stahl, however, did not leave at all. He called one of his servants, who returned shortly with a package.

"So, your sportswear was beyond saving. Because of the blood, you understand … but we got something for you."

Adam took the package.

"It's best if you change your clothes, and then my driver will take you home."

Stahl said goodbye and retreated to an adjoining room. In the package, he found a brand-new tracksuit and running shoes of GDR manufacture. Just as he had imagined before. So now, he was finally entirely the line-loyal worker without Western relatives and Western products.

He left the room and went to the front door. On the spacious square in front of the house, the driver was already waiting for him, having set up in front of a black sedan of Soviet manufacture. He opened the rear car door for him and closed it again after Adam took a seat in the car. Then they drove off. From the back window, he glanced at the house where he had just eaten. However, house was not accurate. It was a mansion. And he hadn't eaten. He had dined. The two-story building was whitewashed and sported a thatched roof. It looked like a cross between a hunting lodge and a fishing hut. Amazing. Quite amazing, as Schabowski would say. Just then, he could see young Immanuel coming out of the building before he disappeared from his sight. What was the young man carrying under his arm? Was it a loaf of bread with which he hastily ran into the forest? Strange boy, he thought and turned back in the direction of travel. After minutes of driving, they reached a gate. The next day was waiting for him. Uneventful and alone with the cold coal.

Adam looked out the window. They were driving on a country road lined on both sides by dense forest. Every now and then, he caught a glimpse of the lake lying quietly there, followed by a grassy landscape, some fields. They drove up a hill. In the distance, he could make out the next body of water. The road wound its way toward Grimnitzsee. At the fork, the driver turned toward Angermünde. Here, there were only a few yards between the lakeside road and the water. After a few hundred yards, the road made a turn inland and a cast-iron fence sitting on top of a brick wall began, behind which stretched a spacious park. On it, facing the lake, was a whitewashed villa. The target. It lay in the dark and housed a small clinic that no one was supposed to know about. However, there was some talk in the area that the political leadership was being treated there. The doctors were handpicked, came to the clinic for the respective treatment, and were certainly as loyal to the regime as they were proud to be allowed to take the nomenklatura of the state under their knives. These were the whereabouts for the past couple of days of the man he had planned to kill. Now he was no longer there. And the only thing that had died was the plan. Where the man had been before and where he would go after, Adam did not know. And if he could trust his despair, he would not bother to find out. Life was playing a bitter trick on him. He was in the right place at the wrong time. So close, yet in vain. The car left the park behind, along with the villa, and soon they were back in the woods. The only light came from the car's headlamps flickering onto the asphalt.

Chapter 3: BLOOD BEECH

November 9, 1987
VEB Stamping and Enameling Plant Gustav Bruhn
Angermünde
District Frankfurt/Oder
German Democratic Republic

Adam was the first worker at the factory that morning. As always, he sat down in the break room before the shift began. And like every morning, he could choose a table. His table.

He had slept very little. The gunshot wound hurt with every movement. That night he had fallen into light sleep again and again and was awakened by a sharp pain in his ribs every time he turned. He remembered bursting into loud laughter a few times, like a maniac. The drugs still hadn't thoroughly flushed out of his system, it seemed, and the weekend's events were hard to beat for absurdity. But the night had done him good. It hadn't worked any miracles. But his vision was no longer obscured by anger over his failure. Instead, his physical pain was a mirror of his inner life. An honest injury. But despite the insufficient sleep, the despair that had settled in him the previous evening gave way to a new aggressiveness. He was no longer facing a black hole. Even though the situation was bleak and almost unbearable, he just couldn't give up. He did not know why it was like that. But he took it as a silent victory of his will over his emotions.

Adam preferred to sit by the window. All alone. His gaze roamed the room. His eyes lingered on the calendar— November 9. The most German of all days. 1918, the end of the Empire and the beginning of the Republic. A big hooray. However, not coming from the mouths of all Germans. 1923 the failed Hitler coup. 1938 pogroms against the Jewish population. Again a big hooray. Again not coming from everyone. There it was, the new perspective he desperately needed. For he had not been hit as badly as the Jews at that time. But that was all the good news. In addition, people in the GDR did not feel particularly responsible for the crimes of the Nazis because, in contrast to the Federal Republic of Germany to the west, they felt that they had been profoundly denazified. So the looting, beating, and murdering had taken place in another country. Thus you did not have to burden your conscience with your guilt on a daily basis.

He leaned forward in his chair, let the pain hit him, waited until it became bearable, and unpacked his breakfast. Whole wheat bread spread with margarine, topped with sliced cooked potatoes, raw kale, and radishes. More nutritious than tasty. Although in large quantities. In addition, rolled oats with water, dried fruits and apples.

The work of coal shoveling was exhausting. Adam bit into the bread and reflected. He needed a new plan. The first thing he had to do was try to contact his informant. At the end of the shift, he wanted to make a new attempt to enforce justice.

He looked out of the window. It was a beautiful day. As beautiful as this barren stretch of land could be. The wind tore the cloud cover apart again and again and let a little light fall on the earth. He took another bite of his bread and looked across the yard. Behind the factory wall stood a tree. A beech tree. Seventy feet tall for sure. It was bare. Autumn had taken all its leaves. Only one leaf still hung on the tree. It shimmered reddish whenever a ray of sunlight fell on it. The word *blood beech* popped into his head. A word that he had heard somewhere once. A long time ago. Since then, the term had not let him go—blood beech. Although he knew that it was a copper beech that stood there lonely at the factory wall, he thought that the name matched perfectly nevertheless. Gnarled, many-limbed, unruly. The wind tugged at the only leaf that still offered resistance. It danced in the gusts, holding on to the branch with its stem. He felt as if he had been put into a trance by this spectacle.

There was a clatter. One of the painters tapped the metal table with one hand in greeting.

"Hey, Hedman, what are you doing here this early? Did you fall out of bed or what?"

"Morning!"

The man stopped in front of him.

"Where were you this weekend, anyway? Didn't anyone tell you?"

Adam took a bite of his bread and chewed slowly.

"What happened?"

"Well, there was a list. You should have been informed."

"About what?"

"You're kidding me now, aren't you? Anna has disappeared. We were all looking for her this morning. The whole factory was on its feet. The others should be arriving any minute now. They really didn't tell you?"

Adam shook his head and wondered why Anna had still not reappeared. Besides, he asked himself if he would have noticed anything about the search anyway. Even if he hadn't been lying under anesthesia in the villa on Werbellinsee. After all, he lived in the middle of the city, and everyone else lived in the new buildings on the outskirts. And he didn't own a telephone either. Whoever was responsible for letting him know would probably have found it too much trouble and refrained from notifying him.

"Anna had already disappeared on Friday. You didn't notice, did you? And because she didn't show up again all weekend, everyone was informed over the weekend. It worked out well. You wouldn't think so. Exceptions prove the rule, as the saying goes, right?" said the man, standing at his table with a grin.

"I noticed. And?" he asked and continued to chew.

"What?"

"Well, did you find her?"

"Nah. But today, after the shift ends, we'll look again."

"Where is she supposed to be?"

"If we only knew ..."

"Do you think someone would just get lost like that?"

"Anything could have happened."

"Like what?"

"Maybe she twisted her ankle walking in the woods and can't get up anymore."

"But then she would have frozen to death by now."

"Well, or she fell through the ice while skating."

"Drowned? Is she even skating?"

"Well, I don't know that."

"Are any of the lakes frozen over yet?"

"I was just trying to say that anything could have happened."

"She's probably just at a friend's house."

"I don't think so. Evelyn would know that. But you'll be there tonight, right, Hedman?"

"She'll have shown up by then anyway."

"What if she doesn't?"

Adam hunched his shoulders.

"See you around," the man said and left.

In the meantime, the factory canteen was bustling with activity. A group of painters sat down at the table behind him. He overheard their conversation.

"It's strange, the whole Anna thing," said one.

"She'll turn up," said another.

"We should go back out there and look for her right after work," said a third.

"Where are we going to look?"

"Anywhere is best. If we divide smartly, we can do it."

"Even in the woods?"

"There too."

"You'd need thousands of men there, right?"

The forests of the Schorfheide formed the most extensive contiguous wooded area on this side of the Ural Mountains. The men knew that and fell silent.

He turned to them. "Morning, men! Maybe we'll ask that guy who lives in the woods if he's seen anything, right?"

He was not genuinely concerned about Anna. It was a good excuse to approach the men about the old man in the forest. In his experience, the *Uckermärkers* were not particularly eager to provide information when asked directly.

"It's quite a good idea. How do you know him?" asked the first.

"I met him the other day on a walk in the woods. Quite a cranky character."

"You can say that again," said the third.

"Don't underestimate Günter. Fate has played him a dirty trick, but he's not as crazy as he pretends to be," said the first.

"What happened to him?" asked Adam.

The men fell silent and chewed on their sandwiches.

"Come on, guys. Can't be that bad, can it?"

The first one retook the floor.

"So listen. I keep forgetting you're not from around here, Hedman. It's been a while. Before your time here anyway..."

"Leave it, Walter," said the second.

"Why, let him know, Uli," said the first.

The second devoted himself again to the stale bread.

"Well, as I said, it's been a while. But no one has forgotten, I can tell you that. There was a hunting accident. His wife was unfortunate enough to run into the bullets. It was funny that not only she was hit, but also a second woman."

"Walter, stop it now. That's a cock-and-bull-story. It was never solved," said the third man.

"Peter, solved or not, that's the situation. The second woman was the wife of party functionary Stahl. They had just moved into their beautiful estate here in our area, and then a few weeks later, that tragic accident. And not just one woman, but two. Günter never recovered from the shock. Since then, he has only lived in the forest, I think. He's probably still hoping that his wife will come back to him someday."

"Because they never found her body," said the second.

"Now it inevitably sounds like a cock-and-bull-story," said the third.

"What happened to the body?" asked Adam.

"Nobody knows. The authorities have only said that it was an accident," said the first.

"And where is the body?" asked Adam.

"Buried here in Angermünde. But they say that the grave is empty. That Günter has never seen his dead wife. He went crazy over exactly that," said the first.

"Tragic story. Do they know who shot the women?" asked Adam.

"Can't be reconstructed anymore. Too many hunters. And with buckshot, there is really no certainty about who shot. In any case, none of the hunters can't remember anything," said the second. "The gang sticks together, of course," he said in a whisper.

"And what about Stahl's wife?" asked Adam.

"Also buried," said the third.

"But for real, or is there nothing in the grave either?" asked Adam.

"No one has told us anything about that. In any case, Stahl hasn't gone crazy like Günter," said the first.

"Well, I doubt Günter knows anything ...," said the second.

"But it still wouldn't hurt to ask him. Maybe he's seen Anna in the last few days," said the first.

The men nodded. The same thing that had happened to to Stahl's wife had happened to Adam. In her case, however, with fatal consequences. If Anna had also been in the line of fire of the hunting party, then the old man in the forest would indeed have told him about it. He thought about it. Somebody had shot Stahl's and Günter's wives, and the whole town knew about it. It wouldn't make any sense to sweep it under the rug if the same thing had happened to Anna.

Then the factory manager Kletzsch came into the canteen and posted himself between the tables. "Friends, as we all know, our dear colleague Anna Sievers has not been home or here at the VEB for a few days. That's why we've all been looking for her. Unfortunately, we still haven't found her. But if we all pull together, we will find her. So we're meeting again today after the shift to look for her. I'm quite sure that if the whole collective joins in the search, we can have Anna back here in our ranks soon."

He was about to turn around and leave when something else seemed to occur to him.

"Oh, right. Evelyn, do you want to say something too?" asked Kletzsch, looking at the sister of the missing woman, who was sitting among her colleagues at one of the tables.

Evelyn stood up and looked at the floor. It took her a moment, but then she had apparently collected herself and looked at Kletzsch.

"So, it would be quite great if you all could help," she said and sat down again.

The VEB boss took the floor again. "Exactly, there's probably nothing more to add to that. We will meet in front of the gate at the end of the shift. If you can't be there, please let me know in person."

Adam raised his eyebrows.

"Do you mind, Hedman?" one of the painters asked quietly.

"Nah, why would I mind?" he said in a whisper.

But he had a lot against it. He had more important things to do than look for a girl who he didn't really know. But he couldn't tell anyone that. The factory manager left the canteen. Adam got up and went after him. He didn't reach Kletzsch's office door with its glass cutout until he had just closed it behind him. He waited until Kletzsch had sat down in his chair and then knocked. The VEB boss waved him in.

"Hedman, hello, what is it? You're not going to tell me you don't have time to help look for our Anna, are you?"

He stopped in the open doorway.

"Herr Kletzsch, if you could relieve me of my duty, I would be very grateful."

"Oh, duty. It's not a duty, Hedman. We do it because we like to help. That's what socialist people are all about. Helping where help is needed. Don't you think so, Hedman?"

"Of course, of course. But it would still be good if I were relieved of this socialist help today."

"You are never released from this, how shall I say, socialist brotherly service. That applies permanently, you understand? Besides, your girlfriend will be able to wait a little longer for you after all," Kletzsch said, smiling. "Or better yet, she'll just come along."

Kletzsch knew that he had no girlfriend.

"It's not my girlfriend that is waiting for me, Herr Kletzsch."

"What is it, then?"

He thought about what reasons he could give. His own suffering was the safest bet. "You know, I'm not doing so well," said Adam.

Kletzsch tightened his mouth. "What am I listening to, Hedman? An important part of the collective is missing, and you say you feel a little sick, is that right? One might think you have no idea what it means when even one cog in the machine is missing. Because then nothing runs at all. Do you understand that? Then the machine is broken."

"I understand that. Of course."

"Look."

"But ..."

"Hedman, you're standing here in front of me, looking like life in bloom. You can still babble quite well. I think there's nothing physically wrong with you."

Adam wanted to start speaking again. Kletzsch's eyes narrowed to slits.

"Listen, Hedman. You show up at the factory gate at the end of your shift like everyone else. Or do you want a note in your employee file about the disintegration of the collective?"

Adam nodded and left. He'd have to tackle his new plan later in the evening, he thought and closed the office door behind him. When had he stopped making up irresistible excuses? Kletzsch had handled the situation better than he had. The last few days had done him no good. Prepared became impulsive. Smart became stupid. There was only the worker Adam Hedman left. And he would take part in the search operation like any other good citizen of the GDR.

He got back to work as he had already wasted enough time. Now they even started to stop him from shoveling coal. There's a wrench in the works. He went to the coal pile, took his tool in hand, and began shoveling. The loads dragged on. The time did not want to pass. His legs became lazier and lazier, his arms weaker and weaker. He felt the tension draining from his body. Like a balloon losing air.

It was not even noon when he saw the VEB manager coming out of the factory gate. He had two Vopos in tow.

What had they come up with this time, Adam asked himself and threw the shovel into the coal. Either way, the seventeen loads were not going to be possible today.

Surrendering to his fate, he put his hands in the pockets of his overalls and waited for the men. He breathed in the icy air that mixed with the coal dust and tasted bitter. In his head, a thought repeated prayerfully. I'm just a cog in the wheel. I'm just a cog in the wheel. I'm just …

The three men had reached him. Kletzsch stood up next to the coal lorry and looked sternly. Behind him stood the two Vopos. Adam hated the Volkspolizei. Always the same guys. Authoritarian and flabby, pale and power-hungry in equal measure. Not even the color of their uniforms could decide what they were. The color of green vomit or grey puke. The taller of the two had three silver stars on the epaulets framed by a wide silver stripe. The shorter one had a thin silver stripe with a thin silver line running orthogonally to it. *Oberwachtmeister* and *Wachtmeister*, the sergeant and his constable. On second thought, he didn't hate them. They were more of a nuisance, like mosquitoes on a balmy summer evening. Except that it wasn't a summer evening. It was a damn cold day in November. And these pests could not simply be dealt with by the flat of one's hand.

He saw that a crowd of workers had gathered at the gate, anxiously waiting to see what would happen next.

Kletzsch turned to the policemen. "That's him, worker Adam Hedman."

Adam did not move.

"The gentlemen from the Volkspolizei want to ask you a few questions, Hedman."

Adam didn't make a face. "What's it about?"

The policemen stepped forward. The taller of the two opened his mouth first. "We'll discuss that with you at the station."

"We can do that here, too, can't we?"

"That's not your decision," the smaller one said.

The taller one took him by the arm and pulled him along. He thought for a moment whether he should fight back. Should his colleagues get a little show after all?

Adam tore himself away. "I want to know right now what I'm being charged with."

The Vopos stopped and held their hands placatingly in front of their bodies.

"Herr Hedman, just come with me, and we'll sort everything out quietly."

The policemen tried to grab him again, but he evaded them.

"I can walk by myself."

Again they let go of him.

The smaller one turned to the factory gate and noticed that they had spectators. "Herr Hedman, we can do this with handcuffs as well."

"Won't be necessary. Like I said, I can walk on my own."

He went to the car, the two men followed. The VEB boss had not moved from the spot.

The police headquarters was located in the old town, not three hundred yards from his apartment. It was housed in a gray building from the turn of the century. The plaster was peeling off the brick wall. Remnants of this plaster were found on the paved sidewalk over which the Vopos took him to the station. Just to the left of the walkway, the guard went off. The two cops disappeared behind the counter. They sat him down on a wooden bench. On the opposite wall, he looked at a saying that had been neatly painted on. It had to be something like the oath of service of the Volkspolizei.

I swear that, without sparing my strength, even at the risk of my life, I will protect the socialist society, state and legal order, socialist property, the personhood, rights, and personal property of citizens from criminal attacks. Should I nevertheless break this solemn oath of mine, I shall be punished by the laws of our Republic.

He was curious to know if they really intended to protect his socialist personhood and how they would do that. The constable came back with a key in his hand.

"Well, come with me," he said, walking down the hall. "Ever been here before?"

He answered in the negative, wondering whether this was a trick question or if the constable was just trying to make conversation. He stopped in front of a wooden door and opened it with the key. Inside were a square table and three chairs. Two behind and one in front. These were the only pieces of furniture. There were no pictures on the walls or clever mottoes here.

"Go ahead and sit down there. The comrade inspector will be here in a minute."

Adam took a seat and waited. When no one showed up after five minutes, he stood up and stretched his legs. He went to the door and found that it could only be opened from the outside. He went to the window, which was painted opaque, and turned the handle. Also locked. So Adam sat down again, stretching his legs, and let his mind wander.

He must have already traveled several miles of these circles in his brain when the door finally opened. The inspector came in. A thin figure, languid eyes, redness in the cheesy, clean-shaven skin of his face. Not a pretty sight. The man sat down behind the table. He placed the file he had with him on the table directly in front of Adam. The man looked at it for a moment and then opened the file.

"We've had your file sent to us, Herr Hedman. You don't exactly have what you'd call a clean slate."

Adam didn't really know what the file would say himself. But he knew that his stretch in prison would always make him a suspect. No matter in what regard. If someone had stolen a piece of chewing gum in Angermünde, he would have been the first one to be arrested. Even more so regarding the disappearance of a young woman.

The policeman received no reaction and continued to leaf through the file. The kind of turning of the pages when you already knew exactly what information was on them. Just as if the policeman was about to reveal a big secret that would put Adam behind bars forever.

"Didn't think one like you existed," the inspector said.

He looked at Adam again. And again there was no reaction.

"You're quite the Dean Reed."

The policeman alluded to the US musician who had settled in the GDR. An exotic phenomenon in a country from which everyone else fled.

"I can't sing, though."

This time there was no reaction from the inspector.

"And the only instrument I used to have some mastery of is the piano. I've never played the guitar, for example."

The policeman wasn't in the mood for this form of humor. Especially not from a crime suspect who had to answer his questions thoughtfully and honestly and otherwise behave humbly.

He thought about all the things that were not in the file about him. Nothing about his motives for coming to the GDR as a US citizen, about his entanglements with the legal organs of this state, or why he was fluent in German. He concluded that there must be two files on him. One for the ordinary patrolman like the one sitting in front of him and one that was treated as classified information. So secret that even a big shot of the MfS like Friedrich Stahl had no access to it.

"You know why you're here?"

"Because you brought me here?"

The man's mouth remained pinched shut into a thin line. He looked again at the document in front of him on the table. "Until recently incarcerated at the Naumburg/ Saale correctional facility."

"That's right."

"Almost seven years."

The man looked at him thoughtfully. "You put a colleague in the hospital."

"Wasn't a colleague of mine."

"I mean another member of the Volkspolizei."

"I see. That's right. It was a colleague of yours, not mine."

That was apparently his only offense on record. It made sense. Everything else was the responsibility of the state security rather than the police service. He noticed that the man was not carrying a pistol. Was it a precautionary measure because he had a dangerous ex-con in front of him or merely official protocol?

In another state, Adam would be a celebrity, or at least well known. A personality recognized on the street, with a name used with awe in justice-loving circles. But because there was no free press and no independent judiciary, no one knew his name, and no one knew who he was. Not even the policeman in a provincial precinct who had requested his file. And around here, the justice-loving circles were small and kept silent. He lived incognito, although he was one of the most hated persons of the GDR regime. Fortunately for him, they underestimated him beyond measure. Blinded by the naivety of his actions at the time. But that was not going to happen to him for a second time.

The Americans had a saying for it: Fool me once, shame on you. Fool me twice, shame on me. And he didn't want to be the clown in his own story.

Adam had no intention of explaining to the man how it had come to breaking the policeman's jaw. He also didn't want to explain to him that he would have liked to beat him to death on that day over seven years ago because he had felt that it would have been the only appropriate reaction.

So he said only one thing. "Released on good behavior."

The inspector shook his head and cleared his throat. "Herr Hedman, where were you on the evening of November 6, 1987?"

"Friday, you mean? That's when I was here in the middle of town helping to put out the church fire."

"And after that?"

"Well, we were busy all night, into the wee hours of the morning."

"Witnesses claim to have observed something else. You reportedly walked away from the location you described at exactly 9:34 pm."

"Whether it was exactly that time of day, I can't tell you. But once I went home briefly. But I was gone for ten minutes at most. Maybe the person who noticed me leaving was gone by then. So, I mean, when I came back."

"Wasn't gone."

Adam thought about how to get an alibi for the night Anna had disappeared and he then had a chase with the police. He searched his memory for allies and found a single one he could reasonably trust.

"Peter Heyer, my colleague Peter Heyer, can attest to that."

He hoped that he had not put Heyer in the line of fire by doing so.

The inspector made a mental note. "All right, we'll check on that in due course. Where were you last weekend?"

He was relieved. Finally a question he could answer. And people of the highest rank who could testify to his whereabouts. "I was invited to a friend's house."

"The entire weekend?"

"Yes, I was there through the night. From Saturday to Sunday. I didn't get home until the evening."

"And what are the names of these friends?"

"I think they would prefer to remain unnamed."

"Herr Hedman, I must urgently inform you that you are suspected of having caused the disappearance of the worker Anna Sievers. In case of violation, the Volkspolizei of the GDR will place you in preventive detention for as long as the case requires."

"But you have to promise not to tell anyone."

"I'm not going to promise you anything. Go ahead and tell me."

"All right, I was invited to Herr Friedrich Stahl's house."

"I assume you don't mean the comrade from the Ministry of State Security."

"Yes, yes, that's who I mean."

The inspector said nothing. He looked at the file again, leafed through it, and then looked at him again. He could not yet decide whether he had to take the statements seriously. "There's no room for that kind of humor here. Think about where you've been. Until then, my colleague will take you to the holding cell."

"I already told you."

Immediately, the door opened, and the constable came in. Apparently, the inspector had pressed a button under the table that signaled the waiting Vopo in front of the door to go in. Adam had to stand and take his arms behind his back. The cuffs snapped shut. He was taken down the long corridor and had to take the steps down to the basement. Here it did not look like a police station, more like a prison.

The little constable unlocked the iron-barred wooden door. Behind it was a tiny cell with a cot and a stool. Moisture had seeped into the concrete floor, leaving circular stains. Under a grate, a neon tube burned on the ceiling, bathing the tiny room in glaring light. The door was closed behind him. The light continued to burn. He lay down on the cot, crossed his legs, and breathed into the silence. Again he was kept from everything that was important to him.

Chapter 4: FOXHOLE

November 10, 1987
Angermünde
District Frankfurt/Oder
German Democratic Republic

Adam woke up. The light was still on. He tried to estimate the hours that had passed since his admission. But he was not able to make a reliable statement. Adam had lost his sense of time. His injury had caused his body to keep taking sleep, which he needed to recover. He felt a little better. He straightened up on the cot, the pain no longer boring so profoundly into his neural pathways. His dreams hung like a haze in his brain. Vivid fantasies that just wouldn't go away. He saw a young man, almost a boy, who had come to a foreign country with ideals. Who had met a young woman. Who had built a life together with her. Who had a wonderful son who had his eyes and her laughter. Who had been able to locate his ancestors.

Then the memory of the dream left him, and he realized that it was not a fantasy but just the mental continuation of all the things that had happened to him. Full of optimism, without reservations. Except that there wasn't much left of his family, apart from dim memories. As he felt the hatred rising inside him, he jumped up and paced through the cell. Five steps forward, five steps back. He had to get out of here. They couldn't hold him back any longer.

Finally, Adam heard footsteps, the rattling of keys on the lock of the cell door. Hours must have passed, which he had spent wandering through the few square feet of his cell. The door opened. Two Vopos, whom he had not seen before, came in. The same expressionless faces as all the others. Maybe he had even seen them before and couldn't remember because the eye couldn't latch on to anything remarkable. The only difference from the other Vopos was that they had taken off their uniform jackets. One ordered him to turn around. The other put handcuffs on him. A good sign. They would take him upstairs and then let him go. The matter was settled for him. If they had had anything else in mind for him, it would have been without shackles on his hands. He had been there several times before when prisoners were beaten up. And each time, their handcuffs had been removed beforehand. Otherwise, there would be bruises on the wrists, and these would be an unmistakable sign that a prisoner had been mistreated. Wounds or hematomas on the body or face were not so easy to prove as mistreatment. Since this was not only against human dignity but also against any prisoner rights, it was thus actionable in court.

Another man entered the cell. Young, not thirty years old. So handsome that he seemed out of place in this foul place. Black hair, healthy complexion, snow-white teeth. Like an actor who came on a movie set. The actor sat down on the cot and took out a pack of Cabinets. He lit a cigarette and took a deep drag. When he blew out the smoke, he grinned, his eyes narrowing to slits as he did so. Adam felt a chill run down his spine.

The two Vopos rolled up the sleeves of their shirts. Before Adam could even become aware of the new situation, he saw the first blow coming at him. He dodged it and was only grazed on the cheek. The next blow hit home. His upper lip became warm. He tasted blood in his mouth, running from his nose. Again and again, he ducked away. Again and again, the fists pounded him. The man on the cot laughed and laughed and laughed. The beaters were out of breath, sweating, and their hair was falling in their faces. Beating him was hard work, and their lanky statures couldn't do much against him. They worked their butts off on him. Except for a few lacerations, they couldn't hurt him much. They could barely raise their fists, their blows growing weaker and weaker. He laughed from his bloodied mouth. They needed to come at him with bigger calibers to wear him down. Adam was known to be able to take a beating. He wouldn't drop until his life was over. But they didn't know that and continued their pitiful attempts.

The smoking man seemed to have seen enough and got up from the cot, threw the cigarette down, and kicked it out with one foot. He took his time, enjoying the way the cigarette butt was crushed under his sole. Meanwhile, the other two gathered behind Adam's back and held him. The man turned to him, grinned again, and then, without a second thought, struck him twice in quick succession. Adam doubled over in pain. He lost his breath. His knees went weak. The man had hit him first in the spleen and then in the kidney. There was a good chance Adam would be pissing blood for the next few days. But he was pleased that the man hadn't picked the other side of his body with the broken ribs. Adam sank to his knees, and the man walked out of the cell. The other two followed on his heels, insulted him as antisocial, and left the cell again.

Shortly after, the two Volkspolizei officers came in again and freed him from his shackles. One of them had a bucket and a mop with him.

"Clean up your mess. We're not your cleaning crew, are we?" he said and placed the bucket clattering in the middle of his blood splatters.

Then they walked out of the cell, and Adam thought about what had just happened. He had misjudged the situation. They obviously didn't care that he would get bruises on his wrists from the handcuffs. The fact that they put up with it spoke for itself. They had no consequences to fear. Who should he have complained to? There was nobody to deal with it. There were no human rights lawyers in Angermünde who could bring a case of police violence to court. And even if there were, the judges would make sure that the state's line was followed. And the state was infallible, the individual only a cog in the collective. A cog that had to run like clockwork and was not allowed to complain when the organs of the state damaged it.

Shortly after, he was released. Adam did not have to sign and was not given a document attesting to his whereabouts. According to the official reading, he had never set foot in the police station.

Exhausted, Adam walked down the street in the old town—and saw Evelyn Sievers coming towards him from a distance. She waved when she saw him. He raised his hand. No greeting, just the confirmation that he had seen her.

"Adam, what did they do to you?"

"Walked into a door."

"The Vopos did this, didn't they?"

Adam's silence was answer enough. She nodded and did not inquire further. Yesterday's arrest and return from the police station in that state told the whole story.

"You live in a pretty run-down neighborhood," Evelyn said just before they reached his front door.

"This is the old town," he said, pushing open the heavy wooden door.

She followed him. "But this is all just shabby here. Why don't you live out in the modern house estate like we do?"

"I don't like it there too much."

She had to know that the apartment had been assigned to him.

"You actually wanted to see me?" he asked, stopping in the doorway.

"You could go ahead and say thank you."

"For what?"

"Well, that I got you out of there."

"And how did you do that?"

"I went and told them you helped put out the fire with us all night long."

"But that's not true."

"I know you had nothing to do with it, the Anna thing."

"I didn't. Thanks."

"Can I come in?"

"Is it really that important? They didn't let me crash. I'm dog-tired. Otherwise, tomorrow we can—"

"It's important."

He made room in the doorway. After that night, he had no more strength to stand in her way or to look for excuses as to why she could not come in.

"Thank you," she said, slipping between him and the doorframe.

He closed the front door. She stopped in the middle of the entryway and looked around.

She turned once in a circle. "Man, in contrast to this it looks like a mansion from the outside."

Evelyn was right. Just by the look of it, the house needed renovation. The plaster was crumbling, and the facade hadn't been repainted in decades. Once you were inside, however, you knew it was beyond saving. The inevitable decay peeked out from behind towers of milk crates. Bricks lay on the broken floor. Walls had collapsed and were provisionally supported by wooden planks. In addition, it smelled musty. To the right was the stairway. Of the three steps that had once been, there was still precisely one. He pointed the way for her. She took the big step and went into the stairwell without any detours. There had not been a door protecting the stairway from the cold for a long time.

He passed Evelyn on the four steps that led to his apartment on the mezzanine floor. He unlocked the rickety wooden door to his apartment, which was secured with a rusty padlock.

There was no hallway. After entering, they stood in the middle of a large room combination dining room and kitchen. In the corner stood a cast-iron stove. Next to it was another door that separated the living area from the chamber.

"Wow, it's cold here. You don't have a toilet here, do you?"

"Nah, it's through the yard."

"Well, it's not that urgent," she said, sitting down at the table.

The table's wood was barely visible, so many books and notes were spread out on it. If this had been a movie scene from an imperialist foreign country, he would now receive the total empathy of the female personality. Evelyn would have sacrificially cared for him, dabbing his face with water and tending to his wounds. He would have felt her warmth, and perhaps they would have ended up in each other's arms. But the real-life Evelyn paid no attention to his injuries, and he preferred that. Adam hated pity.

"I'll leave my jacket on. Didn't you heat?" she asked.

"Forgotten. But I don't need it that warm either."

"It's so cold here, though, you'd think you were a polar bear."

She looked at the table and nodded briefly in the direction of the books. "Didn't take you for such a reader."

Adam was already folding and stacking the books and arranging the papers.

"Don't bother. I don't mind. Do you have any coffee?" she asked.

"Nope."

"Tea?"

"I could offer you hot water."

"Nah, don't bother, then."

He sat down across the table from her.

"Why are you here, anyway?"

"I need your help. Because of Anna. I'm sure you've noticed that we're not getting anywhere like this."

"I'll help you with the search if I can. Up until now, a lot of things always got in the way."

He didn't tell her about his gunshot wound, and the fact that he had been otherwise occupied yesterday was written all over his face.

"I know, but I don't think that what we're doing is working out. Going door to door like this, asking all our friends, looking in parks and the woods. You know, anything we do without a real plan."

"Don't you think she'll just show up again?"

"No."

"But this isn't the first time she's been gone for a few days, is it?"

"Yes, but this time it's different. There is no money missing from my wallet, for starters," she said and smiled.

"And what makes you think I'm right for the job? I'm not exactly the most law-abiding citizen. Ask the cops. You have your friends, Kletzsch ..."

"I can't trust anyone else."

"But we don't really know each other."

"Now, don't be like that."

"Oh, come on ... what about Sebastian? You can trust him. Or Kletzsch? He's quite a terrific helper, isn't he?"

"Well, they're all ..." She continued to speak only after a moment's thought. "They all don't want what's best for Anna," she said and began to cry.

Adam had not seen this emotion coming. He tried to have as little to do with tears in his life as possible. He looked at the sad woman for a moment. Then he stood up. "Evelyn, I really can't help you."

"You're just as much of an asshole as everyone else," she said quietly, then stood up as well and stormed out the door.

Adam did not stop her. Evelyn had left the door open. He locked it again and took a deep breath. Clouds of condensation formed in front of his mouth as he exhaled. He desperately needed to heat. But before that, he had to clean up. He had become dissolute. If the People's Police had searched his house, it wouldn't have taken much for them to uncover his murder plot. He would have been sure of an interview with the Stasi. And what would have happened then, he did not even want to imagine. He gathered up all the notes, maps, and documents and stuffed them into his backpack. They had to be put away. Sleep would have to wait.

Adam's destination was five miles outside of Angermünde. No trains or buses went there. From the nearest bus stop, it was a half-hour hike across boggy meadows, through a spruce grove, and over a hilltop to a small lake. A stone's throw from the body of water, two birch trees stood like twins in the barren landscape. Adam took the backpack from his shoulders and placed it at the base of one of the two leafless trees. Here he knew every square inch. That helped him find the folding spade in the brush in the darkness, and he got to work. He had to dig into the frozen soil amid the birch trees to a depth of about three feet. After twice the time it usually took him, he came upon a metal chest. Kneeling, he moved to his backpack and emptied the contents into a smaller box he had brought with him. Then he placed the documents from his apartment in the chest, closed it, and buried it again. It was done. He took a deep breath and rested for a moment, propped up on his knees.

"What are you doing?"

He heard a woman's voice that sounded strangely muffled. The woman had to be close. From his kneeling position, he extended his right leg in a flash. He hit the woman in the leg. She fell on her back. He jumped on her and pinned her arms to the ground with his hands.

"Adam, you're killing me," the woman screamed.

He loosened his grip and pulled the scarf from her face. It was Evelyn. He had to make a decision. And he had to do it quickly. Could he take the risk of letting her live? He weighed the odds. Could she have seen something important? Would it jeopardize his plan, and as a result, would he never get justice? Adam got off her and remained sitting next to her with his legs bent. He didn't know if

Evelyn would foil his plans. But that uncertainty wasn't enough to kill her.

"That was close. It could have ended differently, you know?" he said.

She sobbed. He slowly blew the air out of his lungs.

"You hurt me," she said, holding her left hand.

"Let me see," he said, checking the joint.

She cried out.

"It's not broken. Should be good in a couple of days. You'll need to ice it," he said.

He stood up and extended his hand to her.

"What are you doing here?" he asked.

"I've been following you. I just wanted to know what you do."

She reached out a hand to him, and he pulled her up.

"What is all this? What are you doing with it?" she asked.

"With what?"

"All that stuff?"

He was already regretting that he had not taken her out of circulation.

"Trust me. You don't want to know."

She pondered. "Look, if you help me, it will be our secret."

She held her wrist.

"Stay where you are for a second," he said.

She stopped and watched him dig out the box again. Inside, he found a first aid kit.

"Let's immobilize your injury."

He put a bandage around her wrist.

"So, do we have a deal?" she asked.

"All right," he said, thinking about what she had seen and what she couldn't have seen.

He hoped that she would not find her way to this place again. He had to look for a new hiding place for the metal box. And he had to do it the same night. But first, he had to bring the sister of the missing girl back to Angermünde. Again, sleep had to wait. And again, he could not do what he had intended to do. It was not the first time in the past few days that Adam felt cheated by fate.

Chapter 5: FIBER CEMENT BOARDS

November 14, 1987
Angermünde
District Frankfurt/Oder
German Democratic Republic

When Evelyn regained consciousness, she looked as if she had climbed out of a black hole. Anita, Maria, and Susanne were standing around her sickbed. Adam stood a little apart, almost still at the door. His presence seemed out of place. The friends had called him because Evelyn had kept calling his name when she was admitted to the hospital. As if in fever dreams. The other three beds in the room were empty. The female colleagues smiled at her. The kind of strained smile when no one feels like smiling. Evelyn wore a bandage around her head and had a deep blue hematoma where her face had hit the floor.

"Why am I here?" she asked.

"You must have fainted. The Vopos said you let the fiber cement boards come at you way too fast," Anita said, breaking into a laugh.

Tears welled up in Evelyn's eyes. She seemed to remember again that she had been at the police station and had fainted afterward. "Anna?"

The woman did not withstand Evelyn's gaze and looked to the floor.

"Would you like a glass of water?" asked Susanne, walking over to the nightstand where there was a carafe of water.

Evelyn nodded, took the water glass, and drank a sip. Susanne stroked her arm.

"Anna will be back. I'm sure of it," Evelyn said and took another sip.

The women said nothing. Anita sat down on the bed with Evelyn and took her hands with both of hers. Appeasement and containment at the same time.

"I would have noticed it if she had been unwell," Evelyn said.

"Oh, Evchen, we know how bad it is for you. For us, too. We can't understand it either," said Anita, using a familiar form of the name Evelyn.

Evelyn withdrew from her hands. "She certainly didn't do anything to herself," she said, emphasizing every syllable. As if the facts would certainly convince her otherwise.

The women were silent. Maria pulled up a chair and sat down next to Evelyn on the bed. Susanne did the same.

"I just know. I'm her big sister. I know stuff like that. I've always looked out for her."

"That's quite normal, Evchen. It takes a little while for it to sink in. When my grandmother died, I didn't believe it first either. It took a few days. It's really quite normal," said Maria.

Anita nodded at her. "You don't know what's going on inside a person. Gosh, sometimes you don't even really know what's going on inside of yourself. Isn't that right?" she said, looking around.

Susanne and Maria nodded vigorously. Evelyn stared through them. She hadn't paid any attention to him yet. He was glad of that.

Susanne put a hand next to Evelyn's arm. "Anita is right. And you also have to see that it's not your fault. It's always the decision of the person who makes it. Maybe it was better that way for her. You don't know that."

Evelyn wasn't listening. "What time is it?" she asked.

"A little after seven," Anita said.

"Why is it so late already? Did they operate on me?"

"No, why would they operate on you?" asked Anita, looking at her colleagues for help.

"You were just in shock. It just took a little while for you to wake up," Maria said.

"We were informed by Kletzsch that you had been taken to the hospital. He could only tell us that you had fainted. But now we are here. Are you feeling better or should we call the doctor?" asked Maria.

"Yes, that's a good idea," Susanne said.

"No, I don't need a doctor."

"Oh, Evchen, this must all be so hard for you," Anita said.

"Nothing happened. None of what they say is the truth. They're lying. All of them."

"I think we better call the doctor. You're in denial about Anna, am I right?" said Anita.

Evelyn's gaze darkened. "Out. I want you to leave. All of you."

Maria stretched out a hand toward her. "Evchen, you have to understand. Anna was sometimes very overexcited. You've heard more than once about those who appear to the outside world as if nothing is wrong when they're in a particularly bad place. You have to digest all that now."

Evelyn slapped her away. "Get out of here! Just get out of here, all of you, I said."

"Now you're acting crazy," Anita said.

"We'd better leave you alone now," Susanne said and stood up.

"You should fuck off."

Anita shook her head. The women left the hospital room. Evelyn burst into tears after her friends left the hospital room. Hastily, Adam also seized the opportunity to get out of the situation.

Adam had a ritual that gave him pleasure. Every evening, he watched first the official news program of the GDR's state television, then the most important news of the FRG. The differences could not be overlooked. Many things were not reported in the *Aktuelle Kamera* on DDR 1 that took up a lot of space in the *Tagesschau* on ARD and vice versa. And if they were the same topics, then from two different perspectives. Watching both programs, one after the other, played tricks on one's mind. After a short time, one no longer knew what to believe. Adam was not the only one in the GDR exposed to these two truths, and so millions of GDR citizens concocted their own version in their heads. Or they did it quite differently and believed in nothing at all. It was different with him. He no longer believed in the big ideology, the socialist idea. But at least he still had something to believe in. Himself and his plan. Even if he had been held back from it again and again and had been set back perhaps by months, if not years. He stood up and poured himself a sip of hot water into an enamel mug. It was as cold inside as it was outside. Adam still hadn't gotten any coals.

There was a knock. Evelyn was standing in front of the door. She took a drag on a cigarette and blew out the smoke. The woman did not look well. He wondered why she had been released from the hospital in this condition. He hadn't expected to see Evelyn again before the start of the new week. Adam had calculated that his problems would have evaporated by then, her blackmailing him into looking for her sister. What did the woman want, and why was she dressed so eccentrically on this gloomy evening? Evelyn's red anorak made a harsh contrast to her green pants and purple bobble cap.

"I'm glad you're here," she said, walking past him into the eat-in kitchen.

"Where else would I be?" he said, looking her up and down.

"It's freezing again today. And I can see that you still haven't got any coal, have you?"

He shook his head and sat back down at the table.

"Well, I can't offer you anything."

"Leave it, that's not what I'm here for ... well, at least your face doesn't look quite so battered anymore."

"Have they released you already?"

"Sure. I wanted to get out of there as quickly as possible."

Unlike most people, he liked hospitals: the order, the atmosphere of bustling professionalism, the polished floors in which one was reflected. No comparison with the moldy hole he called home.

"What exactly happened?" he asked.

"Not that much."

"But enough to put you in the hospital."

"Yeah, kind of. Shit happens, as they say."

"You fainted and slapped the floor."

She took a drag on her cigarette and made a throwaway gesture. "Nonsense. Now, pay some attention. It was all rather strange at the police station. First of all, I was called straight from work to the station. Everything had to happen very quickly, and then I sit there and wait for hours. Can you imagine that? An imposition. At some point, I asked if they had anything important to tell me. They did, or at least they thought they did. But first I had to wait again. Shithole. Then finally, I was let in front of some newbies. Just out of the police academy, I guess. They acted stupidly, I can tell you. Then they started to talk and didn't really know how to say it. At the end of the day, they finally tell me that they think it's possible that Anna killed herself. They weren't so sure, I noticed right away. I cut them down to size, I can tell you that much."

He did not know if he could believe Evelyn's statements. Her descriptions did not match the statements of her friends and certainly not her earlier actions. She was not the type who had anything to say at the police station.

He was trying to get the truth from her. "What did they tell you at the police station?"

"Only what I already know. That Anna has disappeared."

"Nothing more?"

"And that they think Anna killed herself."

She did not say anything more about it.

"And what do you say to that?"

"Nothing. Because I don't think anything of that. I told them that Anna was happy. That I know that because I'm her big sister. And that I should be the first to know when something like that happens, I told them. Then they didn't say anything at all anymore."

"But the police believe Anna killed herself."

"Think so."

"And why?"

"They said something about her personality profile."

"That's all?"

"No."

"Do you know the names of those who told you about Anna?" he asked.

"It all happened so fast. I can't remember anymore. It's not that important."

"Let's do it again from the top."

She was breathing heavily. "I can't do it all over again."

"Try it."

"All right."

"So the police are assuming that Anna killed herself."

"Yes. But there is no body. And they said that they are searching. But, for example, if she threw herself into a lake, then it may be that the body won't be found for a while, they said. I'd have to wait."

"But you don't think that's true?"

"No."

"And then what happened?"

"Well, then I sat around all day with the Kripo and didn't eat or drink anything."

"So you were with the Kripo and not the regular police?"

"Yes. And, of course, my blood sugar was low. And then when I come out into the cold, my legs gave way."

"Strange story."

"I think so, too. But one thing is clear. They don't know anything at all at the Kripo," she said.

The Kriminalpolizei, abbreviated to Kripo, was the criminal investigation agency within the police forces.

"Why is this actually a matter for the Kripo if it was suicide? Wouldn't the Volkspolizei have been enough? I mean, no crime, right?"

"I'm really not interested in who's in charge there now and who's not."

Evelyn rummaged in her purse and pulled out a stack of paper towels. She stuck the burning cigarette between her lips. Adam had an idea where her intentions with him lay.

"Here, we're working through all that now. I already have clues."

"About what?"

"Who took Anna."

That was it, the reality that Evelyn had set up for herself. So she believed in a kidnapping. Adam could imagine several more reasons for a girl disappearing.

"Are those towels for drying your hands?" he asked.

"Sure. They had these in the hospital. That's where I put it all together and wrote it down."

He looked at her and said nothing.

"You don't believe me, do you, Adam?"

"Does it matter?"

She spread the rough paper towels on the table. "Look, I've written down all the people who could have done this. We need to interview all of them."

"Do you need me for that?"

"Not again, Adam. We've already discussed this. Besides, I don't think you really have a choice."

She was right about that. He couldn't make any mistakes if he wanted to successfully carry out the last plan he still had in his life. Adam was at her mercy.

"Evelyn, seriously, when the police are saying it was suicide ..."

"What then?"

"Have you ever heard any official institution admit that people are killing themselves?"

"What do you mean?"

"Everyone knows that politicians don't admit that there are many suicides in the GDR because it looks bad towards the class enemy. The collective and all that. Do you understand?"

In a worldwide comparison, the GDR took a top position in suicides. Around three thousand seven hundred people took their own lives each year. Fifteen times more attempted it. That was about one and a half times as many as on the other side of the Wall in the FRG and thus a taboo subject for the GDR leadership, which liked to demonstrate the superiority of the socialist system over the capitalist one.

"Oh, nonsense. Not Anna," she said.

He tried to counter Evelyn's thoughts with logic. "But then the kidnapper would have to be in cahoots with the police."

"Why is that?"

"Well, because—"

In vain. She did not let him finish. "None of that matters. I know Anna is alive and I will find her. And you're going to help me. We're going with my system. I've got it all figured out."

Adam gave it one more try. "She could have also fled somewhere, to East Berlin maybe."

"Fled from what?"

"Angermünde, ghosts of the past. I don't know, boredom?"

"Boredom. Don't be cruel."

Adam took a look at Evelyn's notes. On each paper towel, she had written down a name. In addition, the relationship between the respective person and her sister. Adam couldn't keep track of how many paper towels there were. So far, she had shown him six or seven. He didn't know how they were going to work through this list. And if he played the game and thought about it, he found there was still one name missing from the list.

"No, that's nonsense, Adam," Evelyn said, lighting a new cigarette with the embers of the old one.

"Is it?"

"I've known Kletzsch for years."

"So?"

"Yes, he's an old school friend of mine. He wouldn't do anything like that to me."

"Well, if you say so. But I find that Kletzsch had shown interest in Anna from time to time."

"Nah, Adam, give it a rest. It's not Kletzsch. Believe me."

He let her draw him into the vortex of suspicion. Why had he considered another suspect if Evelyn's speculations had no substance anyway?

He took a deep breath, wanting to give reason a voice again. "So suppose we find the man who kidnapped Anna. Where do you think she is, or what did he do with her?"

"I think he kidnapped Anna and is holding her somewhere to do whatever he wants with her there."

"But can't Sebastian, for example, as her boyfriend, do what he wants with her anyway? Or do you think he feels rejected by her?"

"Well, I don't know that. I only know that many men want something from her. And she doesn't want to. And she probably doesn't always want to with Sebastian as well."

"Well, that's not unusual, is it?"

"Exactly. But it's unusual when you can't live with that. And I'm telling you, one of them couldn't live with not being able to get it."

He pondered. "It almost sounds like it could've been anybody but Kletzsch for you?"

"No, you haven't done it either. It's one of the ones on my notes here. One of the six. I thought about it for a long time. I'm sure of it."

"Then why don't you ask Kletzsch to help you?"

"Oh, Adam, don't be like that. You're the only decent guy in all of Angermünde. I've never seen you undress Anna with your eyes."

He was almost flattered. Evelyn was right. All the men were looking at her little sister droolingly. Adam had no idea how it must feel for a girl when grown men are already lining up even though you're still a child. And then with the onset of puberty, everyone just wants to see the woman in you. If men undress you with their eyes at the age of twelve, thirteen, just because nature has given you some breasts, then that must shape the way you look at the world of men, Adam thought.

"I don't know if I'm the only one," he said, "but it's true. I've noticed it too. When did it all start?"

"I think it was always like that, to be honest. You have to grow up fast when your parents die."

"But so did you."

"I was already an adult, at least pretty much. I was the only one there, and I kept her away from everything. She never wanted anything from men or boys. But at some point, it started. Then she realized that she had to participate somehow. But she also got herself into a lot of trouble."

"Why?"

"Well, the usual. She flirted, they gave her presents, but she didn't really want anything from any of them. But you know how it is. If men invest something, they want to be rewarded. And if not ..."

"I see."

She sobbed. "Gosh, Anna was happy after all. Kind of." Then she collected herself again, took a drag from the cigarette, and looked at him piercingly. "So when do we start?"

He tried to buy some more time for himself. By his reckoning, each day brought them closer to the release of the body. "The day after tomorrow," he said.

"You're kidding? We'll start tomorrow at the latest. Better today."

Slowly and audibly, he let the air escape from his lungs. He kept forgetting that Evelyn was serious about the game. What would a real investigator do at this point?

"Okay, Evelyn, listen up. Here's what we're going to do. We're going to Anna's apartment now and have a look around."

Her eyes sparkled. "Adam, that's a great idea."

"Where does Anna live?"

"Just around the corner from my place."

"Well, let's do it."

It seemed to be really cold in his apartment. Evelyn still had her winter jacket and cap on when they left the house and got into her Trabant 601s.

The climate in Evelyn's car was not significantly different from his apartment. Just that the cold and the cigarette smoke were crammed into a smaller space. Anna's apartment was in the new construction area of Angermünde. It was where all the employees of the VEB Gustav Bruhn lived. Except for him. They entered the elevator.

"Tell me why Sebastian was so pissed on Anna's birthday. That wasn't because of Kletzsch, was it? Do you remember?"

"He's always pissed. It's his normal state."

"So it wasn't because of another guy?"

"No, no. She just made that one up to tease Basti."

He nodded and said nothing more about that. They got off the elevator on the fourth floor. Evelyn unlocked the apartment door. Fresh air hit them.

"When were you here the last time?" he asked.

"Before Anna's birthday."

"Seems like somebody just aired the apartment, though."

"Well, I didn't."

"Why don't you see if everything is still the way Anna left it?"

She nodded and walked down the hall.

"You better not touch anything," he said.

She turned to him. "Oh, exciting. I feel like I'm in a movie."

Adam raised his eyebrows. He almost had the impression that she wanted to search just for the adventure or not to be alone in her denial of the truth.

"You can touch something. Just don't move anything around or anything."

"Wasn't planning on it," she said, walking into the living room.

"How many rooms does the apartment have?"

"Two. This one and the bedroom."

"Alright, do you notice anything?"

"Not until now."

"Is it always this neat at her place?" he said, looking around the living room.

It was almost in military order. Nothing was lying around on the sofa, the armchair, and the coffee table. Only one pillow was draped on each end of the couch. The carpet was freshly vacuumed, and the pictures on the wall hung in rows. No photos of friends and family, exclusively landscape photographs.

"Did she take them?" he asked.

"No, I think they're from a magazine."

He moved closer. She was right. In the bottom right corner was the title of the magazine, *Geo*. The photo spread was called *Deutschland ist schön*. And as far as he could see, this Germany was exclusively the FRG. Black Forest, Sylt, Spessart.

"Germany is beautiful," he said, referring to the title of the photo spread.

"Really?" said Evelyn, taking a step toward the framed photographs.

"Could be," she said, shrugging her shoulders.

He looked at her for another moment. She said nothing more about it.

"Where does she keep her things, clothes and stuff?"

"Over there," Evelyn said, making her way to the other room.

A bed. A desk. A chair. There was little furniture in the bedroom.

"Doesn't Sebastian ever sleep here?"

"Why?"

"Because the bed is so small."

"I think they're always at his place."

"Doesn't he still live with his parents?"

"Yes, yes."

Adam went to the desk and opened the drawers. "Did she keep a journal or something?"

"I don't even know."

He found only a few pieces of paper, scribbles, pens. "Where are her clothes?"

"In the hallway."

Adam went back into the hallway and opened a large built-in closet.

"So, what do you expect to get out of looking at her clothes?" she asked him.

"Nothing. But you should check to see if anything is missing."

"How am I supposed to do that?"

"Well, do you notice anything? Any underwear missing? Stuff like that."

Evelyn looked through the piles of underwear, went through undershirts and dresses. She pulled out a black dress.

"What is it?" he asked.

"I've never seen that before."

"So it's new?"

"I can't imagine."

"Then where did she get it?"

She held up the dress sewn with black sequins and showed it to him. It sparkled in the light. Paris in Angermünde.

"What exactly am I supposed to see? I don't know anything about this. Is that made of a special fabric?" Adam asked.

"Nah, check the label."

He looked into the dress. It was from Chanel.

"Must have been expensive. Something like that costs a fortune."

"Someone must have brought her this from the West. Where would you find something like that here?"

She carefully hung the dress back in the closet. "Hey, Adam, I think a few things are missing."

"Like what?"

"Like underwear, bras, pants, whatever one needs every day."

"Are you sure?"

"I think so."

"Maybe she took the clothes to Sebastian's house to spend the night."

"Well, yeah, maybe."

Adam pondered. Evelyn shut the closet doors and went into the kitchen. He followed her.

"Evelyn, what I've been wondering all this time—isn't it unusual for such a young girl to have her own place?"

"I don't know. She applied for one and got it in the end. You know, she's working, after all."

"But with the housing shortage ..."

"She was lucky, I guess."

In the kitchen, the same picture. The kitchen table and two chairs were aligned at right angles, with no used dishes on the table or in the sink. Aseptic. There was only one clue that a human being was living here. There was a note on the refrigerator.

Adam picked up the paper. "Do you know who Miri is?"

"I don't know. If it's a friend of Anna's, then she must be new. Let me see."

He handed her the piece of paper.

"That's on Monday. At seven," she said.

"I guess that must be an appointment. Now we have to find out who Miri is and where she wants to meet her. Maybe she heard something from Anna."

"Yeah, right. Maybe we'll meet Anna there. If she hasn't been kidnapped, it's possible that she ...," Evelyn paused.

"Do you think it could be like last time that she shows up again just like that? But then the Vopos would've been downright clueless to make this baseless—"

She didn't let him finish. She seemed uncomfortable with her own hope. "That's right, you're right. That's nonsense ..."

At first, she wanted to give him back the note. However, after giving it another cursory glance, she decided to let the notice disappear into her pants pocket.

Adam walked toward a sideboard with a record player. "It's not furnished in a particularly modern way."

"She can't afford much, you know. She got everything as a gift or borrowed it."

He bent over the record player. "This too?"

"That's my old one."

"No records?"

"Should be down below."

He crouched down and pushed the doors of the cabinet aside. The entire compartment was filled with records. "Wow, I wouldn't have guessed that."

"There are a lot of old ones of mine in there, too."

He pulled out a disc. "Genesis? They're from the West."

"Yeah, so?"

"Isn't that forbidden?"

"Sometimes I think you are from the moon," she said, taking the record from him, looking at the back. "See, it's from the East."

He reached for the record and looked at it. "That's right, Amiga. That's the name of the record company?"

Evelyn nodded. "Licensed for the GDR."

He closed the record cabinet again.

They had seen everything. It was not much. But it was more than he had expected. The cold air in the apartment, the expensive dress in the closet, and the friend Evelyn hadn't heard of—all of that together didn't add up to a coherent picture. Could it be that Evelyn was right? Had Anna been kidnapped by one of her admirers, who had then covered the traces of his deed? And why hadn't Evelyn been to the apartment since Anna had disappeared?

The girl's sister interrupted his flow of thoughts. "Would you like something to drink? I've gotten thirsty from all this."

"In here? It's kind of weird, isn't it?"

"Well, no, it's my sister after all. Come on, let's make ourselves comfortable."

"All right."

They sat down in the living room. Evelyn poured schnapps and put on a record. Soft synthie sounds glided through the prefab apartment. They toasted each other. He had trouble getting the clear liquid down.

Evelyn didn't seem to face the same problems. She downed the liquor and lit a cigarette. "Nice and warm in such a modern apartment, isn't it?" she said and poured him some more alcohol.

In the meantime, the apartment had been warmed up.

"Tell me, Evelyn, why haven't you been here for such a long time? I mean, Anna was gone. Wasn't it your first idea to come here, to see if she was home? Well, at least, that's what I would've done."

She drained the next shot glass and took a drag on her cigarette. "Under normal circumstances, you'd be right. But because we went searching for her right away, I didn't even think about it. We were all so busy that we didn't even notice."

"Because of the burning church?"

"Exactly."

"And then?"

"Then we planned to toast to her birthday. A small group, just friends."

"And that fell through because she couldn't be found?"

"Yes, she only said goodbye to me for a short time because she wanted to change, and then she wanted to come back to me. She never showed up, though."

"And then?"

"Then I went here. But I didn't go upstairs because Sebastian was already coming towards me. He told me she wasn't at home. After that, I was busy looking for her."

"So it could be that she was there after all, but Sebastian was lying?"

"Well, theoretically, yes."

They talked and drank. Evelyn smoked one cigarette after another. In his former life, he would never have bothered with someone like Evelyn. She had no discernible ideals. She didn't live for a better society. She made the best of what life had given her. In the past, he had despised such people. Now he understood her and felt. The arrogance of a man who had always been able to determine his own life. No duties, only desires.

It was getting late. Evelyn lay tired on the couch. The alcohol had done its work. She looked at him. When she realized he had noticed, she quickly looked away again. But there was so much hope and familiarity in her gaze that he felt understood and caught at the same time. He had been wondering for some time why Evelyn had chosen him of all people. It had begun right after he had started at the VEB. She had greeted him in a friendly and familiar way, almost like a buddy. And he hadn't thought anything of it. But now he realized that Evelyn had recognized him. She must have seen his dismissive shell for what it was, protection from further injury. She must have sensed that they both shared a similar fate even though she could not have known it. Both were alone. Both clung to a person with their imagination, not knowing if therein lay their salvation. She believed that her sister had been taken and was still alive. He thought that the man's death would provide him peace of mind. Her pain was his pain and vice versa. He felt connected to her as he had not felt connected to anyone in a long time.

He stood up and went to the record player. "Now I'll choose something for us."

Adam bent down to the records and pulled out one after the other. He got stuck on a disc. On the cover, three stuffed animals were depicted. A dog, a duck, and an indeterminate brown creature. He stood up and looked at the back. "Who is *Pittiplatsch*?"

She looked at him in amazement. As if she had finally seen what had always been there, but only now was she abruptly aware of it. "You're not from around here."

Some signs that one sent out made it unmistakably clear to others that one did not belong. It was as if a Belgian didn't know *Tintin* or an American didn't know *Felix the Cat*.

"Who are you? Nobody who is from the East doesn't know *Pittiplatsch*," she said with wide-open eyes.

"What do you mean?"

His throat tightened.

Tears welled up in her eyes. "Adam, who are you?"

He stared at her, feeling caught again. She had a nose like a bloodhound. He was playing for time. She could barely keep her eyes open. The realization that he wasn't who he claimed to be had given her another boost of wakefulness. But now she was fighting sleep. She tried to fix him for a moment longer, then fell asleep. And he realized he would have told her anything. To finally be able to share his experiences with someone else. And so he talked about his childhood, his break with the old life and his new life, his arrival in the GDR, and everything that followed. When he was finished, he looked at the sleeping Evelyn and carried her to Anna's bed. He watched her as she slowly exhaled and inhaled again. She looked peaceful and was beautiful in her own way. He felt that he wanted to help her. His own operation had ground to a halt anyway. And after years of waiting, what did a few more days matter? Until the Kripo came up with the body, he also wanted to give himself entirely to the conviction that Anna was still alive. Hope was a nobler impulse than revenge. Then he went back to the living room and listened to the music, letting his mind wander until he fell asleep as well.

Adam woke up in the middle of the night. He had a hangover. Another wasted day, but it didn't feel like one. He felt more sense in his life than he had the previous evening. He got up and sat down in front of the record cabinet. Adam browsed through the albums and pulled out some records. A-ha, Silly, Münchener Freiheit, City, Depeche Mode, Undertones, the Ramones, Karat, Bruce Springsteen, Madonna, the Cure. It was a wild mix of East and West, pop and rock, beautiful and awful. Anna also had some maxi-singles in a smaller format. He grabbed the first record and put it on the turntable. Adam turned on the machine. The needle scraped across the vinyl. It creaked pleasantly before the music started. He had heard the song before. At the time, he couldn't make sense of the lyrics or the sadness of the music. Everything about it seemed like it was from another time, another world. He stood up and looked out the window. Below, Angermünde was asleep in the ice-cold night. Adam listened attentively. An acoustic guitar played a few tender notes. A young man sang the lyrics, almost lethargically.

Stell dich mitten in das Feuer Put yourself in the fire's center

He was captivated by the music.

Liebe dieses Ungeheuer Love this monster

He wiped a tear from his cheek.

In des Herzens rotem Wein In the heart's red wine

He stopped at the window and looked out.

Und versuche gut zu sein And try to be good

The tears flowed down his cheeks. Adam had probably become sentimental from drinking. He felt light and heavy at the same time. After a while, his tears were flowing freely. He lay down on the couch and fell asleep again. A giant shrunk to a dwarf.

Chapter 6: CHILD'S EYES

November 15, 1987
Angermünde
District Frankfurt/Oder
German Democratic Republic

Evelyn woke him up. She was standing in the doorway dressed only in an undershirt and panties. Adam was lying on the couch. To another man, the sight would have probably been sexy. Maybe even to him. In another life. But he was no longer that easily aroused. He sat up.

"Are you hungover like me?" she asked.

He supported his head with one arm. "You bet. You can hold your liquor ..."

"I see you listened to some music yesterday?" she said, pointing to the records scattered across the floor.

Adam grumbled something affirmative and was sure that he had sorted everything properly last night. Then he stood up and bent down to the records. Slowly, he picked them up one by one. She sat down on the couch and watched him from there. A slip of paper fell out of a record's cover sleeve. It was *The Kick Inside* by Kate Bush. He looked at the piece of paper. There was something written in girlish handwriting.

"What is it?" she asked.

"A song lyric that Anna must have translated."

"Really, Kate Bush? Didn't know she'd ever heard that record."

"So, how's her English?"

"Guess."

"Bad?"

"I can't imagine where she learned it. She only had Russian in school."

"Self-taught, maybe."

"Let me see."

He handed her the piece of paper. She read the lines carefully.

"You see, two passages are underlined," she said, showing him the note.

He read them out loud in German. "*Keiner weiß von meinem Mann*" and "*Der Mann mit dem Kind in seinen Augen.*"

He went to the record player and put the record on. Then he took the sleeve and looked on the back for the track numbers. He started the drive and carefully placed the needle on the vinyl. An echoing female voice could be heard saying *he's here* repeatedly. Then piano sounds kicked in.

"This is the song," Adam said, stopping to listen next to the spinning record player.

"Oh, that song is so beautiful," Evelyn said, trying to read along with the lyrics her sister had translated into German. "I never knew what it was about. Is this right?"

"I think so. That's what she sings: *Nobody knows about my man* and *The man with the child in his eyes*."

"A little embarrassing, isn't it?"

"I guess. The English lyrics always sound a little funny when you hear them in German. Any idea who she meant? It'd be strange to translate the lyrics and not mean anything by it, wouldn't it?"

"Well, what you're saying sounds a bit silly to me. You don't actually think that has anything to do with Anna or what happened to her, do you? It's just some lyrics."

"But these are lyrics she translated herself. Couldn't have been easy for her. The lyrics aren't printed anywhere. So she had to listen to all that and then translate it word by word with the dictionary. That's real work, and considering, it's pretty good."

"What do you know about English?"

"Well, it sounds like it, at least."

He could have elaborated on where Anna was not quite right with her translation. But it was much more critical what Evelyn's sister had understood or wanted to understand.

"Well, I don't know, Adam. Maybe she thought of Basti."

"You really think so? I don't. *The man with the child in his eyes*. That must be a childlike man or a man who is loving and generous, with kind eyes. Who could that be?"

Evelyn pursed her mouth.

"Well, okay, it's not Basti," she said, laughing. "But otherwise, it could be anyone. She has enough admirers. I've already told you."

"She never talked about how the song was important to her?"

"Nah, never."

"Then it must be a new thing, I guess."

He put the records back in the cabinet. "Well, it's not likely to be Manfred Lopp," she said referring to a colleague who seemed to be quite the opposite of the man described in the song.

She laughed and walked out of the living room.

Adam looked out of the narrow window of the car. The pane of glass fogged up from the inside. He rolled down the window a bit. The cold air mixed with the smoke from Evelyn's cigarette. He realized that he was beginning to resign himself to his fate. At least for the next few days. And he had to admit that the investigation was already more exciting than he had suspected. They even had interesting clues, little riddles to solve.

There was the expensive dress. Riddle #1: How had an ordinary worker in the GDR gotten hold of this noble piece of fabric from France?

There was the meeting with an unknown friend. Riddle #2: Why did Anna have a friend Evelyn didn't know of and what had she wanted to discuss with this friend on the coming Monday?

There were the translated song lyrics. Riddle #3: What had the lyrics meant to Anna, and who was this man with the childlike eyes?

Three investigative tasks for the next few days, which made the unwelcome distraction from work more interesting. Questioning Evelyn's suspects was going to be infinitely more unpleasant. With the puzzles Anna had left behind in the form of objects or writings, he could silently ponder solutions. In the case of the men Evelyn thought could have kidnapped Anna, even more people were drawn into the spell of a woman who alternated between grief and hope. He was carrying out orders. Like a soldier. A mission that consisted of questioning men about whether they had kidnapped a woman. Simple. There were six suspects. Six, five, four, three, two, one, and the job was done. By Monday at the latest, he should be able to get back to the business of serving the socialist people. Namely, to fuel a fire that was nice and hot, to coat pots and pans with enamel.

Suspect 6: Sebastian Koslowski

The first potential kidnapper of her sister was Sebastian Koslowski, the current boyfriend of the missing woman. By no stretch of the imagination was the tender boy capable of murder. But then again, it wasn't about murder for Evelyn. It was about a kidnapping. Evelyn insisted that Anna's boyfriend was suspect number one. In her opinion, he felt neglected by his girlfriend and was often jealous. Never without reason. For her, motive enough to kidnap her sister.

No lights were on in the gray house in the small residential street. After ringing the bell and hearing no answer, they concluded that Sebastian Koslowski was not at home. So they placed themselves inside the cold car and observed the house. There was no auxiliary heating. Now and then, Evelyn started the engine and rattled around the block until it had become tolerably warm inside. However, Evelyn forbade him to roll down the windows so that the precious heat would not escape. The smoke ate into his brain. They spent hours like that. Waiting until it got too cold. Driving until it warmed up again. Arriving at the deserted house. The day was drawing to a close. If they were going to question another suspect that day, they had to decide soon. It was getting dark. They made round after round.

"He's not coming back today," he said.

"He's coming," Evelyn said.

He did not.

Suspect 5: Manfred Lopp

The next suspect was a man he knew well. His name was Manfred Lopp, and he was a colleague from the factory. The man was around fifty and single. His protruding eyes ensured that he was called *Pop* by everyone. He was supposed to have cast his popping eyes on Anna time and again. Evelyn said that Anna avoided the worker so that she would not be continually gawked at by him. At a party of the company brigade, he was said to have touched her once. Not that unusual. The young women of the VEB often got a slap on the butt. That was common, and no one complained about it. Adam had observed this behavior many times, and each time, he wondered what the men got out of it. Except that they could be sure of the disapproval of the women. Pop, on the other hand, had allegedly put his fat paws on her pubic area. For Evelyn, these were offenses of exceptional gravity, and therefore the man was another potential kidnapper of her sister.

Evelyn parked the car in front of a mansion. The plaster was crumbling. But there was a light on. Adam was glad. At least then, he didn't have to freeze his ass off waiting in the car.

"Are you sure that Pop lives here?" he said in amazement.

"Where else?" she said, getting out of the car.

"I was thinking that Pop was eking out an existence like a hermit."

"He inherited the house. Who cares for such an old box?"

Evelyn pressed the bell button on the garden gate. Nothing happened. She rang the bell again. The door opened.

"Evelyn, what are you doing here?" asked Manfred Lopp, beaming with joy.

"We need to talk to you."

"Just a second. Hang on a minute, please. Ten minutes."

He waved and then closed the door again.

"A little late for visitors," Adam said.

Evelyn said nothing and lit another cigarette. "Look, when we go in, I'll distract him, and you look for Anna in the basement."

"Absolutely not."

"Are you scared?"

Adam didn't think much of the plan. But she was right. What was going to happen? It was his mission. He kept silent and nodded.

"Good. Cold as hell again today, isn't it?" she said.

They stood next to each other in silence and waited until Lopp opened the door again. Lights were burning in every house in the neighborhood. There was a peaceful atmosphere. The door opened again.

"Come on in," Lopp said.

The two opened the garden gate and walked towards Lopp.

"I didn't expect you guys at my place," he said, shaking their hands in greeting.

The man led them down the hall to the dining room. Classical music played in the background. At the table sat a woman. Two little girls were playing on the floor. The woman stood up and bowed slightly to them.

"This is Huong. And the two little ones are Linh and Tuyen." He turned to his guests. "It's Evelyn and Adam from work. You know Huong?" Lopp said, smiling.

"Good evening," Huong said.

"Why don't you sit down," Lopp said, pointing to the two vacant chairs where the girls must have been sitting earlier.

"Thank you. I hope we're not disturbing you," Adam said.

Huong glanced at Lopp. They sat down.

"Evelyn, I'm so sorry about Anna," Lopp said.

"Thank you," she said.

"Would you like something to drink? A beer, maybe?" said Lopp, and he had already opened two beers for them.

They toasted each other.

"I didn't even know you had family," Evelyn said.

"Huong is a good friend of mine."

The woman nodded. Adam felt uncomfortable. He excused himself and went to the bathroom. Right next to the bathroom was the staircase leading to the basement. He went down. Finding Anna down here would be a shock to him. But why shouldn't he change his mind about Manfred Lopp for the second time in one evening? At work, he thought the man was a needy loser. At home, he seemed like a fatherly friend to a Vietnamese family. Was this the kind of person who kept an eighteen-year-old girl prisoner in the basement? Possible, but unlikely. It was cool in the basement. All the doors were open. He flicked on the light. Junk, supplies, coals. He searched the floor for trapdoors and the walls for secret hiding places. What had to be done had to be done. He found nothing. Adam made his way back upstairs. A little girl blocked his way. She looked at him.

"Hello!" he said.

She wore a red dress, white stockings, black patent shoes, looked at him expectantly and said nothing.

"*Bạn tên là gì?*"

He was asking for her name in Vietnamese. He had acquired the basics of the language during the Vietnam War. The only enrichment of life he had taken away from that time. On the other side of the Iron Curtain, she was a communist agitator in the making. On this side, she was a little comrade from a socialist brother country. Reality changes with perspective, he thought.

"Tuyen," she said, thinking. "How old are you?" she asked him in German.

He grinned, finding it almost a bit of a pity that he didn't need to use his Vietnamese any further. "Forty-two," he said.

"Look, I'm already ...," Tuyen said, extending four fingers of her hand to him.

"I used to be four, too. How do you like it?"

"Fine."

"I thought so, too. What did you guys play?"

"Nothing."

"But you've just played with your sister, haven't you?"

She laughed. "No, we were looking at something."

"What?"

"Uncle Manfred gave me a book."

"Do you know how to read yet?"

She shook her head. "No, it's with pictures."

"Shall we go back up?"

There were no more secrets for him to uncover down there. The girl took him by the hand and struggled up the high steps. On the landing, she turned to him and beckoned him to her.

She put her mouth on his ear and whispered. "Do you want to see Anna?"

He felt a shiver run down his spine. Taking her hand, he allowed himself to be pulled further up the stairs. She didn't go back to the dining room but took the steps to the second floor. Agonizingly slow, she climbed the stairs ahead of him. At the top, she opened one of the doors leading off the hallway. It was a child's room. Furnished with a closet, a small desk, and a bed.

"Is this your room?" he asked.

"Yes."

"Do you live here?"

"Sometimes."

The girl walked towards the bed, jumped up, and held out her hand. Adam was relieved. He could already guess who Anna was.

"Here, this is Anna," she said, pulling a doll out from under the covers.

Adam introduced himself to the doll and asked her how old she was. After the key data of the doll's existence had been clarified, they decided to return to the ground floor together. From downstairs came sounds that sounded like a fight.

Manfred Lopp's popping eyes were filled with anger. Tuyen's mother was crying. Evelyn screamed and pointed her finger at the man. Adam rushed into the living room and held her. Then he pulled her away from the dining table, down the hall, and they left the house.

"What did you do?" he asked Evelyn.

"Asking him what he did with Anna."

"I thought you were trying to distract him, not turn him against us."

"Believe me, Pop is dirty. Did you find anything?"

"Nah, there was nothing there. He has nothing to do with it. I really can't imagine that. Look, he has a family with two children. That's not possible."

"Everything is possible."

"Come on, Evelyn, let's go."

They got into the car. He convinced her that they should postpone the investigations until the next day. However, she did not miss the opportunity to drive past Sebastian Koslowski's house once again. There was still no one there. She took him home. He had no more strength to pursue his own research work and immediately fell asleep.

Chapter 7: 133

November 16, 1987
Schwedt/Oder
District Frankfurt/Oder
German Democratic Republic

Suspect 4: Andreas Preiss

The Trabant drove east along the country road. Evelyn had picked Adam up at five in the morning. It was pitch dark. They lacked sleep and breakfast. The two of them sat side by side in the car on the way to Schwedt, the town with the oil refineries right on the Polish border. In this town lived one of her sister's supposedly most dangerous admirers. If Evelyn was to be believed. Like Anna, Andreas Preiss was eighteen years old, and he had loved her since the fifth grade. During their school years, the two were a couple until the girls' mother died, and Evelyn Sievers moved to Angermünde with her little sister. Just everyday teenage tragedy, Adam thought. That was four years ago. Anna's older sister was sure that the boy had never gotten over the breakup and had a bad character beyond that. Evelyn seemed to have that opinion about all of Anna's friends, he reckoned. Evelyn could only confirm that, and was even of the opinion that Anna had unerringly been able to win over idiots. And that exclusively. Evelyn had rarely seen the boy since then. Anna, however, was said to have often reported that he had taken the long way to Angermünde to wait for her at the school gate. If this was true, it was conclusive proof of his love. Precisely because he could only do that if he himself skipped school to do it.

They reached the outskirts of Schwedt. Until then, Adam had only heard of the town in relation to the prison where NVA soldiers were incarcerated. The special detention camp was the only military prison in the GDR. That was why 133, Schwedt's postal code, was a synonym for draconian punishments among NVA soldiers and draft dodgers.

Prefabricated buildings lined the street. Not a soul in sight. They drove to the train station. Evelyn stopped in front of it. The station hall from the sixties was styled in the vein of socialist realism. They went inside. No one there as well.

Evelyn headed for the station restaurant. "Okay, then let's have some breakfast first. Go on inside. I forgot something in the car," she said and went back.

Adam went inside. There was no business at all so early in the morning. He walked up to the counter where a woman in a white kitchen uniform had posted herself, not letting on that she had noticed his arrival. Out of the corner of his eye, he saw a man sitting at one of the tables. He was taking a drag on his cigarette and grinned at him. A cold shiver ran through Adam. It was the man who had brought him to his knees with two direct blows in the holding cell. He was sitting there with a cup of coffee and had his newspaper, *Neues Deutschland*, New Germany, spread out on the table. Adam's mind was racing. Was the man on his heels, knowing his every move even before he made them himself, or was it just a coincidence that he was here? All he wanted was to get out quickly. Preferably without causing too much of a stir. So he went to the counter and took some coins out of his pocket.

"Can you give me change for this?" he asked the woman when he had placed a one-mark coin on the counter for her.

"Do I look like an exchange office or what?"

She fumbled in her purse and pulled some small coins. "Here," she said and put Pfennige, pennies, down for him.

He took the money from the counter, thanked her, and walked out of the restaurant again. The man was still grinning, nodding at him. When he walked out, Evelyn just had the door in her hand.

"What's wrong?" she asked, "I thought we were having breakfast."

"They don't serve anything yet," he said, pushing her out the door.

Reluctantly, Evelyn went along with him.

"And what do we do now?" she asked.

"We go looking."

They went back to the car and continued their ride through the city. Their stomachs growled. There was light in the HO restaurant Centra. They were the only guests who strayed in early in the morning. Not even drunks hung around the counter. The patron nodded in greeting. They sat down at one of the tables by the window. The expressionless man joined them after some time. They ordered two coffees. On the menu was a pair of Bockwürste, boiled sausages, with two slices of white bread. Nothing else. So they ordered this meal twice.

"Where does this Andreas guy live, anyway?" he asked.

"We'll find out."

"How?"

"By asking."

"You don't know where this guy lives?"

She said nothing. After a few minutes, the man brought the coffee and their breakfast.

"Excuse me, I have a question. An old school friend of mine lives here in Schwedt. Unfortunately, I don't have her current address. Maybe you know her by chance," Evelyn said to the host.

"What's the woman's name?"

"Marianne Preiss."

"Doesn't ring a bell."

"Maybe her son, Andreas Preiss?"

"Nah," he said, trotting back behind the counter.

He took a sip of the light brown broth. Adam would have preferred to order hot water. He tore off a piece of white bread and dipped it in this dishwater. He didn't touch the sausages. The pigs had died in vain.

"And now?" he asked.

"Wait."

"On what?"

"Other people."

"That's your plan?"

She crossed her arms in front of her chest and waited. After more than an hour, no people had come through the door of the inn yet. She had eaten all the sausages, he the bread. Only brown crumbs from the coffee-like beverage were still floating in the cups.

"Come on, let's go," she said.

He reminded himself of his mantra, "What needs to be done, needs to be done," and stood up.

"We're going to the police," she said.

Adam admired her courage. His experiences with the Vopos kept him from getting these ideas. But in times of need, the GDR citizen even consults the Volkspolizei, he thought.

"So, what is the plan?"

"We ask them for the address."

"All right."

After wandering around the city for a while, they finally reached the local station of the Volkspolizei. He preferred to wait in the car. It took Evelyn forty-six minutes to come out of the functional building again. She waved at him, beaming with joy. He gave her a smile and raised his hand.

"I got it," she said as she dropped into the driver's seat.

"Do I want to know how you did that?"

"I can only say this much—I didn't have to let myself be touched indecently to get it."

"Does that work? That only happens in movies, right?"

"I don't know," she said smugly and drove off.

They stopped in front of a house with a pointed roof and rough plastering. After they rang the bell at the garden gate, a woman opened the front door and beckoned them in. They opened the gate and walked towards the house.

"You're just what I need now," the woman said, looking at Evelyn as they stood in front of her.

She looked exhausted, and her eyes were puffy from crying. In her hand, she held a crumpled handkerchief. "I need to talk to Andreas," Evelyn said, taking a step to the side.

"That's a colleague of mine. He's here with me."

"I can see that. But you can't speak to Andi."

"It's important, though."

"Well, even if the comrade General Secretary comes by in person, he wouldn't be able to talk to him."

"Where is he?"

"The same place Anna is."

"Nonsense, you couldn't possibly know that."

The woman laughed wearily.

"Sure, and you know it too."

"Then tell me."

The woman shook her head and made room in the doorway.

"Come on in. I don't care anymore."

She walked down the hall toward a door with a life-size poster of Don Johnson. He knew these so-called Starschnitte, *star cuts*, from the West. Every week, a section of the poster appeared in the youth magazine *Bravo*, which readers had to cut out and paste together until they could pin their life-size star to the door. The woman let them go into the room.

"Sit down."

There was only a bed and a desk chair. The woman sat down on it. They took a seat on the made bed.

"I knew exactly that this would happen one day with Anna and my Andi. It started on the very first day at the *POS*, the polytechnic secondary school. Andi came home from school, beaming with joy. How old must he have been then, maybe ten or eleven. And he told me about a girl who was in his new class. He was immediately in love, head over heels. Well, that girl was Anna. He couldn't think of anything else. Gosh, he was just a kid then, a little boy, and he fell madly in love with this girl."

She looked down and was absent.

"So, tell me, what's wrong with Andreas?" asked Evelyn.

He sat next to her on the bed and could not believe that she once again did not want to understand. The woman had already told her where the boy was. Evelyn probably thought he was with Anna. Somewhere in a hiding place that the boy's mother was about to reveal.

The woman looked at Evelyn. "When it came to the two of them being a couple, he almost burst with joy. And he was so proud. Anna had already turned all the boys' heads back then. The long hair, the doll's face, always the best at gymnastics. A real Boginskaya. Yes, he was proud. He fulfilled her every wish. And she never loved him. She laughed at him. Again and again. How often do you think he came home and couldn't sleep because Anna didn't have the same feelings for him that he had for her?"

"Oh, come on, Marianne, give me a break. They were still children back then," said Evelyn.

"Anna was not a child. She thought carefully about who she could manipulate. That was my Andi. And he really did anything for her. Even her homework. He picked her up from home, picked her up from gymnastics, you know that, Evelyn. And how did she thank him? She dropped him. Just like that."

"But it wasn't like that at all. We moved away …"

"Did Anna tell you that? She left him much earlier, didn't she?"

Evelyn looked straight ahead, apparently not knowing what to say in response.

"Sure, now you can say that they were children. But she broke Andi's heart. That never healed."

They were silent.

Then Evelyn retook the floor. "I want to talk to Andreas. We have to find Anna. When was the last time he saw Anna?" asked Evelyn.

The boy's mother got up and left his room. There was a sound of sobbing from the living room.

"Now she's leaving us alone. What's wrong with her?" asked Evelyn.

He shared the obvious with her. "Well, I think her son is dead."

"What? No, she just said he's where Anna is."

Adam looked Evelyn directly in the eyes for a few seconds.

"No, no, no. That's not what she meant. Anna is not dead after all. Andreas can't be with her either," she said and went into the living room.

Adam followed her. The woman sat huddled in an armchair and cried. She looked at Evelyn with tearful eyes.

"What has happened to Andreas?" asked Evelyn.

"He's dead, don't you get it?"

"Marianne, I can't know that. What happened to him?"

"This is all Anna's fault. That little bitch."

Evelyn wanted to go towards the dead boy's mother. Adam held her back. Evelyn screamed.

"What's the point? How is it Anna's fault that your fucking son is dead? Your damned brat didn't play any role in her life at all."

"Oh, Evelyn, you are such a pathetic person. I can tell you exactly why Andi is dead. He couldn't cope with the fact that the love of his life is dead. Don't you think everyone knows that? Anna killed herself and then he killed himself. I can even understand her. Look at you. Just get out of here. I never want to see you here again."

Adam took Evelyn and escorted her out of the living room.

"You'd better go now. I'll try to find out exactly what happened to Andreas," he said to her and opened the apartment door for her. "Wait for me here. I'll be right there," Adam said, closing the door in her face.

He went back to the living room, where the woman still crouched on the sofa. She was no longer crying and staring out the window.

"You're still here. Who are you, anyway? I don't want to talk to you."

"A colleague of Evelyn's from the VEB. She can't believe that Anna is dead. That's why I'm helping her ... with what, actually? Somehow I think she needs that to make peace with herself."

"She's still a long way from that, though."

"What happened to your son?"

"He killed himself when he heard about Anna's suicide, I already told you. He was so romantic. That was probably the greatest thing he could have done for Anna."

"I'm sorry about that."

The woman cried again.

"How did he find out about Anna's suicide?"

She gathered herself.

"How? Word gets around. He should never have met her. The first time he saw her, he was already in love with her. That's not normal. I never understood what it means when you say someone turns somebody's head. But Anna didn't just turn Andi's head. She turned everything in his head upside down. He couldn't think straight anymore. And Anna is the kind of girl who notices right away that she has someone in her hand. She won't let you go anymore, and then at some point, it's all over. I should never have allowed Andi to meet her."

"Excuse me. I'd better go now," he said and turned around.

On his way out, he heard the woman crying softly again. Evelyn was seething with anger. She did not believe that Anna could be blamed for Andi Preiss's death. How could she? After all, she didn't even believe that Anna was dead. For him, it was a human tragedy, but at the same time, there was one suspect less.

Suspect 3: Henrik Vahr

The list continued with a playground friend of her sister. Henrik Vahr only knew Anna when he was a little boy. Still, he had apparently developed a real obsession for the girl over the years. The same clinical picture as Andreas Preiss. Unrequited love. The poor boys, Adam thought.

Later, Anna often ran into the odd man, who now had thick-rimmed glasses, after school. Evelyn recounted that it was only after repeated inquiries and threats of beatings that she was able to find out who he was. The boy was said to have finally admitted that he biked six miles from his home village every day just to see Anna. An effort he wanted to save himself by chaining the girl to her own bed, Evelyn speculated. That made him another possible kidnapper.

The car shook them over the cobblestones. At every pothole, she yanked on the steering wheel to swerve. They zigzagged across the desolate road. The Trabant's suspension mercilessly passed on every bump to its occupants. Adam felt like he was in an off-road exercise in a Jeep. He enjoyed Evelyn's furious style of driving. Schwedt struck him as even uglier than Angermünde. The town's best days were not behind it, as they had never existed. There was no old town here. In any case, they had not yet passed it. The charm of the old and dilapidated was nowhere to be found. Everything was new and still run-down. Now and then, he saw a candle burning in a window. It didn't make the town any friendlier. These attempts seemed downright desperate.

"Where to now?" he asked Evelyn, who was looking spellbound at the road.

"To Henrik Vahr. That creep, you know."

"Anna's playground friend?"

"When you say it like that, it sounds like he's not a disgusting guy. But he follows Anna around every step of the way."

"Have you ever seen him?"

"Anna told me about it."

"And when was the last time you saw him yourself?"

"Quite a long time ago. Maybe sixteen years."

"So when Anna was a toddler?"

"And so was he."

"Do you know where he lives?"

"We'll be right there."

They turned into a small side street and stopped in front of a building with a flat roof.

"Come on, let's get out," she said.

"Are we there?"

"Almost," she said, getting out of the car.

He followed her. She stood in front of the fence and looked at the building.

"It still looks the same," she said.

"Is this the kindergarten Anna went to?"

"Nursery. But yes, this is where we sent Anna when she was little."

Evelyn posted herself right in front of the entrance gate and closed her eyes.

"What are you doing?"

"Thinking."

She moved her arms in the air to the right and then to the left.

"Looks like you're about to start at a one-hundred-meter dash. Have you visualized the track already?"

Evelyn opened her eyes.

"Very funny. I need to figure out how we used to walk back then. Now shut up."

She closed her eyes again. He crossed his arms in front of his body and waited.

"Come on," she said after a few seconds, turning left down the sidewalk past the kindergarten.

"Do you know now?"

"I think so. Used to come this way with Anna when I took her to Henrik's after daycare."

"She could barely walk then."

"By then, she was two and could walk very well."

"When she was only two, you left her with strangers?"

"You're really weird. What's the big deal? Everybody does it like that. Besides, they weren't strangers but Henrik's parents. Nobody could have guessed what a disgusting guy he'd turn out to be. So I often took Anna to the Vahrs after the nursery. Just like everyone else does."

"It was just different where I grew up," he said and had to admit to himself that he didn't know much about childcare in the GDR.

"And where would that have been?"

"Magdeburg District," Adam lied.

"Well, they still have a lot to learn in Magdeburg District," she said, turning right into a street lined with three-story prefabricated buildings.

"I guess so. Are we on the right path?"

"Yeah, sure."

Evelyn walked ahead and crossed the street. She stopped in front of the house with the number nineteen and pointed to the bell plates.

"See, I told you I knew where it was."

She pressed the sign with the name Vahr on it. After a short wait, a man's voice creaked out of the intercom.

"Yes?"

"Hi, it's Evelyn."

"Don't know you."

"Evelyn Sievers."

The man's voice could now be heard a little more quietly.

"Ulrike, do we know Evelyn Sievers?"

Through the intercom, it sounded as if the clacking of shoes was coming closer.

A woman's voice could be heard softly talking to the man. "That's little Anna's sister, isn't it? Can you remember? Let me give it a try."

Now the woman could be heard louder. "Evelyn, what are you doing here?"

"I want to talk to Henrik."

"You should have come yesterday when we were all here together."

"I do have to talk to him. Where does he live?"

"Why don't you come up for a moment?"

The man's voice could still be heard briefly, complaining about Evelyn being let up. Then the door opener buzzed.

"Do you want me to wait?" Adam asked.

"You're coming with me."

A man wearing glasses welcomed them at the apartment door in a robe. Beads of sweat shone on his forehead. His wife came into the hallway with a tray.

"Come on in," she said, advancing to the living room.

The three sat down. The woman put the tray with half a marble cake on the coffee table. Her cheeks were red.

The man peeked through the door. "I'll just put some clothes on," he said and disappeared.

"I forgot to bring plates," the woman said and stood up again.

They waited until the woman was out the door.

"I guess we just disturbed them," Adam said, grinning.

"Why?"

"Didn't you see him in a robe and her pink cheeks? They must have ..."

The woman came back with plates in her hand.

"Ugh, that's disgusting," Evelyn said to him quietly.

"What is it?" the woman asked, setting the plates down in front of them.

"Nice place," he said.

"Thank you," the woman said.

"Dig in."

They served themselves, and he devoured his piece in one bite. The woman laughed, cut him another bit, and put it on his plate. Evelyn did not touch the cake.

"I forgot the coffee," she said, standing up again.

By the time she was out the door, Evelyn wanted to have seen evidence of the family's decrepitude everywhere.

The man came into the living room dressed in corduroy pants and a sweater and sat down on one of the two armchairs. "So, you are friends of Henrik?"

"Nah, not exactly. My sister knows him from her nursery days," Evelyn said.

"I see. All right. So that was quite a while ago. Cold today, isn't it?"

The two nodded. The man got up and went into the kitchen. Shortly after, he came back with his wife and a pot of coffee.

"Could I possibly have a glass of hot water?" he asked.

"Try the coffee. It's good," the man said.

"Came with a *Westpaket*," the woman said.

"Jacob's Krönung," the man said, referring to a brand of ground coffee from West Germany.

She poured him a cup. To his surprise, it tasted like coffee. Adam nodded with satisfaction. The couple smiled at each other. They filled up all the cups and sat down.

"I think you've already heard ...," Evelyn said.

"Yes, we did. I'm sorry. She was so young," the woman said.

"Oh, that's the little girl's sister who killed herself," the man said to his wife.

"Peter!"

"We heard about that. Ugly affair," he said, looking at Adam.

"It's not that simple. She disappeared. She's not dead," Evelyn said.

"Is that right?" the man asked.

"We heard it differently. First Anna was missing, and then she was found dead."

"Yes, the Vopos told me that too. But Anna is not dead. I know that."

"Good, well, and how can we help you? I haven't seen you in years," the woman said.

"I need to talk to Henrik."

"He moved out. Now works at Petrochemisches Kombinat," she said, referring to the petroleum refinery in town.

"And where did he move?"

"He lives here in Schwedt with his girlfriend, Petra. What's his connection to Anna these days? They haven't seen each other since forever."

The man poured himself some coffee and looked out the window. But there was nothing to see.

"Henrik saw her a lot. After school and so on, you know?"

"When?"

"Over the last few years."

"I don't think so."

"And what does Petra say about that?" the man asked.

"Oh, that's nonsense, Peter. Evelyn has a bit of an imagination."

"That's not nonsense. That's the truth. Henrik was lying in wait for her after school, bringing her flowers and stuff."

"How could he have done that? He had to go to school himself. Besides, we would have heard about it. And you were living in Angermünde by then. That's much too far away. Evelyn, this is all far-fetched. What do you want to know about Henrik?"

"What he did to her."

"What is he supposed to have done to her?" she asked.

"I guess they didn't really see each other, then?" the man said.

Adam took the precaution of saying nothing and ate the second piece of cake.

"Do I get Henrik's address, or not?"

"Evelyn, how pretty you were. Your long blond hair and you were so sporty. You always had a new beau with you when you picked up Anna from the nursery. I didn't even recognize you at first ..."

"Oh, that's Evelyn. She really did look different once," the man said.

"That was fifteen years ago," Evelyn said.

"What makes you think Henrik has a thing for Anna?" the woman asked.

"She told me."

"If anything, Henrik had a crush on you as a toddler. He didn't want to leave your side, remember? The second word he could speak was Evelyn. I wouldn't have been surprised if he had chased after you. Or if he wanted to see you again after all these years."

"But he has Petra now," the man said.

"That's right. I just mean theoretically."

"I see."

"Did your son ever tell you about Anna?" asked Adam.

"No, never," the woman said.

Evelyn jumped up and stormed out of the living room. "Okay, then, I'll find Henrik on my own."

The woman went after her. Evelyn yanked open doors. Something crashed to the floor. Screams spilled into the living room. The men stood up. The women were tangled up in each other. They were pulling each other's hair and yelling at each other. Evelyn was holding something in her hand.

"Give that back to me," the woman yelled, tugging on Evelyn's hand.

The men intervened and separated the women.

"What have you got there?" asked Adam, looking at Evelyn.

"A photo of Henrik," the woman said.

Evelyn dropped the photo.

"I think it's better if you leave now," the man said.

They left the apartment.

Adam spent the return trip saying nothing to Evelyn.

When she stopped in front of his apartment, she didn't let him out right away. "Wait a minute," she said.

"What is it?"

"I'm sorry. I just want Anna to come back. I know that wasn't good back there. I know that. I really do. I need your help. I can't do this alone. Please!"

He felt sorry for her. But he also needed a breather. Getting up early, the long car rides, and on top of that, his work took their toll. He hadn't gone running since he had been shot. At least the wound was healing gradually, so there was no physical pain left over from the weekend. But apart from that.

"Fine, but I can't deal with that and work at the same time. Saturday again," he said.

"All right."

Adam got out of the car thinking that she could not see people alone in her condition. So he had to take more responsibility in the interviews. He gradually realized that Evelyn would not let go until she found Anna's killer or kidnapper. Until then, he could write off his own life. The thought relieved him for the moment.

Chapter 8: ROCKET TROOPS

November 21, 1987
Vogelsang
Potsdam District
German Democratic Republic

Suspect 2: Andrei Gabulov

The penultimate on the list of admirers was a Soviet soldier. More precisely, the son of a general of the Soviet Armed Forces Group in Germany. Andrei Gabulov had allegedly seen the girl at a military parade. He was said to have been in love with her ever since. He expressed this affection by personally handing her bouquets and Soviet-made chocolates. Anna apparently iced him out. But this had not diminished his commitment and therefore made him a suspect for the crime.

The two-cycle engine worked itself through the forest-lined concrete slab road in the forbidden zone. They had already left the metal sign with the inscription Запретная зона, *zapretnaya zona,* several hundred yards behind them. So that was what he had gotten himself into by taking on more responsibility in the interviews. He thought about Evelyn's plan and imagined it in the most dazzling colors.

Adam had to shoulder his backpack and then progress along the forest paths, which were partly frozen and partly muddy. Soon he should be able to see the wall of the barracks between the trees. Then he had to orient himself toward the west, where the main access road was. Striking through the undergrowth within sight of the road. Hiding from time to time from the Russian military vehicles that drove along the road. Using that as the best way to enter the compound undetected. Continuing to walk for a few hundred meters. Stopping in sight of the main gate and crouching down. Hoping all was quiet at the front gate. Preferably only encountering two guards with a muzzled German shepherd. Taking the luggage off the back. Swapping the sneakers, jeans, and parka for heavy army boots and a Soviet winter uniform. Hiding the backpack. Walking along the road a bit more out of sight of the sentries. Hiding again in sight of the guardhouse. Finding a tree that provides sufficient shelter. Hearing the two men at the gate talking to each other. Being lucky that the dog doesn't strike. Seeing a four-by-four with an Army truck in tow approaching the gate. Letting the vehicles drive slowly past the hiding place. Seeing the tarp on the back of the truck standing open. Spotting a handful of soldiers sitting on wooden benches and chanting loudly. Deciding there is no chance of sneaking into the barracks. Making a backup plan. Watching the short column for a few moments, seeing it stopping at the gate. Maybe discovering a possibility after all. Seeing a soldier getting off the bunk, staggering right at one. Hearing a dog bark. An attempt to escape? Waiting and seeing. Watching the young man unzipping his Army pants and pissing into the woods. Hearing the soldiers from the truck calling after him and then continuing to sing their songs. Watching a whole squad of drunk Red Army soldiers watching the pissing soldier falling over and all laughing again. Shifting one's attention back to the guards walking toward one's hiding place. Leaving one's position, making a circuit through the undergrowth. Feeling safe again. Stepping out onto the road at the height of the Army truck and walking to the tailboard. Jumping onto the truck bed in one leap and sitting down between the soldiers. Briefly waiting for the reaction. Feeling relief about the pat on the back.

Saying *upal*, with a slur, which should mean as much as *I fell*.

Receiving идиот, in response from one of the soldiers, *idiot*. Hearing all the other soldiers laughing.

Slurring *p'yanyy idiot*, to top it off, *drunk idiot*.

Hearing the men laugh even louder and then starting to sing again. Then wondering why the comrade with the weak bladder is pushed back onto the cot by the guards. Guessing that this is the end of his burglary attempt. Waiting again, staying calm, slurring the words. Relieved that they take their comrade back to their midst, without being surprised that they are now one too many. Rumbling shortly after through the barracks gate, which is again closed behind them by the guards. Leaving the sea of trees behind. Finally arriving on the island. No longer seeing the fences. No longer being reminded of being locked up in the barracks area. Looking from the truck. Finding that this is what a city in the GDR looks like. Concrete slabs pave the streets, on which larger and smaller houses with earth-colored plaster stand. Here and there, the architecture is interrupted by a bit of vegetation. Deciding that the only difference is that there are no fences in front of the houses, some massive halls stand around and only Red Army soldiers in uniforms of coarse cloth walk the streets. Having the convoy stop in front of some barracks. Sitting down with the other men. Not going into the building like the others, but passing it on the left. No longer turning around. No longer reacting to questions, jokes, and insults. Counting on soon disappearing from their field of vision and thus from their alcohol-impaired memories.

Going around the building. Finding another barrack behind it. Saluting with hand on cap to the soldiers coming out as they pass by. *Dobryy den'!*

Gladly noticing being saluted back by the soldiers and reaching a parallel road. Recognizing huge halls at some distance. Letting curiosity run free and checking the assumption that the mobile launching pads of the nuclear missiles are located there.

Reaching the hall complex soon after that. Finding the gates locked. Checking to find a door on the long side of the building that can be opened. Carefully poking one's head through the crack in the door and looking down on a battery of olive-green monstrosities. Seeing four of the eight-wheeled Uragan trucks directly in front of him. Each with one of the forty-foot missiles containing a nuclear warhead perched on top. Closing the steel door and walking around the trucks. Wheels so high that they stick up to one's shoulder. Putting one hand on the metal. Taking a few steps back. Picking up the microcamera, triggering it and taking a picture of the SS-12 Scaleboard nuclear missiles. Knowing that the weapon fired from one of these mobile launchers has an explosive power of five hundred kilotons of TNT, which is forty times the Hiroshima bomb, with a radius of six hundred miles. Enough to fatally strike the entire FRG, eastern France and southern Scandinavia all at once.

Adam forced himself not to think about it any further. He wondered where his imagination had conjured up a winter uniform and a microcamera. He possessed neither and realized that it was simply impossible to get into the barracks. He could not afford to come into conflict with the authorities again. Especially not with the Russians, who considered the GDR their front yard and would override any official GDR authority if it served their interests. So, in practice, it was impossible to find and then question Andrei Gabulov, one of the fifteen thousand Soviet soldiers stationed in Vogelsang. Besides, it was probably easier to get into the barracks than to get back out again. Every year about four hundred soldiers tried to escape. But very few of the Red Army soldiers were successful. Most of them got nabbed, arrested, court-martialed, sentenced, and put in prison forever or executed. Two years earlier, a soldier who had made it to the Jena train station had been riddled with eighty bullets while trying to break through a roadblock. By his own people.

Adam looked out the window and let the frozen fields pass him by. Once again, it became clear that he was getting his orders not from an accomplished detective but a desperate workingwoman. He couldn't blame her. It was not her fault. She did what she had to do. And he had to do what she thought was right.

Maybe Adam had to look at the whole thing with a competitive mind. Like a mountaineer who wants to conquer Mount Everest. A runner who wants to survive the New York Marathon. Or a swimmer who wants to cross the English Channel. There is no more profound reason to it. The climber doesn't bring a radio antenna up the mountain. The runner doesn't deliver letters to New Yorkers. And the swimmer doesn't install buoys for passing container ships. They all have only one goal, and that is to master the task they had set for themselves. His mission could be to take an undetected stroll into one of the GDR's most closely guarded security areas. Innocently enough. Admittedly, it wasn't the plan Evelyn had in mind. But he was going to try it anyway. She didn't need to know about the fact that he wasn't even planning to find Gabulov. Even if he couldn't help her with that, he could at least do a little to calm her nerves. All he had to do was get out of the car, walk around in the woods a bit, and later he would be able to explain to her that he hadn't made it to the compound because anything else would amount to a suicide mission.

Evelyn and Adam had not encountered a human being for miles. No walkers strayed here. Especially not in this cold. The Trabant reached a fork in the road.

"Pull in here on the right," he said.

Evelyn steered the small car into a forest path.

"A bit further. Up ahead, where the path widens again, you can stop."

She stopped the car. The two got out and pushed the 1,356-pound vehicle into the undergrowth between the rows of trees.

"Grab some branches, too. We need to camouflage your car so that no one will see it from the road."

Evelyn started with him to collect fir branches and spread them on the Trabant. After a quarter of an hour, the work was done.

He took a look at their work. "That's enough," he said.

"Now what?"

He pulled a map out of his jacket pocket and spread it out. "The area where I need to go is here."

He pointed his finger at a white spot on the map surrounded by a green area. The area was like an unexplored island in the middle of a green ocean.

Evelyn frowned. "This area where you can't see anything? Well, that's just great."

He tapped on a spot inside the green area with his index finger. "It's not a problem. We should be about here."

"And how far is it to get there?"

"I'm guessing about two miles."

"That we have to walk?"

"Yes. But I'd better do it alone. I'll walk down the country road up to the barracks. If everything works out, we'll meet back here at exactly two p.m." Adam pointed to a spot on the map that was beyond the forbidden zone. "And you wait for me right here."

"And that's where I'm walking to?"

He nodded.

"Stupid idea. I'll just wait here by the car," she said.

"What if someone spots you?"

"Then the car has just broken down. Poor little *Fräulein*, you know?"

The rationale was simple enough to work, he thought. He nodded. "Then why did you help so eagerly with the camouflage?"

"That's when I still thought we were going together."

"Well, my fault. You've got plenty of time to get all that fir stuff down now," he said, grinning.

"Thank you very much."

Evelyn didn't make much of a fuss about waiting out in the cold for hours. Apparently, her will was more robust than any sensitivity toward the weather. He was not surprised that Evelyn did not try to dissuade him from this breakneck plan at the last moment. Then again, it was her plan, and she hoped to find her sister that way.

He folded up the map again and put it in his pocket. Then he looked around. It was the middle of the day, but there was no daylight. It was once again bitterly cold. Parka, jeans, and sneakers were not the proper clothing for this day, and a backpack with a winter uniform could not be conjured up as easily as in his imagination. He set off on his way. Between him and the barracks still lay a security area a couple of miles wide. Only then would the fencing of the site begin, where heavily armed guards with dogs patrolled day and night. The watchtowers were equipped with machine guns and searchlights. But that was not to be his problem. He was just an innocent walker. He turned around. He could no longer see Evelyn's car.

"*Kto ty?*" a man's voice yelled in Russian at his back. *Who are you?*

Then he heard a metallic noise. The sound of a Kalashnikov being loaded. Adam put his hands over his head.

"I am just taking a stroll," he shouted in German.

The man came closer. He stopped directly behind him and scanned him with one hand.

"*Dokumenty?*"

"*Nyet.*"

Adam was grabbed by the shoulder and turned around. He looked directly into the muzzle of the assault rifle. The soldier couldn't be a day older than eighteen. Beads of sweat had collected in the blond fuzz above his upper lip.

"Where is *dokumenty?*" he said in broken German.

"Home."

The boy took the rifle out of Adam's face. Not his best idea. With two moves, he disarmed the boy, who now looked at him with frightened eyes. Adam patted his cheek. The young soldier didn't know whether to cry or laugh and tried both at the same time. It clicked again. A Russian rarely comes alone, Adam thought. Another young guard soldier stood in front of him with a Kalashnikov at the ready. He must have been hiding behind a tree. Adam put his hands up. The boy took his rifle again and pointed it at him. With the barrel, he poked him in the side. Adam groaned in pain and, after another thrust, started to move. He had misjudged the situation. Now it was time to be creative. Running was no use. They would gun him down. And even if he were to risk it, the terrain was against him. Here he was game that would be hunted to death without the outside world noticing. So he resigned himself to his fate and let himself be led away.

After a long walk, they arrived at the commandant's building. This did not bode well for him. He had hoped that they would take him to their direct superior or first lock him up in their room. But to be led directly to the commander made matters almost official. Adam was led into an office.

At a desk sat a soldier at a typewriter. The two young soldiers described the case to him. The man nodded silently. When he had heard enough, he got up and went through a door into a room behind this anteroom. Shortly after, he returned, sat down, and gestured to the two soldiers to leave the office. After the two were gone, Adam stood alone in the middle of the room. The soldier paid him no attention and typed on the machine.

Adam cleared his throat. "May I sit down?" he asked in Russian.

The soldier did not answer. He did not even look at him.

Adam gave his thoughts room for a moment. "Who is your superior?" he then asked.

The soldier did not respond to this either. Adam took a step toward the desk, the man looked up. Adam continued to walk. Then the soldier stood up. When Adam still kept walking, the soldier came around his desk. But Adam kept walking. The soldier put out his arm to stop him from reaching the door to the room behind the desk.

"Stop right there," the soldier yelled.

"Don't touch me," Adam yelled back.

Suddenly, the door opened. A young man in uniform stepped out of the door. He beckoned Adam to come to him. Adam took a step toward him. Then he received a resounding slap, and the young man closed the door again behind him. The desk soldier sat back down and grinned. Adam felt his cheek grow hot.

"Stand back there," the desk soldier said. "Now!"

Adam went back to the middle of the room and did not move.

After a few minutes, which felt like an eternity, the door opened again. The young soldier stood in the doorway, lighting a cigarette. "What's all this monkey business?" He waved Adam in and went back in again himself. Adam did not move from the spot. "Well, go on in!" the desk sergeant said.

Adam entered the commander's office. The man in the mustard-green uniform was not older than him. And judging by the epaulets, he did not have a general's rank but a simple officer's.

He pointed to the chair in front of his desk. "Sit!"

After the man with black hair and dark eyes had taken a seat in his leather chair, he sat down as well. Above the man's head hung a framed picture of Lenin, next to it one of Gorbachev. Adam thought about what he could say to the man as he could not pretend to be someone else because there were no papers to confirm it. Anywhere.

"Who are you?" the man asked him.

"Adam Hedman."

"*Nemetskiy?*"

"*Da,*" he replied to the question of whether he was a German.

"You speak Russian?" the officer asked in German with a barely perceptible accent.

"*Nemnogo,*" Adam said in Russian, which meant *a little*.

"What are you doing here, German Adam Hedman?"

"I was out for a walk."

The officer pulled up the corners of his mouth.

"I like you, German Adam Hedman. How did you get here?"

"Walked."

"Are you saying you went all this way on foot?"

Adam nodded. The officer said nothing.

Then he lit a cigarette and looked at him for a long time. "You're under arrest for now," he finally said.

After that, he called the soldier from the anteroom to him. The door opened.

"Soldier, take this man to the holding cell."

"Understood," he said and saluted.

"And soldier …"

"*Da?*"

"Lock him up well."

"Very well, comrade Gabulov."

Gabulov? That could not be. Or could it? What had Evelyn said, that Andrei Gabulov was the general's son?

"Andrei Gabulov?"

The two men looked at Adam. He received a slap in the face from the soldier who was about to lead him to the cell block.

"How do you know the *tovarish's* first name?"

The officer stretched out an arm. The soldier let go of Adam.

"So?" Gabulov asked.

"I'm a friend of Anna Sieversa," Adam said, using the Russian version of her name.

The officer sent the soldier out. Adam was signaled to sit down again.

"What do you know about Anna?"

The man's eyes lit up.

"She sent me," he lied, hoping that news of her disappearance had not spread to the Russian troops.

"How is she?"

"Fine, but she has something to tell you."

"What?"

"I can't say. I'm here to deliver this message only to Andrei Gabulov."

"Out with it, German Adam Hedman. I am Andrei Gabulov. What's the message?"

"She wants to meet with you."

"Where? When?"

"Tomorrow. In Angermünde."

"What time? Where?"

"At the *Stalinorgel* at noon."

"Romantic, very romantic indeed," the man said as if to himself. The meeting spot in the city center where a Katyusha multiple rocket launcher reminded the German people of the Russian victory. The Germans lovingly and fearfully called it *Stalin's organ* for the zinging sound it made when firing its rockets.

"She can be like that," Adam said, grinning.

"I don't know her that way at all. How do you know Anna, German Adam Hedman?"

"From the VEB."

"You're also a worker. Did you serve? Were you in the NVA?"

"No. Bad feet, bad eyes," he lied again.

The officer laughed. "A man must be a soldier. Once in his life, a man must have been a soldier."

Adam nodded. "Yeah, the eyes didn't cooperate, unfortunately. I just can't see clearly."

"I like you, German Adam Hedman."

"I have a question."

The young Russian nodded.

"How do you become a commander at your age?"

"I am not the commander. My father is General Aleksey Gabulov. I am his substitute."

"Where is he?"

"Home. Kaliningrad."

Adam raised his hand in farewell. "Can I go now?"

He wanted to leave as soon as possible. The man had changed from a resolute soldier into a naive lover. Adam had to use the favor of the hour before that turned around again.

"Yes, yes, go," he said absently.

Then he seemed to come back to his senses.

"Just a minute. Can you give Anna a message from me?"

"Sure."

He scribbled something on a piece of paper and put it in an envelope, which he sealed. Then he called the desk soldier to him again. He pressed the message into Adam's hand and looked at the soldier. "Let the man be driven to Angermünde, soldier."

Adam stood up and went to the door. He stopped next to the soldier.

"But, *tovarish*—" Gabulov said to the officer, "Now!"

The soldier saluted and grabbed Adam by the arm. He immediately withdrew from his grasp and went ahead. Adam was in a hurry. The desk soldier called another soldier. He took him outside. There they waited for ages for a four-by-four. Adam drew a deep breath when he took a seat next to the driver. The nervousness had only faded when they had passed the barracks gate. He was back out at sea. Soon the island was only visible in the rearview mirror. The vehicle rocked gently over the pothole-strewn roadway. He remembered that his clothes were hidden in his backpack right at the gate entrance to the barracks, so he convinced the driver to make a U-turn. Adam didn't have a good feeling about it. But he also didn't have a choice as he had no coat to protect him from the winter cold. So he had the man stop in front of the barracks and pick up his backpack. Then he swung back on the vehicle. The soldier behind the wheel shook his head. He had better things to do than drive a stranger around. What this was supposed to be, Adam could not find out even when asked. The man held back and remained silent.

They arrived at the turnoff to the forest path where they had hidden Evelyn's car. He couldn't see the Trabant. Good camouflage, he thought, or the car was already gone. Adam would have liked to make the man stop again. But that would have been too dangerous. The barracks were only a radio call away. A camouflaged car not far from the missile troops would strain Andrei Gabulov's goodwill to the utmost. The driver kept shaking his head. Adam wondered what they had told the man about him. Apparently not much. It was better that way for him, too. And for Gabulov anyway. It was getting dark again. The military vehicle reached the city. He sucked in the cold air.

"*Ostanovitye*," he said to the driver—*stop*.

He stopped the car, turned to Adam, and handed him a card.

"Here! If you ever need anything," he said in almost accent-free German.

Adam took the card. It had a phone number on it, nothing else. "Like what?"

"Like anything," the soldier said, grinning.

Adam thanked him, jumped out, and said goodbye, holding two fingers to his forehead. The soldier stepped on the gas. Adam ran down the arterial road toward the old town. What time was it? He looked at the watch on his wrist—just before two o'clock. He had to hurry to get back to the meeting point at the appointed time to tell her what he had found out. Gabulov, like Henrik Vahr, could be crossed off the list of suspects. All Adam had to do was convince Evelyn. So all that remained were Uncle Alfred and Sebastian Koslowski, whom they had not yet spoken to. And, of course, VEB boss Kletzsch, whom Evelyn didn't have on any of her lists.

According to Evelyn's notes on the sheets of paper towels, Uncle Alfred also had clear sexual intentions. He was not an actual relative but a godfather. After her mother's death, he had taken almost touching care of little Anna. Until Evelyn had once come into the living room and seen Uncle Alfred sticking his tongue down the young girl's throat. That was the last time Uncle Alfred had visited the sisters and the reason for paying the man a visit ten years after the fact. Adam would have to deal with the man sooner or later.

Suspect 6: Sebastian Koslowski

Adam reached the old town. Across the street, he saw a young couple. The man had his arm around the woman. They were looking into the sparse displays of a shop window and laughing. Adam crossed the roadway. The couple did not notice him. He stood behind the two.

"Hey, Koslowski!" Adam said.

Sebastian turned around and let his arm slide off the girl's shoulder. "Gosh, Hedman, what are you sneaking up on me for?" he said, reaching out his hand.

The young woman stood by with wide eyes and smiled at Adam.

"Oh, by the way, this is Ramona," Sebastian said.

They shook hands.

"Can I talk to you alone, Koslowski?"

The woman took Koslowski's hand. "Well, that sounds dramatic. You can speak frankly. We keep no secrets from each other."

"So she knows about Anna?" Adam said, looking at the girl out of the corner of his eye.

"Of course. It's a very tragic thing. But it's nobody's fault," Sebastian said.

The man seemed relaxed, almost relieved. Adam had to think about what to ask him next. The situation was surprising. Officially, he was Anna Sievers's boyfriend, and yet he showed himself quite openly with another woman in town. Didn't Sebastian have a conscience? Adam decided to use a stun grenade.

"Isn't it true that Anna was pregnant by you?"

Ramona let go of the man's hand.

"Can't be," the man said in a calm voice.

"Why not?" asked Adam.

"Because we don't, how can I say ... that's why not. Never."

"That's bullshit, isn't it?" asked Adam in genuine surprise.

"Oh man, does it ever stop?"

Ramona stroked her friend's arm.

"That's a sore point," she told Adam.

"Gee, now don't you start, too," Sebastian told her.

Tears welled up in her eyes. She looked down at the ground.

"*Engelein*, that's not what I meant. It's all good," he said, calling her *little angel* in German and pressing a kiss on her forehead.

She smiled sheepishly. He turned to Adam.

"Okay, then, just to make it clear once and for all, and so everybody knows, we did not have sexual intercourse with each other. Never. That broad was an all-out prude. When you looked at her from the outside, she turned the men on. All of them. But when it came down to it, she was as cold as a fish. She never even gave me a helping hand, if you know what I mean?"

"Geez, Basti!" said the girlfriend.

"Sorry, but that's how it was. Well, people have needs, you know? But Anna hasn't. She only had a headache once. I certainly didn't give her a child, if that's what you mean. And I can hardly believe that someone else was doing it to her. I wouldn't envy him, though. I told you, cold as a fish. Probably doesn't even make a difference if you're doing it to her now or before she was dead."

Sebastian Koslowski turned out to be not only a misogynist but also an asshole with a macabre sense of humor. The man's rage seemed to know no bounds. His girlfriend turned away from him but he didn't notice.

Sebastian took a step toward Adam. "What you should ask yourself is where she was off to when she vanished from the face of the earth for a few days."

"Tell me."

"In Berlin."

"Is that all you know?"

"With a guy."

"That's it?"

"I'm glad I have Ramona."

"Good for you."

"You can give my regards to Evelyn. She should leave me alone. I don't want to have anything to do with her shit."

"I'll tell her that. Who's Anna's guy in Berlin?"

Sebastian shrugged his shoulders.

"That's all you're giving me?"

"Man, I don't know. Some guy who was super nice to her. I have no name, no address, nothing. All I know is that he exists and that he's in Berlin. What am I supposed to do, come up with something to get you to leave me alone?"

Adam smiled at Sebastian. There was nothing more to get from him, he thought and put his hands in his jacket pockets. For Adam, the conversation was over. So much open hostility was simply exhausting. Sebastian had understood. He put his arm around his new girlfriend and left Adam standing there. Another suspect to cross off the list. Two, one. The job was coming to an end. He hoped Evelyn would get to see her sister's body on Monday. Otherwise, he was in for a trip to Berlin.

Adam set out for the appointed meeting place. When he reached the place where he had last seen Evelyn, she was no longer there. Neither was her car. So he returned to Angermünde. Around four p.m., he pressed the bell connected to Evelyn's apartment. Nothing. The job was done for him except for questioning Uncle Alfred. His penultimate official act was to be the messenger of the news to Evelyn. If she had not been taken into custody by the

Soviet authorities, she would report to him the next day at the latest. So there was no hurry.

He reached into his jacket pocket and found the letter he had received from Gabulov for Anna. Adam tore open the envelope and unfolded the small piece of paper. On it was a drawing. A strange sketch in black ink. A bearded man with a club in his hand was chasing a woman in a headscarf and peasant costume. There was only one word scribbled on it.

Разбойник.

Razboynik meant as much as robber. Adam put the paper back in his pocket and went home.

Chapter 9: WOKE RIGOR

November 22, 1987
Angermünde
District Frankfurt/Oder
German Democratic Republic

It was Sunday. Adam woke up. Outside, the day was dawning. He looked at the clock—8:14 a.m. Adam didn't think she'd show up this late and was pleased that he'd gotten more sleep than he'd expected. So he flipped back the covers and sat up. The floor was cold. As it always was. He went to the sink, poured water into a pot, and put it on the burner. He still hadn't gotten coals. But by now, he had gotten used to the cold. He froze less since he'd stopped heating. As the water boiled, he poured it into a cup and drank some. What was better than a sip of this warm liquid in the morning? He brushed his teeth and washed his face. After looking in the mirror, he decided he needed a shave again. He lathered up shaving soap in a bowl and massaged it into his face. Carefully he led the blade over his skin. Stroke after stroke, until every square inch of facial surface was free of stubble. Adam felt fresher than he had in weeks. Was yesterday's adrenaline rush responsible for that? He wiped the foam residue from his face and sprinkled aftershave on it. The alcohol burned pleasantly within the tiny wounds on the skin. He looked at his watch again—8:42 a.m. Evelyn gave him plenty of time that morning. He sat down at the kitchen table and prepared himself a sandwich. Some margarine. A pinch of salt. He took a bite and chewed extensively. Then he went to the closet and took out his new gym shorts, track jacket, and shoes. After putting everything on, he took a big gulp of the now-lukewarm water and left the house.

Tentatively, a few rays of light found their way to earth. He ran down Clara-Zetkin-Straße to the marketplace. From there on to the Mündesee. Half a lap around the body of water until he reached a dirt road. Along with the fields, it went up a slight incline to Pinnow. He crossed the village and ran across the country road to an old oak tree. Halfway there. One of his favorite routes. He felt good. The pace was brisk, the oxygen rushing pleasantly through his blood. On the way back, he increased the speed, incorporated sprints. He did a few laps of the long staircase by the prefabricated buildings on Allee der Kosmonauten. When he reached the old town, he looked at his watch again. It was 10:29 a.m. Evelyn would be at his place by now at the latest. Adam turned into his street. He could not see her yet. She was probably standing in the gateway. But no one was waiting for him there either. He went through the gate and looked around the yard. Nothing. He unlocked the apartment door and grabbed a towel. He wiped the sweat from his skin and sat down at the kitchen table. From a stack of papers, he pulled out an old newspaper in which he had marked articles and read. Then he looked at the clock again—12:08 p.m. He put on a pot of potatoes and stared into the boiling water. Now and then, he poked the firm flesh of the field fruit with a knife. When they were finally cooked, he ate them with a bit of salt and margarine. Then he pushed the plate away from him and looked at the clock again— 12:32 p.m. He threw on a pair of jeans and his parka, walked out of the house, and went to Evelyn's. When he got to her place, he looked up at her apartment. There were no lights on. He rang the doorbell. No one answered. He looked at his watch. 12:51 p.m. He was getting nervous. So far, he had been able to suppress the feeling that something was wrong. He wondered if they had maybe missed each other by a few minutes. Suppose she was standing at his locked door, as he was now at hers? He was about to leave again when the door lock buzzed. She was home, after all. He ran up the stairs. The door was ajar and he entered. The apartment was dark. He closed the door behind him and went down the hall to the living room. It was dim and smelled sweet. Evelyn was lying on the sofa with her legs drawn up. Her face turned to the wall. The curtains were drawn. He went to the window and pushed them aside. A little light spilled into the room. The coffee table was strewn with handkerchiefs and empty liquor bottles.

"I was beginning to think the Russians had captured you," he said.

She did not answer.

He went to the kitchen and came back with a glass of water. "Here, drink this. It will do you good."

She did not move. He put the water glass down on the coffee table.

"I talked to Gabulov," he said.

"He didn't do it," Evelyn said quietly, without turning to him.

"And I met Koslowski. There's supposed to be some guy that Anna met with."

Evelyn turned a little toward him. She looked at Adam.

"In Berlin. That's who we should be looking for," he said.

She sat up and took a sip of water.

"Adam, give me a break."

"Hey, we can find that guy. It's a lead."

"It doesn't make any sense. I'll never find Anna. I was at Uncle Alfred's yesterday. It all makes no sense. My Anna is gone. Nobody did it. I'm not going to find out what happened." She looked him in the eye. "Will I? Will I ever find out, Adam? Tell me."

She cried.

He didn't move. "Evelyn, there's still the friend Anna wanted to meet—you know, Miri? The one from the note we found at Anna's."

He didn't know why he was encouraging her. His job was done at this point, and he was free again. They had questioned all the suspects. But he probably didn't want to see her in this condition. However, he knew that Evelyn's grief was inevitable, as soon as the next lead would also come to nothing. But then he probably wouldn't be with her, he thought.

"We don't even know who he is," she said.

"Then we'll just have to ask around. Talk to her friends, maybe."

"No, we won't find out anything. We never find out anything."

"Tell me her friends' names. I'll find out for you. I promise."

Evelyn cried. He talked to her for a long time. Finally, she gave him three names with corresponding addresses. He had gotten himself deeper into the mess just to let her nibble a little longer on the dangerous fruit of hope.

"Can I leave you here like this?" he asked.

Evelyn nodded and smiled a little. Then he left the apartment.

The first address was just around the corner. With a bit of luck, he could find out who Miri was that very day. And then? He didn't know. As always in seemingly hopeless situations, he took one step after the next, hoping that solutions would occur to him along the way.

The girl was standing in the doorway. In the background, he saw her boyfriend. She closed the door a little behind her and stepped out into the hallway.

"I'm a friend of Anna's sister, Evelyn," he said.

"And what do you want?"

"I'm looking for a friend of hers."

"Who?"

"Miriam."

"Don't know her."

Adam already wanted to turn around and leave again. But he tried again. He had the feeling he was dealing with a young woman who wasn't putting much effort into searching her brain for answers. "Are you sure there isn't someone named Miriam in your circle of friends? A girl you might call Miri?"

"Nah."

"Okay, fine, thank you."

He went out of the house. A window opened.

Her boyfriend looked down from the first-story window. "Wait a minute, dude."

"What is it?"

"Miri is not a girl."

"Then what is it?"

"It's a place."

"What do you mean?"

"You know that old steel mill just outside Schwedt?"

Adam nodded.

"There's a little shed on the site. It was used by the Russians a while ago for exercises or whatever. Anyway, that's the place we call Miri."

"Bit weird, isn't it?"

"Nah, it's a bit funny. At first, it was called *MIR*, like the space station of the Russians. Do you understand?"

"I see."

"And what's there?"

"You'll see," the young man said with a broad grin and closed the window again.

Adam looked at his watch—2:17 p.m. For the first time, he had a real lead in a case in which there had been no progress so far. What was this old Russian shack all about, and who would Anna want to meet there, he asked himself. He felt his ambition take hold of him. The timing couldn't have been worse. Because his employer was curled up on the couch, not giving a shit about his investigative skills.

Chapter 10: MIRi

November 23, 1987
Angermünde
District Frankfurt/Oder
German Democratic Republic

Shoveling coal was as arduous as any other day. The cold did not make it easier or harder. Even the onset of the snow-bringing east wind did nothing to change that. Neither did the prospect of Evelyn's search drive soon dying out or the adrenaline-fueled trip to the Soviet barracks. It was business as usual. Adam worked his shift coal-haul after coal-haul. He existed in the knowledge that this day, like any other, would end eventually. He wondered if he had seen Evelyn that day. At any rate, she was not in the workshop. But it didn't matter. He had done his job, and now he had returned to everyday life. That very evening he wanted to resume the search for the man he had to kill. He dumped the shovel on the coal pile and pushed the coal lorry into the factory building. The workstations were deserted. A crowd had gathered around a woman. There she was.

Workers in smock aprons squeezed and caressed Evelyn on her first day of work after her sister's death. He moved closer.

"Poor you, we feel so sorry for you," said one of the workers.

"Have you heard anything about how it happened? I mean, that's what you want to know, right—what she did to herself? At least I'd want to know," said another.

"I don't know anything. That's why I can't really believe it. For me, she's still alive," Evelyn said and began to cry.

Her colleagues looked at her with tilted heads and stroked her back and arms.

"We still can't believe it either. Anna was such a ray of light. You just liked to look at her. That somehow always put us in a good mood. It hit us like a blow when we heard about it," said another.

Evelyn wiped the tears from her face.

"And you know if there's anything, we're always here for you. If you need help ... you know what I mean," the woman continued.

Her friends Susanne, Maria, and Anita were nowhere to be seen. She sat at her workstation and didn't lift a finger, just stared into space. Adam stopped in front of her. She seemed to take no notice of him. Then she pulled a folded piece of paper from her smock apron and placed it in front of him. He took the paper, unfolded it, and read.

Angermünde, November 6, 1987

Dear Sis!

I am very sorry for everything, and you must know that I will always keep you in my heart. You are the best sister a person could ask for. I am so sorry because I can't take all this anymore. It has become so hard. It just doesn't go on for me in this life. Do you remember how we used to say that we would stick together forever and ever? Maybe you don't remember, but I remember it clearly. And we always will, but now I can't go on. I'm pregnant, and I don't want to get rid of it. But he wants me to, and I can't ask anyone because he's threatened me with beatings if I tell anyone. I can't even tell you. I just can't. I'm so sorry. By the time you read this, I won't be there anymore. But don't worry about me. I'm somewhere better now. I'm sure it's best for me and both of us. Please don't be sad.

Your little sister

His hopes had not been realized. A suicide note would make no difference to Evelyn. As long as she hadn't laid eyes on her sister's body, she wouldn't believe it. Of that, he was sure. As hard as her disbelief was to understand, she was right about one thing. The story left a sour aftertaste. Why hadn't Evelyn received the suicide note earlier? Why couldn't the body be found? Above the women, the VEB boss stepped onto the gallery and, a cup of tea in hand, watched the goings-on one floor below him. When the workers noticed Kletzsch, they made their way back to their stations. As they did, they avoided looking up. Evelyn remained alone at her workstation. She blew her nose with a handkerchief and dabbed the tears from her face. She glanced around the factory floor. All the women had returned to work. She looked at Adam.

"Who gave you this?" he asked.

"The Kripo came to my house this morning."

"Is it authentic?"

"I don't know. The handwriting seems to be right."

"Did they say why they didn't show you the letter until now?"

"Something about meticulousness, the post, I don't know."

"You're saying that Anna sent the letter in the mail?"

"Yes."

"And now the Kripo has it."

"Right."

"Why would Anna send her suicide note in the mail? Couldn't she have just left it next to her body?"

He himself was surprised by his rudeness.

"I don't know. It's not like there's a body."

Nothing about it added up in his mind. Why had the Kripo held the note back at first and then handed a copy out to Evelyn?

"What's going to happen now?" he asked.

She just shrugged her shoulders and then looked up. Kletzsch was taking a sip from the cup. Their eyes met. He looked at her for a long time and then came down to her. As he did, he still held the teacup in one hand and the saucer in the other. He blew into the hot liquid. The steam dispersed in front of his mouth. He took a sip. Adam went to the canteen for lunch.

Adam had brought eight coal runs behind him. Almost half of his daily workload was done. He spooned around in the lentil stew.

"Don't you want your sausage?" asked a workingwoman who had just sat down at the table and pointed to the Bockwurst on the edge of his plate, lying next to a piece of dry white bread.

"Nah, you can have it," Adam said and was about to push the plate over to her when she had already bent over the table and was putting the sausage between her teeth.

"Thank you," she said with her mouth full.

"You're welcome."

"Sad story with the pretty little sister of Evelyn, don't you think?"

"Yes."

"Did you know her well?"

Adam shook his head.

"I did. I chatted with her a few times. Only during the break, of course. Smoked and stuff."

He nodded absently and took another spoonful of the stew.

"You want to hear something? It'll make you fall off your chair. It's about Anna."

"Mm-hmm."

"Listen, but you must keep it between us," she said, taking another bite of the sausage.

"I know why Anna killed herself. She told me several times during a smoke break that she was quite happy with Koslowski. But somehow, she was missing something. Listen, she was pregnant by him. I'm sure of it. Have you noticed how she's been in different moods lately? So bitchy. And then totally happy again. Full of changes. Typically pregnant, I tell you. What do you say now?"

"Then why would she have taken her own life?"

"Hold up. Now you want to know, don't you? Sebastian didn't want any children. He was strictly against them. Nasty guy, I say. Who doesn't like children? He must have put her under a lot of pressure when he found out. So much so that she wanted to have it removed. And she couldn't take it anymore. And that's when she put an end to it."

"Did she tell you about the pregnancy?"

"She didn't need to. Women sense things like that."

Adam leaned over to her. She leaned her upper body forward as well. He spoke more softly. "Do you know how she killed herself, too?"

The woman nodded knowingly.

"She threw herself into the Oder. Do you know how cold it is at this time of year? You don't just drown. You freeze to death."

She put an index finger over her mouth and leaned back again.

"Hell's bells," he said and smiled inside.

"She was such a sweetie. That was really not necessary if you ask me."

A woman in a dark blue costume came to their table. The worker fell silent. She was the secretary of the factory management.

"Hedman, the boss wants to see you."

"Now?"

"Nah, you can finish your dinner," she said and left again.

The worker put the last piece of the sausage in her mouth. Adam went on his way and considered what the woman had just been gulping down her throat with such relish. Cartilage, tendons, fat, salts, binders, intestines, water, and a little muscle meat. He knew why he always left the sausage on the edge of the plate.

Adam left the factory canteen. He gave no further thought to whether there was a shred of truth to the worker's story. He went up to the second-floor offices. The VEB boss propped his elbows on his desk as Adam sat down in the chair in front of him.

Kletzsch folded his hands together and looked Adam straight in the eye. "My dear Hedman, what am I to do with you? First, you don't really cooperate in the search for our Anna, and then I hear that you're turning the whole of Angermünde upside down with Evelyn."

"Where did you hear that?"

"The collective has many eyes and many ears. And, of course, many mouths. But that's not important. What's more important is that Anna could still be alive if we had found her in time."

"True, maybe."

"You see? That's why we all have to pull together. A real worker doesn't let anything stop him. And a real worker also knows what is required of him. If there's a search to be done, there's a search to be done. With all our strength. And with a bright mind. And if a girl takes her own life, a real worker also knows what he has to do then. Namely, to put his work again fully in the service of the common cause, and not to search around for clues. There's no sense in that. I don't even want to know how you attracted the attention of General Gabulov's son. But he was not pleased when I had to tell him that Anna Sievers is no longer with us. He could not believe it. He cursed you. You are lucky that comrade Gabulov is such a reasonable man. Do you even realize what you're getting yourself into?"

Adam nodded.

"I can't hear you."

"I get it. I won't do it anymore."

"What are you not going to do anymore?"

"I will not forget to put all my labor into the service of the collective."

"Good, that's right."

Kletzsch pondered. His face relaxed. "I'm just glad Anna fell asleep peacefully. An overdose of sleeping pills. There was nothing more that could've been done. You know, it does give me a better feeling that I know it wasn't a cruel death."

Tears welled up in the man's eyes.

"This is hard for all of us, Herr Kletzsch."

"Evelyn received her sister's suicide note today."

Why had the man told him that?

"We all have to be brave now," Adam said.

"You're absolutely right, Hedman."

"Did she see Anna's body?"

"I don't know ... no, I guess she didn't."

The VEB manager regained his composure and lowered his voice. "And not a word of this to anyone. Especially not to Evelyn. She's a little unstable. Understand?"

"Roger that, Herr Kletzsch."

"Well, get on with it, then, you hero of seventeen loads," Kletzsch said, grinning again.

Did the man have what it took to kidnap one of his workers and hold her captive? Was he smart enough to make a murder look like a suicide and forge a suicide note? Adam decided to find out the answer to those questions. Evelyn had infected him with her suspicion. He got up and left.

The hero of seventeen loads had done his work. He changed his clothes and left the factory. He looked forward to the solitude of his apartment. Eat, read, be left alone. Kletzsch would have to wait. He could still spy on him the next day.

When Adam reached the factory gate, he heard a honk and saw the little car. What needed to happen had happened—Evelyn appeared. He walked toward the Trabant. She leaned over toward the passenger door and opened it for him. He got in.

"Don't make that face," she said.

She was back to her old self. Evelyn had an unshakable will to push reality aside again and again.

"Feeling better?"

"I was a bit rattled. But they can't do anything to me."

"I thought maybe because you already weren't doing so well yesterday ..."

"Nonsense, that was just the typical Sunday tristesse."

"You sure?"

"Sure."

"I was actually just going home."

"I'll drive you. You still have to tell me what came out yesterday.

He thought about it for a moment. Could he keep from her what he had found out? But in the mood Evelyn was in right now, he couldn't get rid of her that evening anyway. Adam looked out the window. Evelyn possessed the peculiar quality of drawing her motivation from the fact that the situation was hopeless. Adam could not explain otherwise why she wanted to rejoin the investigation. She didn't mention anything about the suicide note. She didn't want to face the fact that her sister was dead. Anna's sibling needed more evidence. She wanted to know for sure. If she wasn't going to get to see the body, she at least wanted to get a picture of the circumstances that had driven Anna to suicide, Adam thought. Was Evelyn so different from him? The most precious human in his life had been dead for over seven years. Until that day, he still couldn't comprehend it. Sometimes it seemed to him that she would show up behind the next corner. Adam knew it couldn't happen. Still, this apparition would be more common to him than never seeing her again.

Adam perceived scraps of words and realized that he had not been listening to Evelyn. It was probably about something at the VEB. Maybe the female colleagues. He didn't know and mumbled agreement so that she wouldn't ask if he had understood everything.

"I know who Miri is," he said.

"Excellent, who?"

He told her. She was thrilled with the results of his investigation and wanted to leave immediately. He tried to talk her out of it. As always, in vain.

She stepped on the gas. He was glad that they were in a GDR-made vehicle. Otherwise, they would be shooting through town at one hundred twenty instead of forty. They left the city behind them. On both sides of the road stretched snow-covered farmlands. Only now and then did a bare tree stand lonely in the landscape. They drove east along the country road. The trees became more numerous. They crossed a forest. Directly behind it was the old steel mill. A seven-foot-high wall of bricks surrounded it. They parked the car directly in front of the wrought-iron gate. The two got out and rattled at the front gate. Locked. In one place, the iron struts were pushed apart. They pushed through the gap and entered the former factory premises. The factory lay silent in the darkness. They saw little and had to move carefully across the site. Then they passed a huge hall and a cooling tower. In the pale light, it looked as if the last worker had just left here after his shift. But no steel had been rolled here for years. Behind the plant, the view opened onto a concreted area. Evelyn slipped on one of the frozen puddles. She held on to Adam's arm. Together they walked toward a cube. They reached the corrugated metal shack and walked around. Adam pointed to the Cyrillic letters painted in red paint on one of the walls.

Мир. *MIR*.

They were at the right place and walked around the building. There was no sound. Was anyone here? Bicycles were leaning against the back. Two mopeds stood next to them.

"This is where it's supposed to be?" whispered Evelyn.

"Yes, yes. We just need to find the entrance. Are you still sure you want to come?"

She squeezed his hand. "Well, sure, it's a great adventure."

There it was again, the adventure, Adam thought and pulled her to the tin cube. There was an embedded door. He tried to open it, but it was locked.

"Should we knock?" she asked.

"There must be another entrance. I'm sure of it."

They searched the ground around the crate. On one side they found an iron hatch in the concrete surface.

"I don't believe it. That's not the entrance. No way. That's much too narrow," said Evelyn.

He bent down and pulled on the hatch. It moved. The two stood in front of a hole in the floor and looked inside. There was nothing to see. They listened inside. There was just as little to hear. Were they going to let this hole swallow them? A metal ladder led down into the depths.

"Do you want to go first, Evelyn?" he whispered, winking at her.

She looked at him and shook her head, so he descended into the darkness in front of her. Twelve rungs later, his feet reached solid ground. He groped into the darkness and found a door in the shaft. It could be opened. He called Evelyn to him. She also descended the ladder. He ducked through the door. She was now close behind him. In front of them was a narrow corridor. The ceiling was less than seven feet high. Dim light leaked from the wall openings along the corridor. A whispering sound flowed through the rooms like a steady murmur. Was it the wind that found its way underground, or was it human voices? Evelyn stayed close behind him. She tugged at his sleeve. He stopped.

"Pretty cold down here. And a little damp. Like in a crypt," she whispered.

"Are you scared? We can go up again."

"Nah, nah, move along."

She pushed him further through an opening in the wall. It was a small room. A candle burned in the corner. Two figures were sitting on boxes. He saluted into the room. The two seemed not to notice him. Were they asleep? The candle on top of the beer bottle flickered and then burned out. All of a sudden, it was pitch black. They turned around, left the room again, and stepped through the next opening that led off the hallway. More sparse candlelight. This room was empty. Across the hall, they found a young man sitting alone in the corner. Adam bent down to him. He did not seem to be conscious. Adam shook him. The boy moved. He looked up from glassy eyes.

"Do you know Anna?" Adam asked him.

The boy did not respond.

He shook him again. "Anna? Do you know Anna Sievers?"

No answer. He let go of him.

"We won't get anything out of him today," he said to Evelyn and left the room again.

From the end of the corridor, they heard soft voices. They went to the source of the sounds. The ceiling got even lower. He ducked his head as he walked. They peered around the corner into the room. One, two, three, four, five figures were sitting in the room, spread out on boxes and crates. Adam moved closer. In the candlelight, he could make out three young women and two young men. One of the girls took a deep breath and moved her head upward. It seemed to take her great effort to make this movement. But she looked happy.

The girl next to her tugged at her sleeve and pointed at the two intruders. "What are they doing here?" she asked.

The other one just shrugged her shoulders in slow motion, sucked in air through her nose, and leaned her head against the wall. The young men and the third girl seemed to take no notice of them at all.

"Ahoy!" he said to the crowd.

Evelyn grabbed him by the shoulder and pulled him back.

"You know, I know those girls. One of them, anyway," she said, gesturing with her head to the two young women in the corner.

"Do you want to talk to them?"

Evelyn nodded and walked past him. He stopped in the opening in the wall. The girls saw Evelyn and pretended to be engaged in conversation. One was wearing a tattered NVA jacket. Her ash-blond hair was peeking out from under a bobble hat. The other had on a coarse wool knit sweater, which she paired with a scarf of the same material.

She wore her long brown hair loose. Evelyn sat down with the two girls.

"Evelyn, what are you doing here?" asked the girl with the hat.

"Hi, Renate!"

"You know that's only what my parents call me," she said, turning back to her friend.

"Renate, I need to talk to you."

The girl pretended not to hear Evelyn.

"It's about Anna," Evelyn said.

She turned a deaf ear. The girl in the knit sweater peeked over at Evelyn and spoke softly to her friend. "Maybe it's something important. Why don't you talk to her?"

She ignored her friend too and dug a candy box out of her jacket. Evelyn rolled her eyes.

"All right, Roxy." She emphasized the name as if it were the most childish thing she'd ever said. "I need to talk to you ... about Anna."

Roxy turned to Anna's sister and popped one of the candies into her mouth. "Well, ma'am, how can I help you?"

"Anna has disappeared. Do you know where she is?"

"Interesting. But don't you want to say hello properly first?"

"What? Sure! Good afternoon!"

"Nah, not to me. We already know each other. My friend here."

Evelyn reached out her hand to her friend. "Good day!"

The girl held out her hand as if expecting a kiss on the hand.

Roxy pulled up the corners of her mouth until her pointy little teeth were showing. "Don't you even want to know her name?"

"But of course."

"Well, go on, then."

Evelyn hesitated. Roxy nodded encouragingly at her. Evelyn looked at the other girl, who was inspecting her fingernails. "Uh, yeah, and what's your name?"

"Freiheit," she said without looking up. Her self-chosen name meant freedom.

The girls giggled.

"Bullshit, nobody is called that."

Roxy and Freiheit turned back to each other.

Evelyn tried again. "Man, now listen to me first. I haven't done anything to you."

"You being here is bad enough," Roxy said.

"But it's about Anna."

"We already know. But guess what, she's not here. You see."

Freiheit pulled at Roxy's sleeve. "Don't talk to her. You know what Anna used to say about her."

"What?" asked Evelyn.

The two girls said nothing and grinned at her. They pretended not to know that Anna was dead. There they were completely in line with Evelyn. Otherwise, nothing seemed to connect them. Or they were just playing a mean game with her. He had been watching from a distance and walked over to the women. Then he pulled Evelyn away from them.

In the hallway, he took Evelyn aside. "It's no use with you and those two," he said.

"But I know them. They're friends of Anna's."

"That seems to be the problem here. They don't seem to like you very much. It's a big-sister thing, I guess. There's nothing you can do about it."

"They're antisocial. They'd better make sure not to end up at a *Jugendwerkhof*," said Evelyn, referring to GDR works yards where teenage delinquents were taught obedience.

"Do you want me to try talking to them?"

"You can do that. I'll wait for you outside."

He nodded. Shortly after, she had disappeared into the darkness. He went back into the room and sat down with the group around the boys.

"You guys got a smoke?" he asked.

"Nah, we don't," said one.

"Fire hazard," the other said, laughing softly.

Shortly after, the other one started laughing and slowly closed his eyelids. The kids were not alright. They seemed far too calm, as if wrapped in clouds. Even the girls' hatred for their friend's sister was muted. And it was fleeting. They appeared to be content with themselves and their surroundings again.

"You want some?" said the one boy, holding out a small bottle to him.

"What is it?"

"You'll see."

The boy poured some of the liquid on his sleeve and held it under Adam's nose. It smelled beastly. Like pharmacy and gas station at the same time. Adam breathed through his mouth.

"Nah, keep your piehole shut," the boy said, pouring some more from the bottle on the same spot.

Again he held it under his nose. Adam closed his mouth, exhaled, and drew air in through his nose. The liquid evaporated, and the gas bit into his forehead. It rushed through all the convolutions of his brain. He felt hot, and then a chill washed over him. He had to lean against the wall. A cloud brought warm rain over him. Dimly he could see the two girls coming towards him. His knees softening, he sat down. Roxy sat down on his left, Freiheit on the other side. The young men had disappeared. He had not seen the third girl in a long time either. Adam was alone with the two who had taken him into their midst.

"Hello, sir!" said Roxy.

"Hi!" he said and contorted his face into a grimace that should have been a laugh.

He couldn't wipe the misshapen grin off his face. It simply remained as it was.

"Hi," Freiheit said in a long drawl.

The girls laughed.

"Say hello properly. It's like bedlam in here," Roxy said.

Adam extended his right hand in front of him and opened it. "Good afternoon, ladies!"

They shook his hand. He leaned with the back of his head against the cold wall and looked straight ahead. He felt like singing.

"*Stell... dich... mitten... in... das... Feuer...*" He spoke softly to himself, repeating the first line of the song he'd heard in Anna's apartment. *Put yourself in the fire's center.*

"What's he saying?" asked Freiheit.

"I know this, I think."

"Do you understand him?"

"Not a word."

"Me neither."

"*Liebe ... dieses ...Ungeheuer.*" *Love this monster* he sang in German.

The individual words of the song lyrics tumbled out of his mouth. Why did it have to be this song?

"What's his name?" Roxy asked her friend.

"Why don't you ask him?"

"Who are you? Do you have a name?" she asked, nudging him on the shoulder.

"I'm Adam, first of men," he said in English.

"*Ädem*? Englishman or what?" said Freiheit.

"What are you doing here, *Ädem*?" asked Roxy.

"I'm looking for a murderer. You can call me Adam," he said in German with a severe face, indicating that it was okay for him to pronounce his name the German way.

The girls laughed.

"No, that's not what I mean. What are you doing here with Anna's sister? Isn't she a bit old for you?" asked Freiheit.

Adam realized that Evelyn was roughly the same age he was but she looked older. Much older.

"We're looking for insights," Adam said.

The girls laughed again.

"Insights into what?" asked Roxy.

"Anna."

The girls laughed briefly. Then they fell silent.

"But Anna is dead, isn't she?" said Freiheit.

"Seems so."

Freiheit looked past him at Roxy. "I think he's had a little bit too much of that stuff."

Roxy nodded. He was still smiling.

"I could use another nose of that. Where are the boys?" he asked, trying to sit up.

"You don't need them for that," Freiheit said, pulling out a vial from her jacket.

She unscrewed the cap, pulled her sweater down to the base of her chest, and dribbled some onto her bare skin. Freiheit put a hand in the back of his head and pressed it to her chest. Adam sucked the evaporating liquid in. The thrill was harder than the first time. It flung him backward. He leaned back against the wall. He grinned. And grinned. And grinned. The girls giggled somewhere in the distance and dribbled the liquid on their arms. Then they breathed in the vapors.

"You were still a virgin with that stuff. Right?" said Roxy.

He moved his head slowly up and down.

"And why are you helping Anna's sister? I mean, that's stupid. Anna killed herself. What else do you want to find out?"

He moved his shoulders slowly up and down. "I don't know. But if I don't help her, she's got me by the balls."

"You're afraid of Evelyn?" asked Freiheit, spitting on the floor right in front of him.

"Are you being blackmailed or what?" asked Roxy.

He laughed silently to himself and searched the room for the others. He could not find them anywhere.

"What did you do that she has you by the balls?" asked Freiheit.

"The truth and nothing but the truth."

The girls laughed again.

"You're funny, Adam," Freiheit said.

"Yeah, I'm funny," he said slowly to himself.

"By the way, do you know Sebastian, Anna's boyfriend?"

"Sure. What about him?" asked Freiheit.

"Well, you know. Was she unhappy with him? Did he ever hit her ... or get her pregnant?"

"Do you think Basti is to blame for Anna's suicide?" asked Roxy.

"I don't know. You tell me."

"No way. Basti is a poor bastard. He always was. He wasn't allowed to get close to Anna. That's what he always said. Even though she was always pretending to be an erotic star. I believed him. She had no idea about fucking," Freiheit said and laughed.

"And you do?" Roxy asked her friend.

"Totally. I do it all day long."

"I saw him with another girl yesterday," he said.

"Ramona," Freiheit said.

"That's right, Ramona. It's weird."

"For you, maybe. Or for Evelyn. But not for us. It hasn't been going well between Basti and Anna for a long time," Roxy said.

"But with Basti and Ramona," Freiheit said.

"Anna was quite happy about it, I think. Basti was always so jealous. Not without reason, I'd say," said Roxy.

"Sebastian told me that Anna doesn't let anyone get close to her. Cold fish and all that. So that she's not up for men at all. Not like that, anyway."

"He said that?" asked Roxy.

"Anna just wasn't into him," Freiheit said.

"So you don't think she was pregnant by Sebastian either, and that's why she took her own life?"

"No, definitely not by Basti. And why should she want to kill herself just because she's pregnant? She could have it removed just like that. I know a few people who have done that. There's nothing to it," said Roxy, looking at her friend.

The brunette gave her a kick against her leg. It could not have been more obvious.

"Okay, then who got Anna pregnant?"

"She didn't tell us anything about that," Freiheit said.

"Let's assume she was pregnant ..."

"Nah, not by anyone that we know. Maybe you'd better ask someone who knows," Roxy said.

He looked at her first. Then her friend. Neither of them said anything.

"Well, who knows?"

"You don't," Roxy said, laughing.

"Quite funny. But ..."

"It's all right. But you didn't hear it from us. Understand? We promised Anna we wouldn't say anything. Especially not to her ugly sister," Freiheit said.

He nodded.

"Sandro. Sandro knows," said Roxy.

"What's Sandro's last name?"

The two shrugged their shoulders.

"And how can I find him?"

"You can't," Roxy said.

"Have you guys ever seen Sandro, like with your own eyes and stuff?"

They shook their heads.

"Any idea where he might be?"

"In Berlin. At Alex. He's out there with the punks," said Freiheit, referring to Alexanderplatz in the center of East Berlin.

"In Berlin?"

"Where else? In London or what?"

"What does he look like?"

"Blue eyes," Roxy said.

"And black curls," the other followed up.

"Are you sure you didn't dream about that?"

"Ha ha," Freiheit said.

"Could Sandro have bought her an expensive dress?"

"Why?" asked Roxy.

"Because she has an expensive dress and Evelyn doesn't know where it came from."

"Maybe she sewed it herself," Freiheit said.

Adam had not yet thought of that. It was possible. Inventiveness knew no bounds in the GDR. Maybe she had sewn the dress herself and then gotten the original Chanel label from somewhere. He decided to ask Evelyn if that could have been the case.

"Do you two know Kate Bush?"

"Sure," Freiheit said.

The blonde nodded.

"There's a song, *The Man with the Child in His Eyes*."

"It's so beautiful," Roxy said.

"Is it possible that she meant Sandro?"

"How would Kate Bush know Sandro?" asked Roxy.

"Well, I found a translation of the text in Anna's records. It seemed important to her. That's why I think Anna might have meant Sandro."

"That may be so," Freiheit said.

"But she never said anything about it being him?"

The girls shook their heads. Freiheit took the vial out of her pocket and dribbled some more of the liquid onto her arm. The three took turns inhaling the vapors and dropped backward one by one.

Falling.

Falling.

Falling.

Chapter 11: CRIMEAN CHAMPAGNE

November 24, 1987
Angermünde
District Frankfurt/Oder
German Democratic Republic

Adam woke up to the clatter of the cooking pot. Everything hurt.

"What time is it?" he asked Evelyn, who was standing in her underpants at the stove in his kitchen, boiling water. She wore nothing else and didn't seem to mind the cold.

"A little after six," she said, looking at him over her shoulder.

"Aren't you a little cold?"

"I'll be right back in bed."

He felt as if a whole division of the Red Army had marched over his skull. As he pulled the blanket away, he realized that he was naked. Usually, he didn't sleep like that. He looked at Evelyn.

"Would you mind telling me what happened yesterday?" he asked, remaining seated on the bed.

"I could ask you the same thing," she said, turning to face him.

Evelyn filled two cups with hot water. Even though he had never wondered what the woman looked like naked, he now had a good impression of it. She sat down on the table and put her legs on a chair.

"You left me there waiting for quite a while. It was freezing in my car. After hours, I mean literally after hours, you came back out. Well, not so much walking, more like staggering. I had to help you into the car because you could hardly walk, and then I brought you here."

"And then?"

"Well, you can imagine."

He said nothing. She took a sip of the hot water. Was it possible he'd had sex with Evelyn? All the signs pointed to it.

"Can't remember?"

"Not really."

"Too bad."

"Let me ask you a dumb question. Was that even technically possible? Me being fucked up like that, you know?"

"No doubt."

He nodded and thought for a moment. "Did I say something?"

"Well, you didn't really say anything. It was more like noises."

"What kind of noises?"

"I would say like a chicken?"

"Did I crow?"

"Nah, more like clucking or cooing."

"What?"

"You kept saying *gack-gack*, *gack-gack*. Just like a chicken. But as high as you were, I wasn't surprised at all."

Adam had no idea what had happened. However, he was not ashamed of it. Two warm bodies, closeness and desire. That could happen. Only he could not believe it yet. He was almost glad if it should be accurate. This behavior seemed so human to him that he hardly recognized himself in it. But the probability was small.

He tried to remember last night again. But there was nothing. The sleeve of the boy with the acrid liquid was the last record of his memory.

"Can you hand me my pants?" he said to Evelyn.

"Yeah, might be better if you put some clothes on," she said, handing them to him across the table.

He pushed the thoughts of the possible sexual intercourse with Evelyn out of his head and pulled his pants over his legs. Then he reached into his pockets and found a few crumpled pieces of paper.

"Did you get the number from one of those bitches?" she asked.

He uncrumpled the pieces of paper. There were two phone numbers written on them in different handwriting. It was surprising that both girls were reachable by phone, since almost no one had a phone line. He had written the girls' hair colors next to each of the numbers. And he had written down something else.

Sandro Alex Punk

Adam handed her the note. "Does this mean anything to you?"

"Nah."

"Maybe it's Anna's guy in Berlin that Sebastian was talking about."

"I can't imagine that. Punks and other lowlives hang around on Alexanderplatz. Just that sort of people. Anna has nothing to do with that."

"So we don't have to interview him?"

"I don't think so."

It was terrific that Evelyn always thought a lead was of no interest when he had just taken the bait. Sandro had made it onto his investigation list. Right behind Lothar Kletzsch. Evelyn got up and got dressed.

"I'm off now. Gotta put some fresh clothes on when I get home," she said, heading for the door. "See you later at the factory."

Once again, Adam was not sure whether he had given himself the right task. The head of the Volkseigener Betrieb Gustav Bruhn was walking a few yards ahead of him. It felt strange to follow his boss after the end of his shift. But he couldn't resist. At least he wanted to stay on his heels until he reached his front door. See where he lived, how he lived. Get a sense of how he celebrated the end of the day.

Lothar Kletzsch walked from the factory to the city center. It was shortly before closing time. Passersby hurried into Konsum, the standardized market for all daily use goods, which carried only domestic products or those from friendly brother nations. The man went to the Exquisit store that was next to it. Sometimes they had goods that could be considered a luxury—sparkling wine from the Crimea, caviar from Beluga, cigars from Havana. Adam stopped in front of the store and looked through the shop window into the salesroom. Kletzsch was waiting in front of the counter. A woman was taking his order. Shortly after, she disappeared into the back rooms and came back after a while with a bottle of champagne. The man paid. Adam went across the street and watched Kletzsch hastily enter Konsum. Shortly after, he came out again with a bulging bag. Right in front of the store, he stopped and looked in the bag for something. He found it and put the bag down. In his hand, he held a pack of cigarettes. He tore off the silver foil and fired one up. Then he took a drag and exhaled the smoke with relish. He had never seen Kletzsch smoke before.

The man grabbed the shopping bag and continued down the main street. Without detouring or stopping again, they reached the neighborhood where Pop also lived. There was no one but them on the road. Adam let the distance increase. On either side of the cobblestone street, single-family homes and city mansions watched over the neighborhood. Bald sycamores, Wartburgs, and Volvos lined the street. Kletzsch stopped in front of a garden gate. He took out his key and unlocked it. The house was plain and lay in darkness. No one seemed to be waiting for him. Until the man had climbed the three steps to his front door and disappeared into the building, Adam remained across the street. Behind the windows of the ground level in the two-story low-rise building, it became bright.

Adam crossed the road. He saw Kletzsch in his kitchen, unpacking the groceries and stowing them in the cupboards. Adam stood in front of the garden fence. With the lights on in the house, the man would not see him outside in the darkness. He looked around. Not a soul was out on the street. No nosy neighbors were standing behind the curtains. He jumped over the fence and ran through the garden and then around the building. Behind the house was a terrace that looked out onto a sprawling lawn that was framed by a row of evergreen bushes. His chance for a hiding place.

Light spilled into the garden. Kletzsch had come into the living room, which was behind the large glass windows overlooking the terrace. He had turned on the overhead light. Adam lay down flat on the ground. The man left the living room again. Crouched, Adam ran to the row of bushes and found shelter behind them. From here, he had an unobstructed view into the living room. He could even see Kletzsch standing in the kitchen through the hallway. He had just taken the champagne bottle and put it in the refrigerator. Then he left the room and could no longer be seen. On the second floor, the light came on. Behind a frosted pane, Adam could see him undressing.

He spent about half an hour in the room, which could only be the bathroom. Then he turned out the light again and came down to the ground level in a housecoat. Kletzsch went into the kitchen and checked the temperature of the champagne. Apparently, he was expecting a visitor. The man put the champagne back in the refrigerator and sat down in the living room. He turned on the television. But

Adam couldn't see which program he had chosen. He would have loved to know if the head of the VEB was watching forbidden Western channels. At least Kletzsch had a remote control in his hand and switched between channels at intervals of a few seconds. It was unlikely that he alternately chose between DDR 1 and DDR 2. At intervals of a few minutes, he stood up, looked out the window, and then sat down again.

After about an hour, the doorbell seemed to ring. Kletzsch straightened his coat and hair and went to the front door. Adam's knees ached. He squatted down and could see Kletzsch taking the coat of his visitor. Who it was, he could not see. The man blocked his view of the other person. Then Kletzsch went into the kitchen, got glasses from a hanging cupboard and the champagne from the refrigerator. When he got to the living room alone, the light came on again on the second floor. It must have been the only bathroom in the house. Upstairs, a woman appeared to be combing her hair. Downstairs, the man was distributing alcohol among the two glasses. He sat down on the couch and waited. For a brief moment, he picked up the remote control. But he immediately put it back on the coffee table and looked around the living room.

Suddenly, the lights in the living room went out. A woman came through the door. She was only illuminated from behind by the light from the kitchen. He could not make out her face. She was wearing a coat. That was strange. Hadn't Kletzsch just taken the coat off her? Adam knelt again. He still couldn't make out anything. Should he move closer? Then it became bright again in the living room. He saw Kletzsch move back from a table lamp he must have just flipped on. Then he leaned back on the couch and looked up slightly. The woman stood a few feet in front of him. Her slender legs peeked out from under her coat. She wore fishnet tights and high-heeled shoes. Her red hair fell almost to her bottom. Adam was struck by lightning.

The woman stalked toward the man. He opened his coat, under which he was naked. There was no mistaking that the man was aroused. The woman spread her legs and bent forward. Kletzsch grabbed her by the shoulders and pulled her to him. She knelt in front of the man and bent over his lap. He put his hands on her head and pushed her down. Rhythmically, her shock of red hair moved up and down. Kletzsch leaned back and closed his eyes. Adam stood up. He took a step closer to the house. Anna? The woman looked like Anna. Had he just watched a missing person having sex with the head of the VEB? Impossible. His mind must be playing tricks on him.

If he had found her locked in the man's cellar, he would have been astonished. But the fact that she was apparently consorting with the VEB boss on her own free will was beyond the limits of his imagination. The woman moved her head up and down a few more times, and Kletzsch grimaced. She stood up and turned around. A second flash hit him. The woman stood in front of the window and looked out. It was Evelyn. She wore a long red-haired wig and lingerie. Adam remained glued to the spot. The man got up from the couch, removed his housecoat, and embraced her from behind. She put her head to the side and let him kiss her on the neck. Evelyn's gaze seemed to meet Adam's. The man clutched her breasts and kneaded them. She fixed on the spot where Adam stood and smiled. No, she was laughing. He wanted to turn away, but he couldn't.

Adam heard a bark and was jolted out of his trance state. Slowly, he took a few steps backward, turned around when he reached the garden fence, and jumped into the neighbor's garden.

He had known the two knew each other from school, but he hadn't thought they had a relationship. He had the feeling he had been watching a party where people indulged in an immoral fetish. Evelyn played her sister Anna. She filled the void for Kletzsch that her death had left. Had Anna only allowed herself to be gawked at from a distance? Now, with Evelyn's help, he was able to turn his fantasy into reality. Why was she doing this? What had Kletzsch promised her to get her to go along? He no longer trusted Evelyn. First, she pretended to have slept with him, and then she had sex with the man at the top of his list of suspects. Or was he looking at it from a completely wrong angle? Could it be that the dead woman's sister and the head of the VEB were in cahoots?

Adam just wanted to get away, and he ran through the gardens until he reached a street again. In a few minutes, he reached home. He closed the door behind him and left the lights off. At some point, he would have to confront Evelyn. But that day, he didn't want to see anyone else. All he wanted was his own life back.

Chapter 12: WORLD TIME CLOCK

November 25, 1987
Berlin
Capital of the GDR
German Democratic Republic

Adam took the train to Berlin and left Angermünde behind. After seeing Evelyn and Kletzsch together, he could no longer bear the sight of them and had called in sick. The compartment was unoccupied except for himself, and he looked out the window. Why was he still investigating at all? He had done his job. None of the suspects had anything to do with Anna's disappearance. But something had grabbed him and wouldn't let go. There was a disturbance in the relationship of forces. An injustice that was unacceptable. He knew he couldn't let go until the person responsible for Anna's disappearance was brought to justice. Or at least he had to find out what game was being played with him. He had already put too much blood and sweat into the search to stop until he had followed up on the last clue. And this clue would bring him closer. He could feel it.

The train stopped in the next major district town. An old man with a boy got on in Eberswalde. The boy sat down at the window and grinned at him. Not smiling back at children, even if you didn't feel like it, seemed cold. And so he smiled. That was all he had to do. Amazing how simple some things were. After a short ride, he said goodbye to both of them at Berlin-Lichtenberg station and changed to the Stadtbahn heading west. The S-Bahn coaches from the twenties rumbled into the station. He got on and sat down on a free seat on one of the long wooden benches.

It was only a few stops from here to Alexanderplatz. If he was honest with himself, he had to avoid the center of East Berlin by all means, as it was swarming with police officers and secret service agents. He let his gaze wander through the car. Expressionless faces on a dreary day. In the corner, a man held a newspaper with both hands and laughed loudly. Around him, the seats were unoccupied. He sat alone at a great distance where the rest of the car was nearly full. The laughter grew shriller. The man took down the newspaper. It was the man from the holding cell, whom he had already seen again in Schwedt in the station restaurant. This could not be a coincidence. Or could it be? Yet again a cold shiver ran down his spine.

When the next station announced itself with the braking of the train, Adam stood up. When the car had stopped, he opened the door and walked out as quietly as he could. The man's laughter echoed down to the platform. Then the doors closed again, and he had the feeling that the man was glancing over his shoulder at him as the train exited. Should he cut short his investigative journey? Was he risking betraying his real goal by chasing a phantom?

He waited for the next S-Bahn and reached Alexanderplatz after a few stops. This was the hub of the GDR. Directly adjacent was the political epicenter with Palast der Republik, Palace of the Republic, Rotes Rathaus, Red City Hall and Staatsratsgebäude, State Council Building. The inhabitants of the capital met here to stroll, to see, and to be seen. In the square, they were proud citizens of the only socialist republic on German soil. They buzzed busily around the tallest building in Berlin. The 1,207½-foot-tall Television Tower looked like a needle fired from outer space, smashed into the concrete slabs of the square. Adam walked through the underground passages of the station, which were like a foxhole under the square.

The citizens passed him grimly or did not dignify him with a glance. The women wore dresses, the men suits. Both wore overcoats. Adam had adapted his clothes to the weather conditions but not to the local style. He wore a wool sweater, a parka over it, jeans tucked into work boots, and a wool cap. A typical dress style for city dwellers in the Western world put you under suspicion of antisocial tendencies in the GDR. He did not look like a well-behaved GDR citizen but like a worker from the province with a criminal record. So, the disguise was perfect. Evelyn had spoken with disgust about the people you could meet here. But where were his brothers and sisters in spirit?

As Adam walked up the stairs from the subway station, he was struck by the icy wind that swept the square during the cold season. This time stretched from October to April in bad years. He walked across the yard. It was emptier than he had imagined. He walked toward an architectural concrete block. It was Centrum department store. A few passersby hurried into the flagship shopping temple of the socialist planned economy. To his left was an underpass connecting the department store to the high-rise Interhotel Stadt Berlin. To his right was the World Clock, which displayed the times of the socialist metropolises of Pyongyang, Moscow, and Kabul, and those of the less socialist New York, Hong Kong, and Sydney. He saw some figures sitting on a staircase. Were these *that sort of people* Evelyn had talked about? He didn't see any beer bottles in their hands. It just couldn't be fun to drink outdoors in Berlin's cold months, he thought. Those were summer pastimes.

Adam walked up to a couple. The young man was sitting one step above an even younger-looking woman and had his arms around her. They were smoking and didn't look like antisocials or punks.

With one foot on the stairs, he stood in front of them. "Do you have another one left?" he asked, pointing to the cigarette in the young man's mouth.

The man in the leather jacket and long hair pulled out a cigarette, Karo brand, and held it out to him. He took the cigarette from him and thanked him with a nod.

"Where do you come from? I've never seen you here before," the man said.

"Angermünde."

"Did you run away?" she asked.

"Nah, why?"

"Well, because you look like you just escaped from the NVA. Always the same shit. They don't know where to go, so they come here first. So, you didn't escape. That's good for me, too. Do you have a name?" asked the young woman with the dyed blond strands in her brown hair.

So that's what they looked like, the punks and lowlives, he thought. He was in the right place.

"Adam," he said.

"I'm Jessi. And this is Speiche. And that one over here is Andri," she said, pointing to the tall man next to her on the stairs.

The man raised his hand casually.

"Hi! Do you know where the punks hang out around this place?" Adam asked.

They grinned.

"What's so funny?"

"Well, you've come to the right place, then," said Speiche.

"Disappointed? What did you expect?" asked Jessi.

"More people."

"It's just too cold today," she said.

"Come on, sit down," the young man said and explained to him the lay of the land in the punk scene at Alex. There were the foster children who didn't know where else to go. There were delinquent youths who would otherwise have to slave away in Jugendwerkhöfen if they didn't have a beer here on the steps. There were children from academic families who rebelled and dyed their hair in wild colors. They all came together on Alex. A society of those cast out of the socialist family. Jessi and Speiche couldn't stop talking. They visibly enjoyed explaining to the stranger the nature of the terrain on which he was moving. Were they trying to show him how beautiful it was or help him so he wouldn't stumble? He was about to find out.

"Do you know a guy called Sandro?" he asked.

Andri seemed interested in the conversation for the first time and joined in. "Why do you want to know?" he asked.

"Asking for a friend."

"And does the friend have a name?"

"Evelyn."

"Is that her whole name?"

"Sievers. Evelyn Sievers."

"Don't know her. Why is she interested in this guy?"

"It's her sister's boyfriend."

"Really?"

Andri looked astonished. Adam thought it was funny that the man couldn't believe that Anna was dating Sandro.

"I think so," Adam said.

"And what do you have to do with it?"

"Her sister has disappeared. Sandro is her last hope, so to speak."

"Poor thing," Andri said, grinning.

"Something wrong with Sandro?"

"Just to be sure—do you know what this Sandro looks like?"

"Black curls, blue eyes."

Andri nodded. "Maybe I know him. If we're talking about the same guy, you should see for yourself. And then I'll be asking you if there's something wrong with him."

"It's all right. Do you know where I can find him?"

"Could get complicated. I'll see what I can do."

Then he got up and left.

Adam looked at the other two, who just shrugged. "What happens now?"

"Just wait and see," said Speiche.

"Is he always this tight-lipped?"

"Sometimes. He's South American. They actually like to babble, I heard. But with him, it's different somehow. Chile, you know? Terrible dictatorship over there. He's a refugee. Who knows what he's seen?"

Adam nodded approval. He had already heard of Chilean exiles who had fled to East Germany after Pinochet's coup, but Andri was the first he had ever met.

Adam waited. Over an hour later, another man approached him and handed him a piece of paper. Shortly after that, he knocked on the apartment door of the address Andri had relayed to him. He found the apartment in a sterile new construction area just a few miles from Alexanderplatz. Nothing happened. He knocked again. Adam heard footsteps on the other side of the door. Andri opened it and nodded in greeting. Adam had not expected to see him. Andri walked down the unlit hallway and told him to lock the door behind him. He didn't know whose apartment he was in or what he was doing there. But he was about to find out, he thought. Andri opened the door to a room darkened by rugs hanging over the windows. A candle was burning. A figure with a sack over the head sat on a chair in the middle of the unfurnished room.

Andri stood next to the seated man. He grabbed the end of the bag and looked at him with a serious expression. "Can he see your face?"

"Why not?"

"Your choice."

Andri tore the coarse cloth from the figure's head. He looked into the bloodshot eyes of a skinhead with a gag in his mouth. His eyes were swollen shut, and his face was split open in two places. The blood had already dried up on his skin.

"There's the ugly maggot," Andri said.

A thick vein emerged from the young man's forehead and stretched across his shaved head.

"Is that Sandro?" asked Adam.

"Why don't you ask him yourself," Andri said, opening the gag.

The man spat a mixture of saliva and blood on Andri's pants. Adam took a step back. Andri gave him a hook. Something in his head cracked. Blood spurted from his mouth. Sandro spat out a tooth.

"Don't knock him dead. Don't forget, I wanted to ask him something," Adam said.

Andri let go of the man, who gave them both a look full of anger.

"What's your name?" Adam asked him.

"I'm the one you're looking for, I hear."

"I thought you were a punk."

The young man smiled with his mouth smeared with blood. "Doesn't look like it, does it? *Frei und national*. I don't have anything to do with these dirty punks anymore."

Sandro had just cited the Nazi motto, which meant something like free and *völkisch*. Adam looked at Andri. He gave him a resounding slap in the face. The young man was still smiling. Pretty tough, Adam thought.

"Do you know Anna Sievers?"

His facial expression changed. The smile disappeared from his face. His eyes flashed. "Who wants to know?"

"Her sister."

"That stupid cunt?"

Andri shoved his fist into the man's neck. Sandro groaned. Adam looked at Andri. He understood and took a step back.

"Do you know what's going on with Anna?"

"Nah, do you?"

"She disappeared, probably took her own life."

That was still the official version, and Adam stuck with that for questioning her friend.

"You're kidding me?"

"That's what the Vopos, the Kripo, says. But her sister doesn't want to believe it."

"I don't care." Sandro laughed contemptuously. "She should keep her mouth shut."

He received a blow from Andri on the back of his head.

"What does she know already?" said Sandro.

"What do you know?"

"Nothing at all."

He got another one on the back of the head.

"You tell that monkey to cut that shit out. Next time I catch him, it's his ass anyway."

The next thrust hit Sandro with full force in the neck. He groaned again. Something in his spine had cracked. He had bitten his tongue and spat out the blood. Adam looked at Andri piercingly. The man then walked out of the room.

"Yeah, fuck off. It's better that way," Sandro called after him.

Adam took two steps toward the bound man and leaned forward slightly. "Now you have to be a good boy, too. It'll be over in a minute. Be good, don't talk back, and tell me what I want to know. Then he'll leave you alone."

"I'll never be good. Besides, you don't know shit about what's going on here."

"And you don't know shit about who I am. So when was the last time you saw Anna?"

"Must have been a long time ago."

"So you're not together anymore?"

"Did we ever date?"

Adam shrugged his shoulders. "Her ex-boyfriend Sebastian says so."

"Don't know him."

"Do you know Kate Bush?"

Sandro looked at him questioningly.

"There's a song, *The Man with the Child in His Eyes*. Did you ever listen to it together with her?"

Sandro's facial expression had not yet changed. "Now where did that come from? Maybe, maybe not. I don't know."

"So you were never a couple and the song has no special meaning to you. Got it."

"Look, with Anna, you never knew for sure."

"What didn't you know for sure?"

"One day she was like kissing and touching, and then you weren't allowed to touch her at all. Anna wasn't easy. And then I didn't see her for a while."

"What happened?"

"I don't really know myself. Once when she was with me, she just packed her things and left. Just like that. I thought she might have wanted to go somewhere else here in Berlin. But actually she didn't know anyone in Berlin except me and a few of my buddies."

"Maybe she just went back home ..."

"I don't think so."

"Another guy?"

Sandro didn't look angry anymore. Disappointment and sadness mixed into his voice. "Guys."

"Do you know any of them?"

Sandro shook his head. He didn't want to talk about it anymore. It seemed that no matter who Adam was talking to, whoever had once fallen for Anna wouldn't get her out of the head for months or years, or forever. The poor little neofascist was no exception.

"So when you were with Anna, you both were in the punk scene, am I right?"

Sandro nodded.

"And then you changed your mind. Anna too?"

The young man shook his head. "Anna has never been a real punk. I just took her with me. I guess she thought it was cool to go to the concerts and stuff."

"And then what happened?"

"I don't know."

"Look, I found a dress at her place, an expensive dress. Could it have something to do with it? Did she get it from a man?"

Sandro looked at the ground and said nothing.

"Look at you. You're a real sensitive guy. Aren't you, Sandro?" Adam said.

"Hey, shut the fuck up. If you want to know where Anna was, then ask at Café Moskau," he shouted.

Adam waited for Sandro to calm down.

"What's there?" Adam asked.

"That's where she got her admirers."

Adam nodded and wanted to leave the room. He had all the information he could get from the young man, he thought. Sandro looked puzzled.

"You're not getting in there," Sandro called after him.

He stopped and turned to the bound man. "And why?"

"For Bonzen only."

"And how do I get in there?" he asked, annoyed.

"I'll tell you if you don't send that beanpole in here again."

"Let's hear it."

"Through contacts, I guess."

"And where am I going to get these contacts?"

"Man, I don't know about that. Do I look like I have contacts to Bonzen?"

Adam left the room. The young man shouted something behind him, but Adam didn't hear it anymore. In the corridor, he met Andri. Wordlessly they passed each other. On his way out, he heard Andri's fists hit the young man's face. Adam let the apartment door fall into the lock behind him.

Chapter 13: CAFÉ MOSKAU

November 26, 1987
Berlin
Capital of the GDR
German Democratic Republic

The officer of the Bulgarian People's Army was walking down Karl-Marx-Allee. Amid the magnificent buildings, he spotted the cube-shaped building with the glass front and the mosaic entrance. He walked towards the building and straightened his uniform.

The lady at the reception greeted him kindly. "Welcome to Café Moskau! Do you have a reservation, sir?"

"*Da*! *Leytenant* Dimitar Popov," he answered in Russian.

The woman took the menu and walked ahead of the man in the pale green uniform to a seat by the window. Popov looked around. About half of the tables were occupied. Mostly with older couples. The gentlemen in suits, the ladies in fine dresses. Military men from the brother republics of Poland and Czechoslovakia were dining at two tables. The man ordered a Bulgarian cabernet,

Beluga caviar and *pelmeni* with *smetana*. The officer liked the food and the service, and he let the waitress know that. The tip, paid in Soviet rubles, was lavish. He asked the lady in Russian where he could have a good time nearby that evening. She didn't seem to understand what he was saying and replied in broken Russian that the restaurant would close at ten o'clock. Popov ordered a vodka and looked out the window. A group of military men got out of a Volga and walked along the wide sidewalk toward the building. Then they disappeared from Popov's field of vision. Gradually, the Russian specialty restaurant emptied. The Polish People's Army officers passed by his window seat and disappeared just like the military men before. He thanked the waitress and had her bring him his coat and briefcase.

Behind the restaurant, there was an iron gate. Popov took position in front of it and waited. A little later, it opened as if by magic, and a young woman welcomed the *leytenant*. She led him down a flight of stairs to the basement. Popov was led through the nightclub to a round table where an orange lamp provided sparse light. The music was not too loud and not too soft. The women dancing on the stage in the middle of the hall were not too naked and not too clothed. The men sitting at the tables around the stage were not too serious and not too boisterous. Popov ordered a bottle of Crimean champagne and lit a cigarette. The smoke mingled with the cigar smoke from the neighboring table. The jackets stretched over the bellies of the two men. Popov greeted them with a nod and clapped to the dancing ladies. Men disappeared into the back of the club. Even after several minutes, they did not reappear. Popov gave the waitress a large-format ruble bill and let himself be taken there as well. She opened the door to a separate room and left the man alone. He made himself comfortable on the velvet upholstery. The door opened again, and Popov looked into the eyes of a young woman. She moved her hips slowly to the music. As she undressed, she kept her gaze on the Bulgarian officer the whole time. She was dancing in front of him in nothing but her panties. He pulled her close to him. The woman sat down on his lap and moved her lower body rhythmically to the music. He smoked his cigarette. She took it from his hand, took a drag, and blew the smoke in his face. Popov laughed. Then she got down from his lap and sat next to him. Her hand wandered down his legs to his fly. She looked deep into his eyes and pulled down the zipper. Popov laughed again and took her hand. In Russian, he ordered her to dance. She moved in front of him again to the music. He asked her about a young woman with red hair and an angel face. She asked him if he was not attracted to her. He said that he did not want to break with old habits. The woman left Popov alone.

Shortly after, two men came in and accompanied him to the door. He lit a cigarette and cursed them in Bulgarian and Russian. The men went back inside. Popov threw the cigarette on the ground and squashed the butt with his sole. The *leytenant* changed sides of the street and waited in a building entrance. He must have been there for three hours. Then he saw the woman who had danced for him coming out of the nightclub. Popov took up the pursuit. She went down the stairs to the train station and got on the subway heading east. Three stations later, she got off again. Popov followed her until she disappeared into an apartment building. He watched the windows of the apartments from the street. A few seconds later, he registered a light being turned on behind one of the windows. He went into the house, stripped off his uniform, and put on civilian clothes. With a few practiced moves, he opened the apartment door. He entered the apartment hallway and heard the pattering of water from the bathroom. The woman was taking a shower. So he sat down in the living room and waited for her. With a towel knotted across her chest, she walked down the hallway on her way to the bedroom. She screamed when she saw the man sitting on her couch in the living room. He put an index finger over his mouth. She fell silent and stopped in the doorway. The man did not move. She dropped her towel and stood naked in front of him.

"That's not what I'm here for," he said.

She bent down, picked up the towel again, and held it in front of her chest. "It's you. I danced for you earlier."

"That's right."

"You speak German," she said as if to herself.

She looked at the ceiling and then back at the man in her living room.

"You look different," she said.

The man said nothing about the fact that he was sitting in front of her in jeans and a blouson instead of an army uniform.

"What do you know about Anna?"

The woman shivered. "Can I put some clothes on?"

The man nodded. She went into the bedroom and came back shortly dressed in a bathrobe. The man patted on the seat next to him and looked at her with an inviting smile. She sat down next to him.

"I haven't seen Anna in a long time," she said, taking the pack of cigarettes from the table.

"Why are you still shaking?"

"I don't know."

It took her a while to free a cigarette from the pack. Then she took it between her lips and leaned forward. The man was faster. He took the lighter from the table and held the flame in front of her face.

As soon as the tobacco ignited, she took a deep drag. "Well, actually, I don't know anything."

"No one knows anything. So when was the last time you saw Anna?"

She took another drag from the cigarette. "I don't know. Maybe two months ago."

"In September?"

"Hmm, maybe it wasn't that long ago after all. Must have been around mid-October."

"You sure?"

"I don't know."

"Why didn't Anna come anymore?"

She shrugged her shoulders. He grabbed her by the wrist. She tried to pull away from his grip. "Stop it. You're hurting me."

But he did not let go of the woman.

"She met someone," she said.

"Who?"

"I don't know."

The muscles in the man's hand tightened around her joint. "I think you know."

"It's okay. A young officer."

"What's his name?"

"I don't know."

He gripped tighter again.

"I really don't know."

The man loosened his grip. "What did he look like?"

"Normal, I would say. Nice. Different from the old farts that come to us."

"That could mean anything. Hair color, eyes, height, special features?"

She moaned. "He was blond, like you, I'd say. Blue eyes. Like you. A little over six feet, I guess. Maybe taller, too."

"So he looked like me?"

"Nah. He was younger. And a good dancer."

"Good dancer?"

"Yeah, he was a good dancer."

"How do you know?"

"Anna told me."

"He danced for her, is that what you mean?"

"Sounded like it. Or together. I don't know."

"So this was a soldier dancing for a hooker?"

"We're amusement ladies."

"Fine, amusement ladies it is. But your story sounds strange. The same goes for *amusement lady*, by the way."

"If you say so."

"So, he danced well ..."

"Yes, she told me. Ask her yourself if you don't believe it."

"It's all right. Do you know what Anna called him when she talked to you about him?"

"She didn't call him anything. I knew who she meant. I saw him, after all." She pondered. "Once, she said that all men are disgusting. And that she'd finally found a man who wasn't spoiled yet. With eyes that can't lie, she said. That meant something to her. He had lovely eyes."

"Was this guy around a lot?"

She shook her head. "One time with a group of other men. Lots of Bonzen. Stasi, NVA, that lot. She danced for him. But he didn't want to, you know, just like you. But then he came alone every night. At some point, she left with him."

"Did you see that?"

She nodded and took another drag from her cigarette.

"Has he been back since?" he asked.

She shook her head.

"Would you recognize him?"

"Yes."

"Do you know what happened to Anna?"

"No."

The man stood up.

"What happened to Anna?" she asked.

He walked out of the living room.

"What's with her?" she called after him.

"I'll be back," he hollered, taking the briefcase containing the Bulgarian officer's uniform and leaving her apartment.

Andrei Gabulov's driver had not promised too much. He was indeed able to get anything. In Adam's case, a uniform with officer rank that was not Soviet. Because that made you one among many and, above all, too easy to track through the dense network of Soviet military authorities. As a Bulgarian, on the other hand, you flew under the radar. The uniform and a few other niceties had cost him almost his entire foreign currency stash. Adam hoped it was worth it.

He had worked through his list of tasks. But he did not feel that he had made any progress. He knew Anna was no longer with her boyfriend in Berlin, or maybe she'd never been. Instead, she had a new boyfriend. One with eyes that couldn't lie. But what did that have to do with her disappearance? He knew she wasn't a punk. That had become clear at last in the nightclub. That also explained the expensive dress. And he had found out that Anna had recognized a real young man of flesh and blood in the song and had not just indulged in a dream. But was it worth finding out who the young man was? Would he find Anna with him, alive? Did he really want to find out what game Evelyn and Kletzsch were playing with him? He could not answer any of these questions and decided to let things take their course. And the course of events, for the most part, meant him becoming fixated on something.

Chapter 14: PEACE OF THE GRAVE

November 27, 1987
Angermünde
District Frankfurt/Oder
German Democratic Republic

Sleet set in. The cemetery was covered with a layer of frozen slush topped with ice-cold water. Mourners moved cautiously along the narrow path that led from the chapel to the grave. All was quiet. Only the precipitation splashed through the bare trees onto the ground. The VEB staff, friends, and family gathered around Anna Sievers's grave. He remained at a distance. It was only that morning that he had learned of the funeral and walked to the cemetery. The factory management had given all mourners time off to attend the funeral. A grand gesture. Adam saw only a few black suits, but apparently, everyone had chosen their best clothes for the occasion. He wore jeans and a parka. The men had dug ties out of their dressers and placed them around the collars of sturdy linen or cotton shirts. They wore slacks in muted tones over their freezing legs and their soggy work boots on cold feet. The women had traded their smock aprons and tired eyes for dark dresses over opaque tights and eyeliner.

Only the dead woman's sister stood out from this picture of restrained festivity. Adam had not seen Evelyn that morning, and at first, he had not recognized her at all. She was dressed in black. From head to toe. Wearing high-heeled leather shoes and black nylon tights. Over them, a knee-length sheath dress and a cape of suede. Around her neck was a scarf, on her head a hat, above it a veil. Her jet-black appearance seemed surreal in its clarity against the mottled gray sky and muddy brown earth. The widow of a mafia patriarch at the grave of a GDR teenager.

She stood close to the pit. The coffin lay in the depths, just a step away from her. Across from her, the parish priest had set up. The men and women stood in a cluster around the grave, close together and in several rows. A barely perceptible distance had formed between them and the woman. The clergyman spared a few words on the life and passing of the eighteen-year-old. From dust, you were born, and to dust, you would return. The woman's face was seamed with black tears. The VEB boss rushed to her to support her. Each individual from the mourners' congregation walked past the grave and threw a shovel of sand on the coffin. Gradually the gravesite emptied. Adam silently joined the column of mourners. He scanned the procession for Evelyn but could not find her. After a short time, not a soul was to be seen in the cemetery anymore. When he came to the cemetery gate and still had not spotted her, he turned back. She had to be at the gravesite still, Adam thought.

There he found a figure that had nothing in common with the woman he had seen only a few minutes ago. Evelyn seemed to melt with the background. An extinguished fire in a moonscape. She was covered with earth and dirt. Her hat and veil lay in the mud. Sweat appeared on her forehead. She was up to her knees in the hole in the ground. She was lifting the earth from the freshly filled grave with a shovel. Even when she saw him coming towards her, she continued. He stopped in front of the grave and watched her work. For minutes, she conveyed damp soil out of the pit.

Then she set the shovel down and looked at him. "When will you ask if you can help me?"

"Never."

She got back to work.

He squatted down next to the grave. "What are you trying to prove here, anyway?"

Evelyn ignored him.

"I know that you're pulling some sick shit with Kletzsch," he said.

Evelyn set the shovel down and stared into the soil. Then she began again to stick the shovel into the earth and move the brown mass out of the hole. If she continued at this pace, she was bound to hit the coffin soon. For a brief moment, it looked like the woman was grinning. He heard a thudding sound. The shovel had hit wood. Evelyn paused for a moment. She didn't seem to know what to do next. Then she threw the shovel into the mud and knelt on the coffin. With her bare hands, she wiped the earth from the wooden plank.

"Are you sure you want to do this?" he asked.

She bent over the coffin. With both arms, she tugged at the lid. Nothing happened. She tried again. In vain. Then he bent down to Evelyn and grabbed her shoulders with both hands. She wanted to shake him off and continued to hold on to the coffin lid. He let go of the woman and helped her. With their combined efforts, they opened the coffin. The wooden box was empty. Evelyn wiped the sweat from her brow. He stared into the emptiness. Suddenly, Evelyn's legs slumped away. She fell to the ground. He bent down to her. She did not move. He crouched down behind her and supported her head.

After a while, she opened her eyes again. "What happened?" she asked quietly.

"You tumbled over."

"Anna?"

"She's not in the grave."

"I'm never going to see Anna again, am I?"

Adam stroked her head with his hand. The woman straightened up again and remained sitting on the ground. He squatted down next to her and reached under her arms. She did not move.

"Let go of me. I'm not coming."

She pulled the sleeves of her dress over her hands and folded her arms in front of her body. Then she leaned forward and looked into the empty grave.

"I will not see Anna again. I don't know what happened to her. Where is she?"

He put an arm around her. Tears ran down the woman's face.

"I'm sorry, Evelyn."

"You're not sorry. You just want to get rid of me. Everybody wants to get rid of me. You don't even believe me that I had nothing to do with Anna disappearing. I always wanted the best for Anna. She was my angel. Everyone loved her. Lothar loved her. I wanted a piece of that, too. You saw how he loved me. I'm not a bad person. Adam, you have to believe me."

Her sobs swallowed her words. She wiped the tears from her cheeks and pulled up the snot in her nose.

"All this shit. You don't find out about anything. You're lied to by everyone. Everywhere it's the same. On the news, they don't tell you what's going on. At work, they don't either. You're only allowed to say what's going on in the quiet. And if you're unlucky, you've talked to a spy. It could be practically anyone. The woman next to you in the factory or in line at the supermarket, even you, Adam. We don't know shit about what's going on here. All of us. I realize that you have nothing to do with us here. That you're not one of us at all. You don't give a shit. One day you'll leave here, and then you won't give a shit about us. Isn't that right? But we have to stay here. We can't get out of here. I'm so sick of it. The stench of our dirty cars ... the slop that's sold to us as food ... the lies that are served to us every day. I'm not going to eat any more of it." Evelyn screamed the anger from her soul. Then she became very calm and looked at him. "Adam, I just want to see her again. I want to hug her one last time."

"I know."

"Surely no one can deny me that …"

They sat together on the cold ground for a while. Both were wet to the skin from the sleet.

"Come on, Evelyn. Let's get going. We're going to catch our deaths."

"Let me sit here for a minute. I'll be right there."

"Promise?"

She nodded. He left her alone at the grave that wasn't one.

The empty coffin gave him a headache. He could think of no reason why the authorities would not put the body of Evelyn's sister in the ground. Unless they still hadn't found the body. The only thing they had found was nothing. But they knew all about that in the GDR, about nothing. Because what shouldn't be in the GDR, wasn't there. There was a lot of nothing. No AIDS, no hookers, no car accidents, no drugs, no demonstrations, no porn, no suicides, no Nazis. There was none of that. A huge pile of nothing.

When he had already left the wrought-iron cemetery gate a few steps behind him, two black limousines and an ambulance stopped before his eyes. For a brief moment, he thought that a corpse was being taken here to its final resting place. Then men in leather coats got out of the Soviet-made cars, and he knew what was going on. Typical intelligence operatives. With expressionless faces, they walked past him through the gate. Only two men remained in the ambulance.

Had they followed Adam and then called for reinforcements after his encounter with Evelyn? He turned around and followed the four men. They went straight to the place where Anna Sievers's false grave was. He could already see the gravestone. The tomb lay dug up. The shovel lay next to the grave as Evelyn had left it. Only her, he could not spot anywhere. The men looked around the grave. They had already seen him, so he just kept walking like a regular cemetery visitor, greeting the men as he passed by. They did not greet him back and looked for possible traces that Evelyn had left behind. Only a few more steps and he could step onto a narrow path to his right. Then the men would not see him anymore. Adam had to control himself to avoid walking any faster. He strolled toward the fork in the road.

Right before he reached it, he heard the voice of one of the men. "Hold it right there."

Adam did and turned around.

One of the men looked at him. "Come here."

Adam walked up to the man.

"A little more briskly, if you will."

Adam walked faster and stopped a few yards in front of him on the path.

"Come over here and take that shovel right there."

Adam breathed a sigh of relief. He went to the grave and grabbed the shovel.

"Take a look at this mess. Fill it back up."

Adam put the shovel into the soil and conveyed it onto the coffin, which had been closed again in the meantime.

He had not seen whether the men had done so or Evelyn before them.

"Stop what you're doing for a minute," the man said, approaching him.

Adam paused his work and looked at the man who was giving him commands.

"Do you dig graves often?"

"No."

"But you're doing it because someone asked you to do it?"

"Yes."

"Well, that's interesting."

Adam continued to look at the man. The other men had built up behind him.

"Identification papers!"

Adam placed the shovel on the ground and held it by the wooden handle. He knew how to handle shovels. With his other hand, he reached into his jacket pocket and pulled out his wet ID card. The man from the group who looked the youngest approached him and took the papers from him. He took them to the man who had asked for them. But he didn't take them off him. "Read them out," he ordered instead.

The man did. After reading out the information on the ID card, he asked Adam if the information was correct. He answered in the affirmative. His nerves were tense to bursting. But obviously, they didn't know who he was and didn't get suspicious when hearing his name. The man put his hands in his coat pocket and looked at him.

"Well, then, tell us what you're doing here, Herr Hedman."

"Today was the funeral of a colleague from the VEB."

"Yes? Go on!"

"And I was at the funeral service, too."

"So, where are the others now?"

"Back at VEB, I'd say. And that's where I'm going right now as well. Shoveling coal."

"You're making fun of us?"

"No, at work, I shovel coal. Maybe that's why I wasn't baffled that I should start shoveling here, too."

The man nodded. "Luther, why don't you give Herr Hedman back his identification papers?"

Adam got his papers back and put them in his jacket.

"Go on, get on with it."

He continued to shovel earth into the grave.

"And if you notice something, get back to us," the man said, pulling out a small card from the inside pocket of his coat.

He waited until Adam took it from him. Adam looked at the business card of Major Kolja Kremer.

"But first, you finish here," the major said as he walked away, pointing to the pit.

Shortly after, the men were gone. That was his start signal.

1984 yards. Zero steps per second.

Adam threw the shovel into the dirt. Across the slippery paths to the long side of the cemetery. Past the graves from World War II. A few from 1940 and 1941, the majority from 1942, 1943, and 1944. Adam reached the cemetery wall and leaped over it in a single bound.

2.3 steps per second.

His gaze turned to the cemetery gate. The men had not yet reached their vehicles.

1840 yards. 3.5 steps per second.

He landed on his feet in the garden of a family house. A man was taking a bucket of kitchen scraps to the compost pile. Adam couldn't even hear his curses by the time he had jumped the fence to the adjacent property. Even before he had reached the ground, he saw the beast rushing toward him. A Rottweiler latched onto his heels, bared teeth on display.

4.5 steps per second.

He heard the laughter of the man from the neighboring property. His legs drummed in staccato into the frozen ground. The dog's muzzle touched his calf. Just for a moment. The dog snapped. Once, twice. Then he yelped. A chain tightened around his neck. Three, two, one, jump. He landed in a pasture.

1801 yards. 2.5 steps per second.

The terrain was slightly sloping.

3.7 steps per second.

It was slippery. Adam stumbled and slipped off with his left leg. He was just able to break the fall with his right. Then he stretched his legs out again.

Zero steps per second.

Go on! Run, run, run.

Still 1678 yards.

Picking up speed again. He ran through bushes and shrubs.

1.2 steps per second.

His heart was hammering in his chest. In front of him was Mudrowgraben. In summer, a trickle of water a handsbreadth wide. In winter, an ice stream as wide as a full-grown man. Should he jump or trust that the ice would carry him and just keep running? No trust. Not even in the subzero temperatures. He stepped off, took a leap, and landed on his butt.

Zero steps per second.

That should leave a big bruise. He got himself up again.

1323 yards. 2.1 steps per second.

He crossed a dirt road.

3.4 steps per second.

Through bushes and shrubs again. Pushing through.

0.4 steps per second.

He reached an open grassy area. Picking up speed again. Let the blood pump even more oxygen through the arteries.

1110 yards. 3.5 steps per second.

Another fence. Jump. Passing the house on the left. Don't run into the woman with the cat in the cage. Through the gate of the veterinary practice out into the street.

1085 yards. 2.0 steps per second.

Finally asphalt under the feet again. Spurting across the road. No cars far and wide. Up onto the field and plowing over the hard furrows. Finding the right pace. Determining the optimal stride length. Don't stumble.

707 yards. 2.4 steps per second.

His thighs burned with exertion. His muscles had to compensate for every step on the uneven ground. Tense and relaxed, again and again. An ordeal for the musculoskeletal system. The road lay ahead of him. Only a few more steps. Feeling level ground underneath him again.

651 yards. 2.8 steps per second.

Down on the left. Past the pale green, ash-gray, matte orange Trabants and Wartburgs that were parked at the roadside. There were only a few hundred steps left. He was running for his life. Actually, he was running for her life's freedom. Would he be running faster if it were for his own life? Adam pushed the thought out of his mind and concentrated on his movements. He could already see the factory gate ahead of him and sprinted past the coal mountains. He reached the gate, yanked it open, and reached the canteen. Everyone looked at him and interrupted their conversations.

Zero yards. Zero steps per second.

He had staked everything on one card. But his assumption was wrong. No one at the VEB had seen Evelyn. After she'd left the cemetery, she must have had a different destination than her workplace.

Adam walked along the path paved with square stone slabs to entrance B of number 186. As he reached the glass door enclosed by aluminum sheets, he peeked into the hallway and rang the bell. Nobody answered. So he rang the bell of the neighbors. Success. The buzzer of the bell system sounded, and he pushed the door open. He took the stairs up to the second floor and knocked on the door of unit

2.23, made of particleboard. Nothing. Adam turned around as the door of the opposite apartment opened.

A young woman stepped through the doorway, arms folded. "They took her."

"Who?"

"Men in coats. You know," she said, her voice quiet and strained.

"When?"

"Just now."

Adam nodded. She stopped in the doorway. He turned around and pressed one hand against the door to Evelyn's apartment. Unlocked. Slowly, it gave way to a view of the hallway. There were traces of blood everywhere. The neighbor stood on tiptoe to look over him into the apartment. He closed the door behind him. The apartment had been turned upside down. Once state security had been through, he wouldn't find anything anymore anyway. He looked in the bathroom. Blood as well. It looked like a terrible fight had happened. He turned around. There was a boy. Slender with large brown hornrimmed glasses.

"Are you Evelyn's friend?" he asked.

"Yes."

"Good, I saw everything. Four men in leather coats came with two GAZ-24s. And in addition, in a Barkas ambulance van, there were also two more men. They were waiting downstairs and smoking. So there were six in total. The men had pistols, of course, Makarov type. They drew them when they were standing in front of the door."

The depth of detail in the description was astonishing. The military science lessons at school and the programs on television had left their mark on this offspring of the GDR. He wondered why the Stasi had brought an ambulance.

"How did you see all this?"

"What a question. I watched. First from my room to the street, then through the peephole in our door. Two ran down the stairs. Two took the elevator. Then they met again here in the hallway."

"From there, you saw everything?"

"No. But when they went in the apartment, I went in after them, and I heard them."

"Isn't that a little bit dangerous?"

"Maybe."

"And then?"

"Then one of them got a little black box and took out a small tool and used it to open the door. It was locked, though."

The boy looked at him expectantly. He wanted to be asked what happened next.

So Adam did. "And then?" he asked.

"Then they got a pair of pliers, a big pair, and they cut the chain. Then they were in."

"And Evelyn?"

"Was in the bathroom."

"Did they speak German or Russian?"

"German. It was the Stasi, as Frau Schneider has already told you."

So the boy had also overheard the conversation with the neighbor. An excellent informer, he only had to shed his childish credulity.

"That's right. I just wanted to make sure again that she saw it all correctly."

"Yes, yes, I see."

"And after that you probably didn't see anything, did you?"

"But I heard them. The men were very quiet. You could hear the water coming from the bathroom. From the sink, not from the shower. The men went in. Evelyn was screaming. The men didn't say anything. But they fought with her. Then one of the men screamed. She kicked him or bit him. Then there was a loud thump, and everything was quiet. Then the men whispered."

"And you heard that, too, huh?"

"*Gee, don't beat her to death*, one of them said. That's all they said."

Judging from the marks, there were two different injuries that had caused the blood loss. One from a blow to the head, probably a laceration, where the blood had splattered, and one from hitting the back of the head on the edge of the bathtub. They must have then dragged the lifeless body from the bathroom down the hallway. Two men, each had grabbed one of the shackles.

"Do you think Evelyn is dead?" asked Adam.

"It's hard to say. I didn't get a look at her when the men left."

"Why?"

"They wrapped her up in a rug and carried her out."

Adam looked into the living room. The carpet was missing. Except for in the bathroom and the hallway, there were no other traces of blood. The boy's narrative seemed to fit the facts offered by the room.

"Then they loaded them into the Barkas and drove away. With sirens and emergency lights."

So Evelyn must be in the hospital or the morgue.

"Anything else?" asked Adam.

"Yeah, hang on."

The boy ran out of the apartment. Shortly after, he came back with a package held together by a cord.

"What is that?" asked Adam.

"Evelyn said if anything ever happened to her, to give this to her friend, who would come over."

"Thank you," he said, taking the bundle from him. "It's best not to tell anyone else what happened here. Especially not that the Stasi was here. If anyone asks, Evelyn had an accident, and the ambulance came."

"As you say."

"Now, you better get out of here before someone else comes."

The boy left. Adam looked at the package. What could Evelyn have for him? He went out of the apartment, closed the broken door as well as possible, and took the stairs that led to the higher floors. Once at the top, he sat down on the steps. He tore open the package and found notebooks in different colors inside. He opened a sky-blue book. They were Anna Sievers's diaries. So there were notes in existence after all. Evelyn must have taken them a long time ago and thus had kept her sister's experiences and thoughts from him. Why? He read through the diaries page by page.

Years of her life were recorded. Starting from puberty until shortly before her disappearance, a total of about three hundred pages. The books were full of tirades of hatred for teachers and classmates, for her admirers, and the parents of her friends. Above all, she puked her guts out over and over again, page after page, about her sister. In the last book, she described a terrible argument she had with Evelyn. Was that already a motive for murder? Only at the very end did the tone become more gentle. In the notes, Evelyn came across as a mentally deranged person who wanted to ruin her little sister's future. Adam could understand why Evelyn had withheld these lines from him.

Then it got interesting. She described meeting a young man. One who was different from the others. Who not only saw her beauty but understood her desires and dreams. One who wanted to help her. It remained vague. He could not find answers to who the young man was and whether he was capable of murdering her. The diaries were of no help to him. He had spent hours sitting on the cold steps for nothing. He felt anger rising inside him. Anger at his own powerlessness. Anger at the cover-ups by the authorities. Anger at the removal of Evelyn. He slammed the book shut. Somehow he had to help her. He owed her that. But first, he had to find out where she was. Or if she was even still alive.

Adam returned home. The door lock was broken. When the state security wanted to search an apartment unnoticed, that was what they did. And if they wanted to intimidate someone, then it looked like it did now. All the books and papers were scattered across the floor. The food supplies had been dumped out, the upholstery of the furniture slashed. It was a threat. Crude but effective. His own home no longer offered safe refuge. Blind rage gripped him. Someone had to be responsible for the fact that the Stasi had hunted down a woman who was grieving for her sister. Only one name came to mind.

He ran out of his apartment. In the courtyard driveway, he kicked aside the milk crates. After a brief search, he found the loose stone in the wall and pulled it out. From the hole in the wall, he took out his pistol. Adam put the Makarov in his waistband and ran out into the street. The darkness wrapped itself around his body like a custom-made suit. It took him less than ten minutes to reach the house of VEB manager Lothar Kletzsch. Adam was out of breath and walked around the house. There was no light in any of the rooms. He stopped in the garden and observed the situation. After a while, there was suddenly light in the hallway. Kletzsch came down the corridor and switched on the lights in the living room as well. Adam went to the front door and rang the bell. It opened.

He pulled out his pistol. "Where's Evelyn?"

Kletzsch looked surprised, but he said nothing. Adam pressed the muzzle into the man's head and forced him to walk backward into the house. Then Adam threw the door into the lock behind him.

"Tell me, Kletzsch, what have you done to Evelyn?"

Kletzsch stood directly in front of him. "Hedman, where did you get that gun? Be reasonable. I've never seen you like this."

Adam cocked the hammer of the pistol. Kletzsch held his hands protectively in front of the gun. Then something happened that Adam had not expected. The seemingly harmless man let his head shoot up. This distracted Adam for a split second, and Kletzsch had his hand on his gun. With the other, he flipped Adam's wrist. Now he held the gun in his hands, and Adam was threatened with it. The tide had turned, but Kletzsch did not know the weapon. And the Makarov had a quirk you had to know about if you were going to operate it. So Adam took a step toward Kletzsch, who immediately pulled the trigger. But no shot was fired. Puzzled, he looked at Adam, who knocked the gun out of his hand and, with the same movement, delivered a blow to the man's ear.

Kletzsch's sense of balance was disturbed. He staggered and fell to the floor. The gun was lying next to his body. With a quick movement, he would have had the gun back in his hands. But he no longer trusted it and instead reached for an umbrella that was in the stand. Kletzsch put the umbrella behind Adam's left foot and jerked it out of position in one motion. He used the momentum to get back on his own feet and run into the living room. Adam scrambled to his feet and chased him. Again the man surprised him. Adam didn't see Kletzsch's leg coming at him and caught a karate kick to the temple. Adam felt woozy, but he managed to keep his balance. He was able to block the second kick with his arms. Then he got hold of the leg and pulled Kletzsch's standing leg away. Again the man was lying on his back.

Adam jumped on him and hit his temple again and again. The man fought off the blows and reached out for Adam's larynx. When he got hold of it, he squeezed. Adam was left breathless, but he still managed to land a well-aimed blow in Kletzsch's arm cavity. He let go of him and leaped down the hall. But Adam caught him with a kick, speeding up his movement and sending the man running headfirst into a glass pane at the end of the hall. There was a dull thud. His skin burst open on his head. Blood ran down his forehead. Adam walked up to him and looked into his hate-filled eyes. The man's resistance was brutal. Kletzsch wiped the blood from his eyes. Adam was here to get information from Kletzsch, not to kill him. But Adam had to take him out as quickly as possible, or his days were numbered. He grabbed the pistol. Kletzsch jumped after him. Adam turned around, unlocked his Makarov and fired a shot next to the man's head. The man stopped dead in his tracks and threw up his hands. Adam stood up and ordered him to sit down on the sofa. Kletzsch did so.

Adam pointed the gun at the man. "Where's Evelyn?"

"Do you even know who you're messing with?"

"My boss."

Kletzsch grinned. "I'm going to kick your ass. Do you think you can set foot in the factory again? I knew it was a mistake to give you a chance back then. Pure philanthropy, that's what it was. And this is the thanks I get? You betrayed everything we stand for. I should have known that you can't expect anything from an imperialist and a Jew."

Adam grinned and shook his head.

"What's so funny?" asked Kletzsch, full of anger.

"Jew. Jew. Whenever there is a problem, I am the Jew. If I'm good, then I'm the hero of the seventeen coal runs, but if I ask one question too many, then I'm the Jew. And you know what the problem is? I didn't choose any of this. I never called myself that. It was always the others. I was born a Yankee because it was the only country that took my father in, and if it had been up to him, I never would have known what he was, where I was from. He did everything he could to make sure I wasn't the Jew to anyone. I don't even have his name. But to you, I am the Jew. Yet I have never visited the temple, nor read the Torah, not believed in this one God. I believed in socialism. As a socialist, I came here because I believe in justice. I believe that everyone is equal."

"Then you betrayed all of us. I know one thing for sure, one socialist does not betray another socialist."

"I have not betrayed a socialist. I have accused a man of being what he is, a liar."

"Oh, I can't hear it anymore. Why can't you let history rest? Instead, you always have to tell us about that again and again. But you have to look ahead, to the future."

"If the past stinks, so does the future."

There was a brief moment of silence.

"Well, that's enough of that old chestnut. Where's Evelyn?" asked Adam.

"I'll tell you in a minute. Not a problem at all. It's not even a secret. Everyone can know. But you really pissed me off, Hedman. Coming in here with your gun pointed at me, wanting to know about Evelyn. About that wreck. You know what I do with something like that Evelyn? Use her and throw her away after. That's all she's good for."

"Nice. Even if she dresses up like Anna?"

"So you know about that. Did she tell you?"

"I saw you guys."

"So you've been spying on us."

"I needed to know if I could trust Evelyn."

"You can't. She's completely nuts. After Anna's death, there's nothing left to do with her. I can't even let her work at the VEB anymore. She just can't get anything done. Nothing else was to be expected from her. Once crazy, always crazy. There's nothing you can do. But with you, Hedman. There was still hope. You did a good job, didn't you? Hero of the seventeen runs. And now you're standing up for this human garbage? That won't get you anywhere. You have to work for your chances in life. You were well on your way. A few more years hauling coal, and then there would certainly have been a decent job waiting for you at the factory. Maybe even something in the office. Do you think my position was just handed to me? That was hard work."

"And on the side, you did some martial arts. Am I supposed to believe that or what? Those who have a gun stuck in their face are pissing their pants in fear, and here's the good-as-gold leader of VEB Gustav Bruhn shitting on the Makarov in his face. It's not the first time this has happened. Am I right?"

"After all, we've all served. When the class enemy shows up, we are prepared."

"Nah, nah, that's a bit more than just having done your military service in the NVA. Or are you really just a colorless guy who was hoisted to the leadership post because he licked the saliva of the right Bonzen in the Party?"

"Your disrespect. I resent that. I was already fighting when you were still in diapers. Do you know what it's like in Afghanistan? Our Russian friends are dying there every day in booby traps laid by the CIA mujahideen pigs."

Adam had been not in Afghanistan but Vietnam. In terms of experience with war atrocities, the two were evenly matched.

"So? You're not even much older than me. You just look like it."

"Whatever. There I was. I saw it all up close, first hand. Lothar Kletzsch is not a colorless guy. He was an excellent instructor of military reconnaissance of the NVA."

"Nonsense. If that were true, you wouldn't just tell me. You were in Afghanistan as a Red Army instructor? No way. And now you're the boss at a stamping and enameling plant? No fucking way. Then you must have been dishonorably discharged. What did you do? Did the Russians have to put red wigs on for you too?"

Kletzsch's eyes filled with hatred again. "You shut the fuck up."

"Or else?"

"I've yet dealt with anyone. Do you think the Spetsnaz were easily impressed? But they were afraid of me. Do you know what they called me?"

"Colorless Lothar?"

"They called me *sumasshedshiy nemets*. Do you know what that means? The crazy German."

"That's crazy. So, I guess I must be really scared of you."

Adam's patience was at an end. He gave Kletzsch a blow on the head with the Makarov. Kletzsch writhed in pain.

He held the muzzle of the pistol to his temple. "Enough chatter. Where's Evelyn?"

"In the clink, where else?"

He took the barrel from the man's head and stood next to the living room door.

"Which one?"

"Eberswalde."

That was all he needed to know. But what was he supposed to do with Kletzsch? The man had been right when he'd said that Adam could not show up at the VEB again. So he had to go into hiding. He didn't know how things would go from there. Kletzsch slumped on the sofa. Adam walked toward the man. Suddenly he let one hand disappear under a sofa cushion and pulled out a pistol with it. Now both had their weapons pointed at each other. Adam had his Makarov, Kletzsch a Tokarev TT-33, the predecessor model of the Russian Army pistol. Not as powerful and not as reliable as its successor. But if a bullet hit you, you were still pretty much dead.

The VEB manager was seething with rage. His head was red. Tears were pooling in his eyes. "I am Lothar Kletzsch. Colonel of the Military Reconnaissance of the National People's Army," he said, full of pathos.

They shot at each other. Kletzsch missed. Adam didn't. The projectile left a circular bullet hole between the man's eyes. The bullet exited the back of his boss's head. Kletzsch was thrown backward and was dead on the spot. His lifeless eyes stared at Adam. What was he to do with the dead man? He went to the window and looked out. Had the neighbors noticed the gunshots? He saw no one and opened the patio door. As long there were no police sirens, he should have ample time to develop a plan. Adam played through the possible scenarios in his head. He ruled out every plan that involved transporting the body. It would be too conspicuous, and it was too complicated. He looked in the basement for chemicals that could decompose a body. Not only could he not find any, but it would also take days. And time was not on his side. So he went with the easiest option.

He took his Makarov and wiped his fingerprints off it with a cloth. Then he went to Kletzsch's body and took the pistol from his hand. Rigor mortis had not yet set in. He sat the man down in the armchair and put his Makarov in his hand. Then Adam tucked the man's Tokarev into his waistband. Not a good exchange. He checked the arrangement in the living room. To untrained eyes, it might look like suicide. Somehow, some time, they would figure out. But not that day. What he needed was time. And with the fake suicide, he had gained a few days.

Chapter 15: INSANE ASYLUM

November 30, 1987
Eberswalde
District Frankfurt/Oder
German Democratic Republic

The sign at the entrance to the grounds of the Soviet Military Hospital in Eberswalde was written in two languages, German and Russian.

Lunatic Asylum.

Enter at your own risk.

Harassment must be expected.

The buildings dated from the midnineteenth century and were scattered over a wide area in the middle of a wooded zone. Adam climbed over the wall. Anyone escaping from the hospital at this time of year would first get lost in the forest and then freeze to death on the forest ground in their thin hospital garb. This side effect of the secluded location was undoubtedly not undesirable for the management, he thought. There were no lights burning in any of the buildings. The hospital town lay as if abandoned in the snowy landscape. Lanterns cast their weak light on the frozen paths.

He still had this one clue to follow up. Adam was firmly convinced that the man with the boyish look was the key to the mystery. Together with Evelyn, he wanted to find him. He had to find the ward where she was housed. Only then could she make her peace, and he could get back to the sad remnants of his life. Besides, he had begun to take things personally as soon as somebody was shooting at him. Adam reached a fence behind which was a barred complex of buildings. He read the sign on the access gate.

Area of exemplary order, discipline, safety & cleanliness

It was locked. So he climbed over this fence as well and went to the entrance of the building. The plaster was peeling off the building, revealing the brickwork. There were no modern surveillance technologies like cameras or motion detectors installed here. Except for a few fences, the facility was in the same condition as when the Soviets had taken it over in the forties. And as he had already expected, the door was also locked. With his door-opening tool, which he had brought with him, opening pins and locking hooks in a variety of versions, he opened the lock in no time.

A musty smell emanated from the building as he entered the corridor. At the end of the hallway, he saw a glint of light on the tiled floor. Cautiously, he walked on, stood next to the open door, and held his breath. Since no sounds were coming from the room, he decided to go inside. It was the station office that was unoccupied. Only a desk lamp was still on. In the cabinets, Adam found the admission file of Evelyn Sievers.

Reason for admission: erratic behavior, resisting law enforcement officers, psychotic disorder.

She was housed in room 3IV. The corridor ended at an iron grate and was secured with a flimsy lock. After Adam opened the mechanism with ease, he went upstairs. A woman in a white nurse's uniform came down the stairs. She had not seen him yet. So he decided to go back to the ground level. There he waited for the woman, who was much smaller than himself but certainly weighed a lot more. He grabbed her from behind and covered her mouth. She did not scream, but she braced herself against him with all her strength. He fell to the floor, she on top of him. Adam could not restrain the woman. So he kept one hand on her mouth and, with the other, squeezed the main artery in her neck until the woman lost consciousness after about half a minute. Then he dragged the heavy body into the wardroom and tied her to the chair with the leather straps that were otherwise used to restrain patients. Then Adam gagged her and took a white gown from the hook. This way, he might be mistaken for a doctor or a nurse from a distance.

He took the stairs up again. Everything was silent in the stairwell. He only heard a breeze whistling through the corridors. When he reached the top, he stood in front of another locked door. As he opened it, a shrill scream echoed through the hallways. He pulled his pistol from his waistband. Silence reigned again. Only a distant hiss could still be heard. But it didn't seem to mean danger. He walked down the corridor and stopped in the first doorway. The moonlight brought in just enough light for him to guess the locale. The hall was crowded with about two dozen beds. In front of each were a chair and a washbowl. Between them was just enough room for an orderly. It smelled of dried saliva. He heard breathing, crunching, and whimpering. Each of the bedsteads was covered with a tightly woven net. Beneath were the asylum patients. Adam was in the middle of a room of people and felt utterly alone. The presence of a conscious mind was not to be felt.

In the bed to his left, a young man was lying stretched out on the cot. His arms and legs were tied to the bed frame. He was breathing heavily with his eyes closed. Adam glanced to his right. A pair of eyes had locked on him. Behind the mesh, an old man with an unshaven face was looking at him with wide-open eyes. He did not move his head, nor did he blink as Adam stepped closer to him. The man seemed to stare into the empty darkness. Adam walked backward and caught his heel on something. It rattled. Adam had tripped over a bedpan. It reeked of feces and urine. From a corner, he heard a burst of pointed laughter. Adam turned and made his way out of the hall. Something slapped his cheek. He grabbed his face with his hand. It was wet. He looked around. In the bed right next to him, a boy had sat up and spat on him. He grinned at him and breathed through his crooked mouth. Adam left the room.

He realized that the Tokarev was still in his hand. Adam put the pistol away and found the section where Evelyn was placed at the end of the corridor. The same nasty smell. Luckily it was cold, he thought. At least this way, the smells couldn't move through the air so quickly and exert their full force. He held an arm in front of his breathing organs and went into the hall. The beds here had iron bars. Adam looked into the first bed. A woman lay curled up on her mattress with closed eyes and tangled hair. At his back, he heard a female voice. A hum, a sound. Not a recognizable word. He turned and looked in the direction of the human-like sounds. He saw the outline of a woman. Her long hair wavered across her face. She was rocking her body back and forth. He stepped closer. She reached her hands through the grating. The hands were darker than the rest of her skin. He stopped in front of the bed. The arms tried to reach him. He took a step back. The woman's white nightgown had a large dark stain at the level of her private parts. He turned away. Where was Evelyn? One of the beds was empty. He walked up to it and looked in the patient sheet hanging at the bed frame. It was her bed. There was only one word on the entry from the day.

Isolation.

He ran out of the room, down the stairs to the ward office. The nurse was conscious again.

"Where are the isolation cells?" Adam asked her.

He ripped the gag out of her mouth. She screamed. He covered her mouth.

"If you tell me where the isolation cells are, I'll let you live."

She snorted, then calmed down. He carefully took his hand from her mouth.

"So?" he asked.

"In the basement. But it's dark there."

"No electric light?"

She shook her head. He put the gag back in her mouth and left her on her own. He found a candle in the office and lit it as he descended the stairs to the basement. The flame flickered. Air sucked its way into the basement. Adam held his hand protectively in front of the light. The stairs had different heights, and he had to keep adjusting his descent to them. At the end of the stairs, he came upon an iron door locked with a bolt from the outside. He opened the door and stepped into a cellar vault.

Once inside, he raised the candle into the air. The ceiling was slightly higher than he was. It was damp. Water dripped from the walls, and it smelled moldy. He could hear his heart beating. There was a door open next to him. He shone a light into it. A hole. No longer than himself and so low that he could not stand tall. A cot against the wall, a wooden bucket in front of it. The cell was empty. The nearest cell door was locked. He raised the light to the level of the viewing slit. A figure was lying on the cot with her legs drawn up and her hands wrapped around them. He unlocked the door and went inside. The human bundle did not move. He shone the candle over the human. It was Evelyn.

Adam put the candle on the floor, put a hand on her shoulder, and pulled her to him. She opened her eyes. From small slits, she looked at him. He said her name. She opened her mouth. No words came out. Only a croak. He told her about his plan. She just stared past him into the black. He shook her. The woman did not come out of her state.

Adam heard noises and jumped up. Footsteps. Men's voices. He was trapped. The cone of a flashlight danced on the masonry. He stopped at the wall. Behind it, the stairs led up to the first floor. They came closer. First, he saw the barrel of a rifle. He grabbed it and thrust it into the soldier's face. Teeth splintered. The man screamed in pain. Adam kicked the other man hard in the side, and he flew into the wall. After several well-aimed blows, Adam had both knocked out. Then he dragged the men one by one across the corridor and locked them in the isolation cell. Upstairs, the woman still sat bound and gagged in her chair. Adam left the building and finally the hospital grounds. He stripped the gown from his body and threw it into the bushes. At a run, he went through the night. Only when he was sure that he was not being followed did he stop.

Adam thought of Evelyn. She was no longer a person. She was vegetating in an unconscious waking state. Trapped in a space without spatial extent and time. A sad animal.

He could literally feel the anger eating through his body. His previous caution was replaced by a new fighting spirit. They can't get away with this. They can't just destroy their own people. Those responsible must be held accountable. Adam wasn't going to let them get away with it again. He was still waiting in the corner of the ring for the next round to be called. But he had to keep waiting. He had taken on a new fight.

Chapter 16: FATHER FROST

December 1, 1987
Angermünde
District Frankfurt/Oder
German Democratic Republic

The operations of the VEB Gustav Bruhn were not disturbed by the absence of its leader. The painters painted, the sheet metal punchers punched, and the coal hauler hauled. The police and the Stasi had still not caught on to him. In the VEB, there was talk of suicide behind closed doors. Most of the workforce could understand their boss's decision. Adam still had no plan for how to proceed. He had had the impulse to leave everything behind. But he didn't know where to escape. So his only option was to go about his work as he would on any typical day. Knowing the boss was away made that possible. Everything had to have the appearance of normalcy. Despite the search of his apartment, the incarceration of Evelyn, and the killing of Lothar Kletzsch. He was like a newscaster on DDR 1. He knew what was going on, but he had to tell a different story in public. When his colleagues asked him about Evelyn, he reacted evasively, concealed the truth, or took refuge in lies.

"Have you seen Evelyn?"

"Not yet today."

"I'm sure she'll be so wiped out from the funeral that she stayed home."

"Definitely."

"Did you see *Polizeiruf* yesterday? Best episode in a long time."

"Wasn't bad."

"Really got goose bumps."

"You know what? Me too."

"That's never happened before, Kletzsch, nonoperational."

"Don't get too excited. He'll be here any minute."

"Don't ruin it for me."

"Well, I have a feeling."

However, the head of the VEB did not come. Instead, he had to interrupt his work in the afternoon because he was called to the secretary's office. The management assistant asked him to sit down on a chair in the anteroom. She couldn't or wouldn't tell him what it was about. She asked for his patience and then returned her attention to reviewing invoices. He didn't have a good feeling about this. Who did he have to wait for? He still had a chance to escape. Then the phone rang. The woman listened into the receiver, said no more than *Good afternoon, Fine,* and

Goodbye before hanging up again. A short time later, two men walked in. She nodded in greeting and pointed to Adam. His opportunity to escape was over. Had his instincts failed him, of which he could usually be sure of in any situation?

The men planted themselves in front of him. Adam rose from his seat. The shorter of the two walked in front of him, the taller one followed. The three of them crossed the factory floor. The workers looked at the group out of the corner of their eyes. No one dared to look directly at them or speak a word. The two men had the appearance and demeanor of intelligence officers. This kind existed all over the world and was the same in any one of those services. They hid in overly large coats and did what was asked of them. On this day, it was apparently their job to pick up worker Adam Hedman from the VEB Gustav Bruhn. Why they did this, they certainly did not know themselves. Their badge and their handgun were enough to legitimize their ignorant self-confidence. Too much information only disturbed the comfortable murmur of pompous cluelessness inside their heads.

The man marching ahead pushed open the gate to the factory floor. The man behind him ordered Adam to stop after the shorter man on the right disappeared behind the factory floor. Adam was alone with the taller man, who looked down on him with any noticeable facial expression. They did not speak a word. Cold air pressed into the hall. The workers mimed bustle at their stations. After they had waited in the cold for several minutes, a black limousine came around the corner, drew a large circle over the icy factory grounds, and then stopped at the height of the waiting men. The driver left the engine running, got out, and opened the rear door of the Volga. White clouds rose from the car's exhaust. The taller one gave Adam a shove. His signal to go to the car. The man followed close behind him. When they arrived at the vehicle, he pushed him onto the leather bench seat and closed the door. Adam immediately tried the door opener. Locked.

The big man opened the door again. "What's wrong?"

"I forgot my jacket."

"Won't need it."

The man closed the door again and waited at the factory gate with his colleague. They lit cigarettes. Adam was alone in the car and could not hear what the men were saying. He only saw their mouths moving. After they had smoked up, they got back into the car. A plastic window separated the driver's cabin from the rear. Again, he couldn't listen to what was being said. As a result, he had no idea where they were taking him or what they intended to do with him. The city roared silently past him as the car weltered over the pothole-strewn country roads. It was warm in the car, but his hands were cold.

After they had driven a few miles, the car turned onto a boggy dirt road. Adam reached behind him. No Tokarev. Not even a waistband where he could have hidden it. He was wearing his dirty work overalls. The car rocked over the uneven roadway. In the distance, lights flashed between the conifers. They were approaching a gate brightly lit by spotlights. A wall enclosed it. As if by magic, the gate slid open to the side when the car was about fifty yards away from it. The Volga drove through at walking speed.

Adam looked up at a deserted guardhouse with a surveillance camera perched on its roof. The gate closed, and the black sedan regained asphalt under its wheels. They drove for minutes on the pothole-free roadway through dense forest until all at once the rows of trees thinned, and the car stopped shortly after that. The taller man got out on the passenger side. The Volga was at the end of the road. Everything that followed was nonartificial. The car's headlights cast their light on reeds in the distance, divided by a well-trodden path. They were on the shore of a lake.

The man opened the door again. "End of the journey."

Adam got out, and the man got back into the car. As he walked down the path, the vehicle remained in position with its engine running and its headlights illuminated. Soon Adam reached the reeds. Darkness fell around him. He turned around. The driver had turned off the car's headlights. He looked up at the sky. Black clouds were pushing past the moon in quick puffs. He kept walking. The path became even narrower. The reeds sprawled across the trail. Adam bent the stalks aside and continued step by step. He turned around. The car was no longer visible, but it must still be in the same place as he had not heard any engine sounds. Suddenly the path ended, and he stepped onto wooden planks. A long jetty was in front of him, with the lake behind it. Adam didn't know exactly which lake it was. The body of water was large. It could be Grimnitzsee or even Werbellinsee. He had been swimming at both the previous summer. Both were too big to swim once around in one go.

The moon shone its light on the frozen floes in the lake. The ice cover had not yet fully closed. Adam wondered if he should attempt an escape. Strip off his clothes and swim across. He calculated his chances. Diving under the ice could be done. But surviving in the cold for long after he got out of the water without dry, warm clothes was more difficult. To make matters worse, he was not safe at home. Adam pushed the thought out of his mind again and walked to the end of the wooden jetty. At his feet, he saw a rolled-up towel. Did the men in the Volga expect him to get into the water? Was the towel to serve as a piece of evidence that he had gone swimming in the freezing lake and not returned? The third suicide after Anna and Kletzsch? But then why this remote spot, which was also sealed off from the outside world by a yards-high wall? It didn't make sense, and that reassured him. One could say a lot about the GDR, but not that its executive organs acted senselessly. Everything followed the dictates of instrumental reason.

He looked out at the lake. On the opposite shore, he could see the lights of two houses. But they were too far away to make out details. Then he heard a noise. Shortly after, something rose out of the lake. It was a man pushing himself naked out of the water onto the dock. The man took the towel and dried himself, blowing clouds of steam from his mouth. Adam hadn't recognized him right away, but it was the same man in whose house he had woken up a few weeks ago after his hunting accident. Friedrich Stahl wrapped the towel around his robust body and put his arms on his hips. Then he looked across the lake, shook himself, and let out a deep howl.

He took a few steps toward Adam and put on a big grin. "That's what awakens the spirits."

He spoke into the vastness of the water. "Hedman, come over here. Stand right here. Take a deep breath. Let some air into your lungs."

Adam got next to Stahl and breathed in the frosty air. Both looked across the lake. Water dripped from the man's body onto the jetty.

He stretched his arms toward the sky. "As far as the eye can see, nothing but ice." He spoke pensively and pompously. "Thousands of feet thick. Under the ice shell, all life is crushed. Century-old trees are snapping like matchsticks. The megafauna is on the run. Mammoths, woolly rhinos, aurochs. The giant beautiful creatures are fleeing from the ice masses that are pushing inexorably forward. They bury everything under them. Mountains are ground down. Stones turn into the finest sand. Under the ice sheet, all life is frozen, seemingly preserved forever. Imagine that force, Hedman."

Stahl grabbed him by the upper arm and squeezed hard. "Feel the cold. Twenty thousand years ago, there was nothing but ice here."

The man stretched his arms northward and spun halfway around. "All the way up from Scandinavia, through what is now Flensburg to Hamburg, Havelberg, Luckenwalde, Lübben, Guben. Everything is under the ice. You have to visualize that. Where Berlin is today, everything was buried under a sheet of ice. The ice pushed huge landmasses in front of it, rolling everything down underneath it. At some point, the icebergs, weighing tons, stopped pushing further across the land."

The man loosened his grip and finally crossed his arms in front of his chest. "Out of the blue, it got warmer. The ice melted. Life was coming back. Where there had been frost for millennia before, the sun's rays brought spring, summer. The ice became water, and the water fed these lakes. These eerily icy lakes."

Stahl shook his head and continued to speak softly, almost imploringly. "Isn't life one of the most damn inexplicable mysteries, Hedman? And yet, it goes on and on. It never stops. Not because you or I or any Neanderthal believes it. It stops when it's over. Not before and not after. If the ice is going to melt, it's going to melt. And it will melt. Be sure of that. But as long as everything is under ice, you keep still. One is a small birch seed that is enclosed in the ice. And what does the birch seed do, Hedman? The birch seed doesn't look for its way out of the ice. The birch seed waits until its time has come. Because the birch seed is smart, smarter than the biologists give it credit for. It waits for things to work themselves out without effort. And the birch seed is right. Because things work themselves out for it, totally on their own. The sun comes, warms the ice until it is free. It lets the wind carry it to a beautiful place and begins what it has been waiting for. It begins to live. It takes root and, as a full-grown tree, laughs at all those who had no patience. Let this be a lesson to you, my dear Hedman. Every ending is a beginning."

The man laughed briefly and then became serious again. "Sounds like an ancient proverb somebody once doodled into a friendship book. But at this point, it's true. This is where my wife died. It was as cold as it is now. Snow everywhere, ice ..."

He paused for a moment and then continued speaking. "But even after winter came spring. Shoots sprouted from under the blanket of snow. I was alone with my two boys. I made the best of it. There's only so much you can do, Hedman. Let others judge us."

He turned to Adam. "Come on, let's go. It's getting cold."

Stahl walked down the pier. Adam followed him. He had the feeling that the man wanted to tell him more than he could understand. Adam sensed a gap between what was being said and the meaning. Stahl reached the end of the footbridge. There was a tin box. The man took out a bathrobe and bath slippers. Stahl put on the robe, and together they walked to the limousine waiting for them at the end of the path. They sat down in the back seat.

The car drove through the night to Stahl's estate, which Adam had left a few weeks ago with a gunshot wound. The thatched mansion. It seemed to him as if his accident had happened years ago, in another life. They went inside, as the two men in leather coats had to stay outside. They entered the spacious vestibule, where a woman in a gray dress met them. It was a different woman than the one last time he had visited. But she had the same austerity. The double doors to the dining room were closed. Stahl excused himself and took the stairs up to the second floor. The woman escorted him into the parlor. They passed a wall of hunting trophies. Red deer and wild boar from the surrounding forests.

They reached the salon. Behind the door, a stuffed polar bear was waiting for Adam. Certainly not from the surrounding area. The fire was burning in the fireplace of the wood-paneled room. He was placed on a sprawling sofa covered in green velvet. The woman left him alone with himself and the white behemoth. The house had nothing at all in common with the sobriety of real socialism. It breathed the spirit of a bygone era. The pompous hideousness of the *Gründerzeit*, when the German Empire fought with the great colonial powers for a *Platz in der Sonne*, a place in the sun. He continued to look around. Except for the ice monster, his eye caught on nothing much. A few paintings, some antique furniture, a chandelier, a fireplace. It looked like a steel baron imitating the old-established nobility. Stahl came in again. He had exchanged his bathrobe for a tracksuit and sat down in an armchair across from him. The woman also came in again. She asked for their drink requests and disappeared again when the host had ordered the usual from her.

Stahl looked at him. "You surely want to know what you are doing here?"

"Right, what am I doing here?"

"I'll tell you about that in a minute."

Then the woman came back with a tray on which she balanced the drinks. She put two glasses on the table and poured into them from a pitcher of milk.

"Please bring the envelope I have prepared for Herr Hedman," he said to the woman, who immediately went on her way.

Stahl took a big sip of the milk. "Try it. It's fresh. You can't get it like this anywhere else."

Adam took a small sip of the warm liquid and set the glass down, nodding his approval to the man.

"Nothing has been done to the milk yet. Not pasteurized, not homogenized, nothing. It comes to us directly from Mother Nature. The real thing, the unadulterated thing. You can taste it, am I right?"

"Yes, thank you!"

The woman came back with an envelope in her hand. She handed it to Stahl.

"You see, what I have in my hand here will reassure you. I have already told you that there is a beginning in every ending. It's just that you have to allow the end to happen first. And the end is in here."

Stahl handed him the envelope. "Open it."

Adam found a photograph inside. Black and white. By all appearances from a morgue. He saw a young woman on an autopsy table. This could only be Anna Sievers. He looked at Stahl.

"That should remove the last of your doubts. Because, as I have heard, you have cast doubt on the fact that Frau Sievers is indeed dead. Well, you have the proof in your hands. Uncertainty can drive a person mad. We have seen that with Evelyn Sievers. If you can't let go, if you don't want to grasp the obvious, the truth, then you get entangled, then you fall. And you have to be careful that the hole is not so deep that you can't climb out again. You do want to climb out again, don't you, my dear Hedman?"

He didn't know what to say. It was a rhetorical question, but he felt it needed approval. So he nodded and produced a timid *yes*. Then he put the photo back in the envelope and the envelope in his overall pocket.

"Good, then I don't have to worry about you anymore. It would have been too bad. Such a strong young man, hardworking. As I've been told, an important part of the collective—we can't lose someone like that. Not for such a stupid thing."

"Is that why you searched my apartment?"

Stahl smiled. At first he left it at that, to say nothing. Then he decided to answer after all. "Just for your own safety. You don't know what kind of stupid things people do sometimes. You have to be protected. From yourself, I should say." He thought for a moment and spoke a little more quietly as if to himself. "Sometimes you have to protect people, from themselves even."

Then Stahl looked at him, smiling again. Adam did not smile back.

"So the whole shenanigans have come to an end once and for all. Can I count on that?" asked Stahl.

Adam nodded and drew air into his lungs, letting it out slowly. Why did Stahl have to make sure of his silence? Being here by the lake with him, the worker with the Stasi district leader, was not ordinary. This courteous treatment could only mean one thing—Stahl was afraid. Of him. But what had scared him? Adam had hit a nerve, a weak spot that made him vulnerable, and he wanted to make sure that he had nothing to fear from him. Not a smart move on Stahl's part. For it was only then that Adam became suspicious and felt that he was closer to the truth than he had thought possible. What made Stahl vulnerable? His family, his two sons, no doubt. Once before, a woman had died when her path had crossed with Stahl's. That could not be a coincidence. Then, as today, Stahl had had his hands in the game. How exactly, he had to find out. He collected himself. Just don't look too suspicious, Adam thought.

He tried an innocent question about his shooter. A wound that had left a scar. "How is Immanuel doing, by the way?"

"Good, he's in school."

"At this hour?"

"It's more like a boarding school. An officer's school in Rostov."

"In the Soviet Union?"

"That's right, in our beautiful brother nation."

"I didn't even know he was a soldier."

"You served, too, didn't you?"

"Briefly."

"I've been preparing my sons to go down this path since they were little boys. So, of course, it's just the right thing to do to encourage them in any way I can."

"And his brother?"

"Ephraim is still too young. But he will get there. I'm sure of it."

Friedrich Stahl finished his glass of milk and wiped his mouth with his hand. Then he escorted Adam out of the house. Adam's glass remained almost completely filled on the table. On his way out, photographs of the children caught his eyes.

"Is that your youngest?" asked Adam, pointing to a boy and girl at a ballet performance.

The man laughed.

"No, it's not Ephraim. This is Immanuel. He was very young then."

He grabbed him by the shoulder and walked him to the front door. Outside, the black limousine was waiting for him. The taller man got out and opened the car door for him. Stahl raised his hand in farewell, and a moment later, the front door slammed into the lock. The car began to move. They drove along the perfectly paved road, passed the gate, and reached the forest path. Adam leaned back in his seat and looked out. The coniferous trees passed him by. His eyes grew heavy. He nodded off.

Suddenly Adam was torn from his sleep. A bad feeling rose in him. He felt sick. Was it the milk? He knocked on the window. "Pull over."

No response.

"Stop the car. I'm going to puke."

The driver groaned and stopped the car. His copilot opened the door. Adam rushed out of the Volga, and immediately a gush shot out of his mouth. He collected himself for a moment. The nauseous feeling was gone. There remained a clarity he had not felt in a long time. With an acrid taste of acid on his lips, Adam sat back down in the back seat. The men grinned. His body had resisted the suspicion his head was forcing on him. The man with the boyish eyes was Immanuel Stahl. All the circumstantial evidence pointed to it. He danced, just as the man in the Café Moskau had done with Anna. He was an officer's candidate, which explained the visit to the nightclub. He looked younger than he was. But the reason Adam felt his guts shooting out of his body was the realization that the young man had attended a military school in the Soviet Union. The place where there was a series of murders of women. Was he not only Anna's murderer but also the murderer of several other young women? Was he the Beast of Rostov, who had been wreaking havoc in the city on the Don for years?

Sometimes the truth was unimaginable, and it took someone to uncover it. But it felt like a bad joke that the truth had allowed itself to choose him to bring it to light.

Without Adam having told the driver his address, he dropped him off at his front door. Adam looked at the dilapidated building and had the feeling that he had never been here before. The house looked different than he remembered. It gleamed a dull green as if a thin layer of moss had covered the crumbling facade. In addition, the glass was missing from one of the windows on the second floor. He walked through the gateway. The sediment had settled black in the empty milk bottles. This was where Adam Hedman lived. But it was not his home. He felt as if it was the last time he would enter this place for all time.

Adam climbed the rotten step to his apartment and inserted the small key into the padlock. Even without turning the key, he could look through the wide crack in the door into his kitchen–living room. It looked just as he had left it. Who would have changed anything? Even a second search of the house could not make it worse. The cushions were still slashed; only the papers and books he had stacked haphazardly. Adam went to the closet and took out his backpack. Then he gathered all the documents, sorted them into an envelope, and put the envelope in the bag. He looked around the apartment. After a moment's thought, he took a stack of books under his arm and went outside with them. Empty-handed, he came back inside and took another dozen books. Adam did this until he had gotten all the books out of the apartment. He grabbed a bottle of methylated spirits and went outside with it. He squirted the liquid into the garbage can where the books were, lit a match, and threw it in. Immediately the books caught fire. Adam felt his conscience blaze higher than the flames. His father's incantations that no one in the world should ever be allowed to burn books again sat too deep. Adam tugged the rational motives for this act into his head. He knew it was the right thing to do, as he had to cover all the tracks that could lead to him. Furthermore, he knew that this burning of books could save lives. First and foremost, his own. Adam looked into the flames for a few more minutes and left the courtyard only when he was sure that the fire had eaten every single page.

When he reentered his apartment, he stuffed his clothes into his backpack and took one last look at the empty room. The table, the chairs, the bed. None of it belonged to him anymore. He walked through the door and left it open. Let the cold creep in, and the weather take more and more possession of it.

Adam was walking down Clara-Zetkin-Straße. He would have taken his bicycle as usual, but it had disappeared in the night, from which Anna Sievers also had not returned. Soon he left the old town behind him, then the new housing estate, and shortly afterward had reached the city's outskirts. He walked along the country road, away from the city that had offered him work and shelter. Adam had the icy wind from the east at his back, whipping him forward. His only job was still to put one foot in front of the other.

After several hours of marching, his trek had come to an end. He had come to the place where a road sign pointed the way to the highway. Adam beat a path into the bushes. From here on, there was no more road, no more paths, no more trails. He had trouble orienting himself on the terrain in the moonless night. After an hour, he reached the group of spruce trees standing alone in the pitch dark on a sandy elevation. On his knees, he slid to the brush where he had hidden the folding spade. Adam began to dig in the frozen ground. After only a short time of working, sweat had already beaded on his forehead.

When Adam's muscles had long since stopped wanting to dig, he came across the metal chest. He opened it and took out the flashlight. Then he made sure the red plastic screen was screwed in front of it and put the light next to the hole in the ground. The flashlight colored a cone around him in dim light. He pulled the heavy chest out of the earth and opened it.

First, Adam took out the Browning and then pulled the Tokarev out of his jacket. He looked at both weapons and weighed them in his hand. Then he decided on the Russian model. Although he had no suitable ammunition for the Tokarev except the few bullets remaining in the magazine, it was the obvious choice. But supplies should be easy to obtain for a Russian make on this side of the Iron Curtain. He tucked the gun into his waistband and the American make back into the box. Then he found the plastic bag with the documents. He put a Bulgarian and a Soviet passport together with the blank visa papers into his backpack. Then he put his ID in a waterproof document case and put that in the box as well. It was already risky to travel with two different identities, so he didn't want to push his luck with a third. What was missing was the uniform, which he had folded impeccably and stowed in another plastic bag. As he found it, he put it in the backpack.

For the first part of the plan, Adam had everything together. For the second, he took out a leather sheath and rolled it up. Aiming, he pulled one of the knife handles and eyed it briefly. It was the right one. A small knife he tucked into his boot. Then he took out another palm-sized tin box, in which he found a syringe and a vial of anesthetic. He put these into the backpack as well and then closed the chest again. Using the spade, he filled the hole in the ground with sand and then put the spade back in the place where he had hidden it before. He hoped that this was not the last time he would dig up his treasures.

Book II

"The belief in a supernatural source of evil is not necessary. Men alone are quite capable of every wickedness."

—Joseph Conrad

Chapter 1: INTO THE HEART OF THE BEAST

December 2–3, 1987
Berlin
Capital of the GDR
German Democratic Republic

The *Ludmilla*, a powerful DR 130 class locomotive, stood in the station with a roar from its diesel engine and was at rest. The day had begun, it was almost minus ten Celsius, and since she was on her way east, the only thing for it was to resign herself to the cold.

The trackbed of the east-west axis stretched before them like the beginning of an interminable railroad track. On the horizon, the earth and the sky were welded seamlessly together, and in the luminous space, the windows of the sleeping cars, sooty from the storm rides, shone as sharply outlined brown glasses, framed by the olive-green paint of the wagon sheets. A haze rested over the plain, disappearing into a landmass of endless expanse. The sky was dark above Berlin, and farther back still seemed condensed into a mournful gloom, brooding motionless over the biggest and the greatest town in the Soviet-occupied zone.

But there was no community. Adam was standing alone on the platform in the Bulgarian officer's uniform amid hundreds of Russian soldiers. Here and there, he saw a Polish uniform flashing olive green through the masses of brown coats and black *ushankas*. It was how he had imagined it. He was the only Bulgarian in a sea of the socialist brother forces. Men crowded to the doors at either end of the seven sleeping cars harnessed behind the locomotive. Women of the Soviet troops walked through the rows of men, blowing their whistles. Chaos reigned. The men pushed, shoved, and laughed. One of the women in an olive-green military skirt approached him and indicated with a sweeping gesture of her hand that he too should stand at the edge of the crowd. Adam followed the request and got to the edge of the hustle and bustle.

There was a clammy smell of wool and adolescent sweat. The young Russians turned to look at him. Not only was he the only Bulgarian, but he was also the only officer among ordinary soldiers. The men did not seem to be surprised by this. A Russian officer would not show his face here, but a Bulgarian, they could explain that to themselves. Those poor Bulgarian dogs. Adam was the last to board the wagon. The narrow aisle was overcrowded. It was loud and hot. He felt the pores under his arms giving off moisture. Little compartments without doors led off from the aisle, with three beds piled up on either side. He found a compartment in the middle of the corridor where five boys were sitting in the bunks, tossing cigarettes to each other. He stopped in the aisle and asked if there was another bed available for him. They waved him in.

Adam stowed his bag under the lowest bunk and got rid of his coat. Then he lay down on the hard mattress and paid no more attention to the soldiers. Outside, a whistle shrilled, and the train began to move. The soldiers in his compartment lit their cigarettes and shouted insults at each other across the bunks. One of them had a bottle of vodka with him, and the soldiers circulated it among them. They passed the Oder River, whose ice had been broken by ships. Below them began the People's Republic of Poland. Border guards came into the compartment. The Russian soldiers reluctantly interrupted their game and stood up. Without speaking a word, the border guards examined the papers of the Red Army soldiers. Then the two young pimply Poles turned to the Bulgarian officer. One was stout, the other slender.

"*Mówisz po polsku?*" asked the slender one. *Do you speak Polish?*

"*Nyet,*" he answered truthfully in Russian.

"*Russkiy?*"

"*Da.*"

The slender stripling said something in broken Russian that was meant to tell him that they had not been told anything about a Bulgarian officer on board. Adam then pulled out his papers.

The haggard border guard studied them and then looked at him over the documents. "What do you want in Moskva?"

"I'm only going as far as Warsaw."

"And what are you doing?"

He already had a story in mind in case of this question. "I'm visiting the *Wojskowe Centralne Biuro Konstrukcyjno-Technologiczne.*"

He could say the name of the institute in Polish. It was the Polish Office of Military Technology and should be a sufficient reason for his destination of travel. The two border guards looked at him penetratingly.

Then the young man gave him back his documents. "It's all right, *Leytenant* Popov."

Adam put the papers back into the breast pocket of his uniform. He had the feeling that the border guard was not entirely convinced of the authenticity of his documents. Maybe he was just too lazy to get to the bottom of it. Whatever the case, he had overcome the first hurdle. There were still higher ones ahead. The border guards saluted and continued their inspection. When they were out of the compartment, the Russians came down again and distributed the cards.

"Dirty Poles," the man next to him said, laughing at him through yellow teeth.

Flat snowy landscapes passed in front of the dirty windows. Kunowice, Rzepin, Boczów, Torzym, Zamęt, Mostki. Adam was getting tired. The wagon jolted comfortably over the sloping rails, and he fell asleep. Shaken by vivid dreams, he woke up. Outside it was still dark. He reached to his breast pocket and pulled out the photo of the dead Anna. Up until now, he hadn't bothered with it but had only ever glanced at it. Now it was time to face the truth. The black-and-white photograph showed the woman lying naked on a tiled counter. A small piece of wood held her head up. She had her eyes closed, and her hair was slicked back. Quite different from the curly mane she was known for. In the background, he could see a calendar. The page showed November 27, 1987, a Thursday. Exactly three weeks after her disappearance. He felt a tear run down his cheek. When he ran his hand over it to wipe it away, his fingers remained dry. His mind was crying. His body was not showing it.

The route to Warsaw dragged on. Kostrzyn, Podstolice, Konin, Kutno, Sochaczew and finally Warsaw Central. Only a few Polish soldiers got off here. The Russians stayed put. Soon Warsaw was in the past, and only snowy plains passed by his sleeping car. They drove past the Mazovian towns of Halinów and Dębe Wielkie without stopping. As the terrain became rougher and hillier, they passed through Mrozy, Siedlce, Łuków, and Międzyrzec Podlaski. Skimming the airport of Biała Podlaska, crossing fields and forests, leaving Małaszewicze behind, they reached Terespol, the last town on Polish territory.

Adam's head was racing. He pulled out the photo of the dead woman once again. Something was wrong. November 27 had not been a Thursday. At least not that year. Because the date had fallen on a Friday in 1987. The day of Anna's funeral. He pondered. The mistake could not be explained. At least not if nobody had manipulated the photograph. But if it was fake, then this wrong detail could quickly be defined as a careless mistake by the retoucher. Assuming he had taken the negative of another photograph of a dead person made precisely one year earlier, the date would fall on a different day of the week. That was the case here. Adam had a fake photograph in his hand. A perfect retouch, but one that contained a tiny logical flaw. He had to turn Immanuel in. Her killer was the only one who knew the truth.

He got up, stood in the hallway, and looked out the window to the south. He knew the area only from stories. Majdanek, Belzec, and Sobibor were only a few miles away from the tracks. It all looked so peaceful.

The border river Bug meandered under the railroad bridge. Brest was the last town with European track width. After that, the rails were a handsbreadth wider all the way to the Pacific because the tsars had feared an invasion from Europe by rail in the nineteenth century. So the safest precaution was to make Russia's entire rail network impassable to European gun trains. From Brest in the far west to Vladivostok in the far east.

On the neighboring track, a train came in from the opposite direction. The soldiers poured out of the sleeping cars. So did the soldiers from the train that had just arrived. Past the border guards and through the crowds of Red Army soldiers, they fought their way across the platform into the other car. Here on the Polish-Belarusian border, it was five degrees colder even than in Berlin. The cars were just as run-down and stuffy as the others. The only difference was that these were on bogies four inches further apart. For the Red Army, it saved more time to move the soldiers from one train to the next than to move the train to another bogie. If something became technically tricky, it could still be solved by sheer human power. He had learned the first lesson in Russian pragmatism.

The train stopped at every Belarusian district town. Each time Adam was awakened by the squealing of the brakes. Ivatsevichy, 10:31 p.m. Lida, 00:45 a.m. Maladzyechna, 3:42 a.m. Minsk, 4:58 a.m. Smolensk, 7:50 a.m. The day had dawned. The light struggled through the gray clouds.

He had arrived in the Union of Soviet Socialist Republics, and he stood up and stretched his legs. Ice crystals had formed on the windows overnight. The most dangerous part of his journey was behind him. The borders. The other stations led as if drawn with a ruler dead straight to Moscow. Vyazma, Gagarin, Mozhaysk, Tuchkovo. In between, there were hours of endless snow-covered expanses.

When the train pulled into Moscow's Belorusskaya Station, almost one thousand two hundred miles were already behind him, and he was still far from reaching the destination of his journey. Adam had to think of Evelyn, without whom he would not be on this train now. It was she who had sent him on this long journey without being aware of it. Evelyn had insisted that he help her find her missing sister. In doing so, she had risked her own life. And lost it. She now vegetated as a mere shell in an East German basement dungeon. He didn't know if he owed it to her or himself. But Adam was sure he was doing the right thing. Everything else was beside the point for the moment. His own life had been waiting for so long that a few more days and a few more bruises didn't matter anymore.

The station was painted mint green and stood out sharply against the gray sky. The thermometer showed eighteen degrees Celsius below zero, minus one Fahrenheit. Adam flipped up the collar of his uniform jacket, opened the door to the reception hall, and found the restrooms. The ammonia-tinged air cut into his lungs. He walked into one of the stalls. On the walls, a few wobbly scratchings of cocks and pussies. *Arte Povera*. He came back out dressed like a Russian farmhand in loose cotton pants, a buttoned work jacket, and heavy boots. He took a look in the mirror. What looked like a cold nose on an officer was already interpreted as a red drunkard's nose on a laborer. His hair was ragged and greasy. Adam covered it with a peaked cap, wrapped a coarse woolen scarf around his neck, and left the restroom as a poor figure.

He used the escalators to get to the Moscow underground. At Komsomolskaya station, he got off and stepped out of the station building. In front of him was a vast square, where three long-distance stations were located. From Kazanskaya station, the trains went to the south. The old diesel locomotive with the red star on the front pulled in on time. Behind her, she pulled a long tail of wagons, some of them sleeping cars. A comfort he was not to enjoy on this trip. Adam entered the third-class compartment to Rostov-na-Donu. It smelled burnt by heating air. Knotted carpets were laid out in the aisle. Adam slid back and forth on the hard bench seat. This was his place for the journey, which was to last twenty hours.

The train jolted off, and he pulled the newspaper out of his jacket. To the left of the *Izvestia* lettering, three emblems graced the newsprint. One with Lenin's head, one with the battleship *Potemkin*, and one with the hammer and sickle. The rest of the sheet was unadorned. Paragraph after paragraph of text. He sat back, read the paper from the first line to the last. It took almost three hours and was good practice for his Russian. But it did nothing for his knowledge of this country. Adam now knew what the government wanted him to think. But he didn't know what was going on. If he trusted the articles, the Soviet Union had to be doing wonderfully economically. But when he looked out the window at the desolate apartment complexes or the pale faces in front of him, they said a hundred times more about the reality in that country than many thousands of words in this official mouthpiece. It was the same in the GDR. But there, at least, he had the opportunity to receive and compare news broadcasts from the East and the West. The Russians could not do that. They had to believe what their newspapers and television told them. Or they had to look away and not listen.

By now, it had become dark. Soon they reached the station of Ryazan. Adam pulled his cap over his eyes, folded his arms in front of his body, and tried to sleep. As they approached Liski, they crossed the frozen Don River for the first time on the journey, which from the little town meandered for nearly one thousand two hundred miles to come through the Russian and Ukrainian SSRs until it poured downstream into the Sea of Azov at Rostov. Every hour the train reached Rossosh, Kantemirovka, Chertkovo and Millerovo. They rattled across the railroad bridge over the Siverskyi Donets, which lay frozen in its riverbed below them. Shortly after, they reached Kamensk-Shakhtinsky and Zverevo. It was getting light. They came to Shakhty and a few hours later to Novocherkassk. On the other side of the glass, he glanced over the endless expanse.

Adam remembered a lesson in physical geography. The class was asked to calculate how far away the horizon was. The answer was surprising. It was fifteen thousand five hundred feet for a normal-sized man. So if he felt that the distance was infinite, it wasn't true because he didn't know what came after fifteen thousand five hundred feet. Perhaps a breathtakingly beautiful lake or the sea. As a student, he had concluded that no human being had an infinite horizon. Instead, all people only believed what they witnessed with their own eyes. And that was a vanishingly small part of the earth's surface. Everything beyond that was a pure abstraction for the human brain. It sounded like trite wisdom, but sometimes you had to be above things to have foresight. Even from a height of one hundred feet, one had a view of over twenty thousand yards. But when do you ever get that high in life?

The train rattled along the icy tracks. He looked at his watch. When they pulled into Rostov Glavny station, it was 3:53 p.m. The train was several hours late. He gathered his things and got off the train. First order of business was to put all his belongings in the station's locker. Anesthetics, guns, and army uniforms were for Bulgarian officers, not Russian farmhands.

Chapter 2: MOTHER RUSSIA

December 4, 1987
Rostov-na-Donu
Rostov Oblast
Union of Soviet Socialist Republics

Adam found a restaurant on the ground level of an apartment building. The interior was as cold as the weather outside. On the linoleum floor were tables without covers and chairs without cushions. Ceiling lamps brightly lighted the restaurant room. But it was warm inside, and there was vodka. The few guests sat on high chairs at the bar. He sat down and ordered a vodka. The host wore a white coat and a bald head, over which he had combed the rest of his black hair. He placed a water glass on the table in front of Adam and poured it full to the top with alcohol. One hundred grams or 3.5 ounces. Adam drank half of it in one gulp and felt the warmth flow into his body.

The man next to Adam looked at him from glassy eyes stuck in a thick round skull from which blond hair grew like bristles. "I have an anecdote for you. Do you want to hear it?"

"*Da.*"

"Listen up, *tovarish*. At the border, an Arab and a Jew are shooting at each other. All of a sudden, the Arab stops. *Hey, Mohammed, what's going on?* asks the Jew. *I'm out of ammunition*, says the Arab. *Come over here. I'll sell you some*, says the Jew."

The man burst out laughing bronchially. The innkeeper and the other drunks laughed along. Adam had heard a Jewish joke or two in his life. But this was not one of the good ones. The men were unabashedly indulging in their anti-Semitism. He wondered if he should tell them that they were looking at a Jew. And a real exotic one at that. For he was a Jew from the GDR. There weren't many of them, maybe five hundred. No one knew that for sure. Five hundred, that was about as many as lived on Cocos Islands. But he decided against it. The mood was just so beautifully exuberant.

"Have you guys ever met anyone from Cocos Islands?" he asked.

"Where would that be?" the host asked.

"In the Pacific. Nice and warm there."

"Nah, have you ever met anyone from there?"

"Maybe."

The host shrugged his shoulders. The others had not been listening.

"Listen, comrades. This anecdote is good, too," said another drunk. He looked around the room. When he had gathered enough attention, he began to speak. "You won't believe what happened to me. I was walking down a shortcut by the railroad tracks, and I found a girl tied to the tracks. I told my friend about it. He asked me if she had sucked my dick. I told him, *But I didn't find the head.*" As fate would have it, the men with their bad jokes had gathered the two subjects that had played the leading role in his life in recent years. His heritage and murdered girls. Accurate drunkards.

The joke sharer laughed and looked around. As the men got up and bore down on him, Adam had no idea what was happening.

The innkeeper came around the counter and stood between the men. "Quiet, comrades. This is just an anecdote. Just a little harmless anecdote."

However, the men did not calm down. So the only thing left for the joke sharer to do was put on his coat and leave the pub. When he was gone, everyone sat down again.

"Shit, comrades. Rape is not funny," said the host.

"Unless you're raping a clown," the man next to him said.

The mood remained depressed. The host poured out the vodka.

"Nobody raped a clown, though," Adam said.

"Nah, nobody did," the man next to him said, looking down at his vodka glass.

"Who was it, then?"

"You best stay out of this stuff, *tovarish*. You got that?"

"I was just asking. It's a free country, comrade!"

All the men laughed. The host patted him on the shoulder.

"You're all right, *tovarish*. That's a good one," he said, grinning and finishing his glass. "The militia is doing everything to make sure this gets cleared up," he followed up.

"The militia doesn't do shit," the man next to Adam said.

"Comrade, it's only a matter of time, and they'll catch this guy. And then they'll cut off his head."

"If you say so, *tovarish*. We don't even know yet whether it's one murderer or several. A crazy, a sick thing is this business. Ambushing women, raping them, gouging out their eyes, cutting open their bodies. It makes you crazy. We all go crazy over it. Give me another water, *tovarish*."

The innkeeper poured him a drink. "They will get him. Soon they will have him. Mark my words, *tovarish*."

Adam said goodbye to the men. He was glad that they did not know who he was. Otherwise, as so often, he would have been one of the suspects. And from suspicion to lynch mob, it was only a tiny jump, one wrong word.

Outside the door, the frost hit him like a blow. By now, it had become dark. He tied his scarf around his head again and walked through the snow across the prospectus. Adam could not go to the *komendatura* to ask where the military academy was. If he did so, he might as well put himself in jail. He walked two blocks, and all of a sudden, he hit a railroad embankment. It seemed as if the city had ended. Only in the distance could he see some apartment blocks. The railroad tracks cut right through the middle of the town. A small pedestrian tunnel ran under the railroad embankment, with a single small light dangling from it.

Snowflakes drifted playfully through the cone of light. He couldn't help but think of the distasteful joke of the man with the headless woman tied to the rails. In the weather-protected underpass, he only noticed how the wind had whistled around his ears. Beyond the tunnel was a wasteland. Adam walked to the end and saw a woman walking along a small path by the tracks. He followed her. She wore a long skirt and a padded coat over it. Her long red hair peeked out from under a bobble hat. She was as tall as Anna, and she moved the same way. Of course, he knew it couldn't be her. But Adam's curiosity kicked in. Besides, if he walked one step faster, he would overtake her anyway. So he did. Adam didn't know if the woman had noticed him yet. She kept walking in front of him and didn't turn around to look at him either.

He called after her. "*Izvinite, izvinite!*" *Excuse me.*

But the snow swallowed all sounds. She continued to walk ahead of him, the wind pushing against them. Adam went even faster. Finally, he had reached her, and they were walking side by side. The woman turned to him. She looked frightened and she was beautiful. But it was not Anna. In order not to frighten her with his disguise, he pulled the scarf from his face. Then something hit him in the back. He fell to his knees. The woman opened her coat and pulled out a pistol. She held it to his temple. Someone yanked his arms up. Handcuffs clicked around his joints behind his back. He didn't know what had happened. But it appeared not to be a good idea to follow a woman in the dark in Rostov. The woman put her pistol away again and stopped as two men in uniform took him to a militia bus. They didn't speak a word or answer his questions. The windows were fogged up from the inside. They opened the side door and pushed Adam inside without releasing him from the handcuffs. He was tossed on the floor of the van. With difficulty, he managed to stand on his knees in the rocking van. There was another man next to him. He sat on the bench and looked at him.

Adam scrambled to his feet and sat down across from him. "*Privyet!*"

The man laughed, nodding as he had done before. "*Privyet, privyet!*"

He had an oval face, and hair came out of his scalp in straight wires. "I'm Ivan."

"Aleksey," Adam said, introducing himself with a false name. "Why are you here, *tovarish*?"

"Why are you here, *tovarish*?" the man repeated the question.

"Didn't you hear me?"

"Didn't you hear me?" the man repeated again.

The man laughed. There was no point in talking to him. The van stopped again. Adam wiped the window with his sleeve to look out. It was still snowing as hard as before, and he could see nothing. The two militiamen brought another man to the van. His face was covered in blood. They were led by the woman in the bobble hat. The bait. The men yanked open the door again and threw their prisoner inside. He fell to the floor in front of Adam and Ivan. As he tried to get up, the driver stepped on the gas. The man was knocked off-balance, and his head rumbled against the seat. He was immediately knocked unconscious. From driving through the blowing snow, the man was thrown around on the ground. Blood spreading, Ivan rocked his upper body back and forth. He was terrified.

Soon after, the vehicle stopped, and when they had to get out, they climbed over the man. Finally, the militiamen each grabbed a leg and then pulled him out. His head hit the asphalt. He was lucky that there was snow, so the impact was at least somewhat cushioned. Soon the man regained consciousness and was pulled to his feet. Shakily, he trotted along behind Adam with Ivan trailing. The militiamen pushed them up the steps. Ivan stumbled. He wailed, tears standing in his eyes. Adam looked around. They had been driven in the van to a courtyard enclosed by a wall. Adam had gotten into a situation he wanted to avoid. He was gambling with his own life, and he didn't know if he could rely on his Russian if he was tortured. Adam hoped he wouldn't have to find out that night. Again, he looked around. If he was going to escape, now was the time.

A heavy wooden door was pushed open in front of them. Four uniformed men received the prisoners. Adam had thought for too long. Maybe he could overpower the men. Perhaps he could even escape from the courtyard. But what was to happen next? He didn't know anyone in Rostov, didn't know anyone in the entire Soviet Union, and was almost two thousand miles from the nearest safe haven. And even then, he could not say with certainty whether he was still safe there.

Adam let the men grab him by the arms and pull him into the building. High ceilings, long corridors, cold walls.

Behind a wood-paneled desk was a militiaman. Indeed the first point of contact for anything and everything at the station. Without having their particulars taken, they had to sit down on a wooden bench in the corridor. One of the handcuffs was removed from each of them, and they were chained to the bench with the one that had become free. Then they were left alone. The man was still bleeding from the nose and mouth.

He looked at the two of them. "What have you done?"

"Nothing. I was just talking to the *devochka*," Adam said.

"And that one?"

"I don't know. He's a little slow in the head."

"Slow, slow," Ivan said, then laughed pointedly.

"And you, *tovarish*?" asked Adam.

"I did nothing at all."

"You look like shit for that, though."

The man coughed, spitting blood on the floor.

"Do you know why we're here?" asked Adam.

"It all has to do with the girls who get killed around here."

"So, did you do it?"

The man showed his bloody teeth and pulled up the corners of his mouth. "Maybe. But I'd rather blame it on that guy," he said, nodding again at Ivan.

"Ivan didn't do it."

"Ivan, Ivan," he said, rocking back and forth.

"I can see that too ... what's your name?"

"Aleksey. And you?"

"Timur."

"Are you from around here?"

He shook his head. "Batumi."

"Where's that?"

"Georgian SSR. But I work here."

"Moskva."

"Well, then."

"Do you know the military academy?"

"Sure, everybody knows it."

"And where is it?"

A man in civilian clothes came down the corridor, followed by militiamen. He did not dignify them with a glance and walked past them. The uniformed men stopped in front of them. They undid their handcuffs from the bench and let them snap around the other joint again. Then they led them into a room where there was only one table and exactly three chairs. After they had removed their shackles, they left the three alone again. It felt good to be able to move both hands again. Ivan stood up and walked up and down.

"Sit down. You're driving me crazy," Timur shouted at him.

But Ivan covered his ears and continued to err around the room.

"Do something. He's driving me crazy, that idiot," he said to Adam.

So Adam went to Ivan, took him by the shoulders, and talked to him. The man turned away and let out another scream. Adam left him alone. It was no use. When he sat down again, Timur jumped up and went after the man. He hit Ivan in the face with his fist. Blood splattered. The man went down. He doubled over and cried. Adam jumped up.

Timur kicked at Ivan, Adam yanked him away. In his gaze, he saw that the man was thinking for a moment about whether he should punch him too. He decided against it. Fortunately for both of them. Adam couldn't afford a brawl in a Soviet police station. Ivan slid to the wall and leaned against it. He held his head and looked at his red-stained hands. "*Krov', krov',*" he kept saying. *Blood, blood.*

They took their seats again and left Ivan sitting against the wall. The door on the other side of the room opened. No one came in. The two men looked at each other. Timur wiped his face with his sleeve. That had to hurt, he thought. Timur stood up.

"Where are you going?" asked Adam.

"See what's going on."

"I don't think that's a good idea."

"Why? Are you scared, *tovarish*?"

"Don't you think it's strange that a door just opens like that at the *militsiya*?"

"You overthink, *tovarish* Aleksey."

Timur went to the door and pulled it open. His suspicion was replaced by curiosity. Then he disappeared behind the door, and the cold streamed into the room. Ivan jumped up and went to the door as well. Adam lunged at him. He squirmed in his grip and screamed. Adam put a hand over his mouth. Ivan bit him, and Adam squeezed tighter. Then they heard a gunshot whipping through the night. Ivan went silent. Adam let go of him.

"Stay here, Ivan. This is a trap. Do you understand?"

Ivan nodded.

"*Lovushka, lovushka,*" he repeated. *Trap, trap.*

Adam walked away from Ivan and sat down again. Ivan slid back against the wall and remained sitting there. Adam had taken a big risk. He had naively approached a woman on the hunting ground of a mass murderer. If he wanted to return alive from this trip, he had to be more careful from now on. After a few minutes, a man in civilian clothes came in. He introduced himself as Major Makunin and had Ivan led out of the room. Then he closed the door that led outside and joined him at the table. Makunin leaned back, crossed his legs, and looked him in the eye. Adam was looking at a middle-aged man with a thick full black beard. He had kind eyes. But what did that mean, Adam thought. Men with kind eyes he had watched killing innocent men. The eyes say nothing about a man, he thought and was torn from his thoughts by the major.

"Name?" Makunin asked.

"Aleksey Ilyich Kokorin."

Makunin pulled out a pack of cigarettes and lit one. "Is that what your ID says?"

"*Da.*"

"What happened here today?"

"I don't know."

"Me neither."

He took a drag from the cigarette. "I only know what didn't happen here," Makunin said after a long pause.

Then a woman came in. She was wearing a militia uniform and stood next to the door.

"Do you know this woman?" asked Makunin.

"I don't think so."

"But the woman knows you."

Adam did not recognize the stern woman. "Why?"

"Because you talked to her earlier, by the railroad tracks."

She looked nothing like the woman he had seen in the blizzard, now in her uniform coat and service cap.

"Then I know who she is. But I don't know her."

"What did you want from the woman?"

He wondered what to say. "Talk to her."

"About what?"

"Maybe the weather."

"And what else?"

"That would have remained to be seen."

"So you think it's appropriate to just approach strange women like that?"

"I don't know."

"Think twice next time."

"Yes, *tovarish* Major!"

Makunin gave him a long look and took a drag from his cigarette. "You can go."

The woman left the room. Makunin pointed to the door through which the woman had just vanished. Adam stood up and left the *komendatura*. He had not seen Ivan again and tried to push the memories of Timur out of his brain.

It was the middle of the night. The storm had subsided. Tiny snowflakes swirled in the icy air. The building was at a wide intersection. It was set back a few yards and enclosed by a wall that ended with the *komendatura*. The entrance was on the corner. Adam crossed the courtyard and passed through the gate. Then he looked down the street. The complex of buildings stretched several hundred yards down the prospectus. Then Adam flipped up the collar of his work jacket and walked along the sidewalk by the building. Every few feet, he passed a barred window that started at his head level. The windows on the four floors above had no bars. But that didn't matter yet because he didn't know if he was at the academy yet.

Adam walked for minutes with no door, gate or entrance. Only brickwork, windows and bars. Finally, he reached the end of the block and turned right again. As before, the view stretched far along the facade of the house. He wondered if he could trust a man who had so naively walked to his death. The cold bit into his face, ate under his clothes, and gnawed at his bones. He walked on until there was a break in the building's sill. Behind it, a spacious square opened up, with bare trees reaching for the sky.

At the level of the building Adam had wandered along, a wrought-iron fence with golden spikes rose up. Walking by, he could see a magnificent building through the iron bars. In the middle of the fence was a gate. He stopped in front of it. A wide tree-lined path led directly to the building. No human being far and wide. Not in front of the gate and not behind it. He walked towards it. Locked. On either side of the entrance pillars was a field gun on whitewall tires. Adam didn't have to wonder for long if this ostentatious building was the military academy. Under the ridge of the roof, it was written in red letters.

Kalininskoye Suvorovskoye Voyennoye Uchilishche

Now, in addition to a plan for getting into the Suvorov Military Academy, all he needed was an idea of where the student housing wing was located. But one step at a time.

As always. He felt at his lower back. No gun. That was good when arrested but bad when you wanted to confront a young officer candidate. Adam pulled up the leg of his pants just to make sure. No boot combat knife either. He was completely unarmed. Adam's head and body were his only weapons. But he was also only dealing with a student. However, a student who was going to be an officer. A student who had a fearsome state security man for a father, had his girlfriend on his conscience, and had murdered perhaps dozens of women.

So Adam decided to proceed with caution. It took him almost an hour to get back to the station. Once there, he put the Tokarev in his waistband, the knife on his ankle and the anesthetic syringe in his jacket pocket.

When he stood in front of the fence again an hour later, the situation had not changed. The area was deserted, and he still had no plan for how to get inside. Adam had to put his safety concerns aside, because the only way he would be on the safe side was if he turned around and went back home. That wasn't an option. Sometimes the most straightforward way was the best way, he thought and climbed the fence, swung himself over the iron bars, and set off at a run for the main entrance. No sirens, no guards, no dogs. Adam stopped in front of the gate, wrapped the scarf around his fist, and smashed one of the small wood-framed panes of the door. The glass was thin, barely making a sound. He opened the door from the inside. No cameras, no trip hazards, not a soul. Easier than he had thought, strangely simple. It wasn't an intelligence facility or barracks, just a military academy. What would there be to steal here, he thought, trying to calm his nerves. The only thing he could steal here was the anonymity of a psychopathic teenager.

Adam looked around. There was no light anywhere. He was standing in a spacious entrance hall that was completely dark. A sign that no one was making nighttime patrols here, he thought. And if they did, it would be announced by the cone of light from a flashlight and the sounds of footsteps. That reassured him all the more. He found the office wing on the first floor. The secretary's office was just to his right at the back of the school building. The door was locked. But here, too, there was glass that he could carefully break through. And here, too, the door was only pulled closed and not locked. Adam went inside and found the file cabinets with the students' files. On one was the name he had been looking for.

Иммануил Сталь

In Immanuel Stahl's file, he found his school performance, a psychological profile, and information about his family. Adam was surprised to find that there was nothing wrong with the boy's psyche. He was described as a well-balanced, attentive, and intelligent young man. But what did psychologists know, he thought. Especially those who were appointed by the military. The file got him nowhere. Adam continued to look around the office. Nowhere did he find the files on room occupancy. So he left the office again and walked through the rooms on the ground level. Everywhere it was quiet. Behind a wooden swinging door, in which frosted glass was embedded, was a large hall. He pushed open one panel of the door and walked through. Adam looked directly at a larger-than-life bust of Lenin that stood on a pedestal at the end of the room, illuminated by street lanterns that cast a little light in. There were long benches on either side, at equally long tables. It was the school dining room. He turned back around and pushed open the door, and a chalkboard mounted on the wall caught his eye. It was a seating chart with the names of all the students. Next to each student was a combination of numbers. The room numbers.

III/X.

Сталь.

Adam memorized the code and went back to the entrance hall. From there, he took the stairs leading up. On the first and second floors, it looked like an ordinary school building. There were classrooms in each hallway. At the bottom of the stairs to the third floor, he came across another door that was not locked. He walked through and looked down a long hallway with a large window set into the end. A little light was cast on the stone floor. Still, he heard only a few sounds in the building. The soft gurgle of the heater and the faint whistle of a draft. Adam listened at the door to his left with the code III/II and heard a steady snore coming from the room. He was right in this part of the building, he thought and continued down the corridor. At the end of the hall, a door opened, and a figure came out. Adam hadn't yet been spotted. So he pushed down the handle of the entrance to the next room and slipped inside. In the small room were two beds, two desks, and two closets, fairly divided on either side of the room. In each of the beds slept a boy, not older than sixteen or seventeen. He held his breath, opened the door again, and looked down the hall. Everything was clear. Then he heard a toilet flush and took a step back into the room. He closed the door again and put an ear to the wood. There was a shuffling in the hallway. He waited a little longer. One of the boys had sat up in his bed and was looking in his direction. He spoke softly into the darkness and then lay down again. Adam opened the door and reentered the hallway. All was quiet. He took a few steps. There was a clatter. At his feet, he saw a toy, a tin tank that he had kicked over. He pressed himself against the wall and listened into the building. Everything was quiet. He saw that he was directly before the room assigned to Immanuel Stahl.

Adam reached behind and pulled out the Tokarev. Carefully he opened the door. Weak light fell through the window into the room. He could not make out much. Outlines, shadows that did not give a clear picture. Something hit him on the hand. His pistol flew to the floor. He tried to duck and reach for his knife when something hard hit him in the back of the head. Suddenly everything went black before his eyes.

Adam became conscious again. It was bright in the room. The bedside lamp was burning. He had been knocked out for only a few moments. But the time had been enough for the boy to sit on his chest and pointed the Tokarev at Adam's face. Only now did Adam's mind clear. Quick as a flash, he extended his hand. The boy had not expected it. Adam disarmed the boy and directly aimed the pistol at his head.

The boy laughed and descended from his chest. "I can pull the trigger. You can't. If you shoot, you won't get out of here alive," Immanuel said.

Adam put the gun down.

"Why did you kill her?"

The boy's expression was unchanged. "Who?"

"You know that very well."

Immanuel looked frozen. "Where is she? I didn't kill her."

The young man looked lost in thought. Then he lashed out and hit Adam right on his temple. Again it became dark around him.

Chapter 3: VIOLENCE MACHINE

December 5, 1987
Rostov-na-Donu
Rostov Oblast
Union of Soviet Socialist Republics

When Adam woke up, the first light of the day came into the room. He blinked and could not move. As he looked around the room, there was no sign of the boy. Adam was sitting tied up on a chair in the middle of the room. On the bed was the syringe with the anesthetic he had retrieved from the station locker. His skull was humming. The boy had beaten him with his own weapons. Literally. He could not call for help. If any of the students found him, it would mean the death penalty for him. Adam tried to untie himself from his bonds. But the knot was tied so tightly that he had no chance to undo it with his muscle power alone. He moved back and forth in the chair. The construction was wobbly. The wood drifted apart, and all at once he was sitting in the remains of the chair on the floor. An endearingly rotten chair.

The door opened, and a young officer cadet with a duffel bag on his shoulders came in. The cadet saw Adam and was about to turn back, but he had already broken free from his bonds and jumped toward the young man. Adam grabbed him by the torso and pulled him to the ground. The boy squirmed under his wrestling grip. Then Adam wrapped his legs around his neck and squeezed his thighs together. Ten, nine, eight, seven, six, five, four, unconscious. Three, four seconds more, and he probably would have been gone for good. Adam pulled the unconscious body into the parlor and closed the door. Then he looked at the syringe. There was still a little residue in it. Enough to keep the young man in this condition for several hours. So Adam squeezed the liquid into the cadet's bloodstream. Then he hoisted him onto the bed, removed his uniform, and tied him up by his arms and legs. Immanuel's roommate was a little smaller than he was, but it should fit. So Adam slipped the uniform on and put a wedge under the door.

He decided against taking up Immanuel's pursuit immediately. Because the boy had a few hours' head start on him, Adam took his time to search the room. His pistol and knife were gone. But he found letters. They were written in a cipher he didn't understand. He searched the boy's bookshelf for a worn book and found a Reclam volume that looked like it had been read thousands of times. Adam pulled out the book and leafed through it. There were no notes of any kind. He looked in the letters. Some sort of code appeared at the end of each letter. Adam looked for the places in the book that the code indicated and found them.

In that way he was able to decode the first line of the letter.

My dear son!

Adam felt the adrenaline shoot into his body. He had found the secret correspondence between father and son and was even able to decode it. Adam packed up the letters and made sure the young officer candidate was sleeping soundly in his restraints on the bed. Then he stowed his work clothes in the duffel bag and left the room.

The hallways were empty. The students were in class. He swept through the corridors, jumped down the stairs, and went out through the main entrance. Soon he had reached the gate. At a run, he set off for the station. He still had no idea if he was going to get back into the GDR without his German documents. He had to hope that opportunities would open up for him. Usually, that was the case, and he drew confidence from this experience.

Adam slipped his ragged clothes back on, miming a Russian farmhand in the station restroom, and left the cadet's uniform in one of the stalls. He didn't know how much time he had left before the unconscious man would wake up again and raise the alarm. But he couldn't hope for much. So he hurried through the station's reception hall, took his things out of the locker, and ran straight to the tracks. Behind the platforms where the passenger trains were dispatched, Adam found the rails for freight traffic. One of the long trains was just ready to leave. He asked one of the workers where the train was going.

"North."

This information was what he had hoped for, and he had not been disappointed. Adam moved away from the man's field of vision and walked past the freight cars on the opposite side. There was only one way to survive on an unheated freight train in subzero temperatures, he thought. So he rattled off car after car until he finally found the ones that contained his survival insurance. Some had cows, many had pigs, and one had horses. The decision was not difficult for him. He jumped on the wagon with the cold-blooded horses, heavy workhorses destined for pulling hay wagons. At least that was how he put it together because it fit perfectly into his image of Russia. Perhaps the animals were instead intended as an attraction for children at a fairground. Adam stroked the good-natured animals, which were unimpressed by his presence. Then he sat down in a corner and waited for the diesel locomotive to start moving the wagons. After a few minutes, which dragged on into infinity, the train set off. The more miles he had put between himself and Rostov, the safer he felt. They would look for him in Rostov, but not in the entire Soviet Union. He reassured himself that the Rostov militia suspected him of being an ordinary burglar, not a GDR worker who had nearly killed an officer trainee from the same country on Soviet soil.

The train crept through the station of Novocherkassk. His opportunity to jump off. Adam did not have to wait long for the next passenger train to Moscow. It was third class, and a wide-body car again, filled with ordinary people who would accompany him during the twenty-hour train ride to Moscow. People with the same expression on their faces. Adam missed the horses and their soothing smell.

After having a seat, he pulled out the letters he had taken from Immanuel's room. To decode the cipher, he opened the Goethe volume and began the transcription work. The already small white space of the pages he smeared with his handwriting. It took hours, which he interrupted for a few minutes only by tea breaks and strolls through the train.

By now, they had left behind not only Voronezh but daylight. The train rattled through the Russian winter night. After he had finished decoding, he could finally start reading. At first glance, only individual words stood out. Some he had only heard from the mouths of people who had already experienced the last German war as adults.

Tinnef, Antlitz, Mumpitz, Kehricht, Wankelmut. Old and seldom used words for *rubbish, face, balderdash, refuse, fickleness.*

Others he had never heard in his life.

Gake, Ingrimm, Ranküne, Labsal. Nearly obsolete words meaning something like *silly goose, ire, rancor, refreshment.*

The Stahls apparently dug deep to unearth the nuggets of the German vocabulary. In addition, there were short passages written in Latin. Adam's second decoding task. He hoped that the meaning would emerge from the context, because his Latin skills had already been bad in school, and the probability that they had gotten better since then without practice tended toward zero. He had picked out a few letters from the conversation. One had been written by Immanuel's father shortly after the events in the forest.

Another was the son's last letter to his father, which he had not yet sent.

Adam hoped to find clues in the letters to what exactly had happened to Anna. Because so far, he only knew that Immanuel had killed her, even if the young man denied it. But Adam didn't yet know why. To make matters worse, he had no idea where Immanuel was right now. He only knew that the man with the boyish eyes had a few hours' head start. Anna had apparently felt safe and secure with him, recognized mildness and tenderness in his gaze. But he had seen the other side of the boy. A fearsome side. One that was capable of hammering a person out of consciousness with the pommel of a gun. But perhaps that was not a particular trait of the boy. In his experience, the ability to transform into testosterone-fueled violence machines from one moment to the next was inscribed in all men.

Adam and Evelyn had suspected many men of having killed, tortured, raped, or kidnapped Anna. In the end, it was none of their suspects, although Evelyn had been rock-solidly convinced of it until the end. Not Andreas Preiss, who had taken himself out of the game by suicide. Not Sebastian Koslowski, who already had a new girlfriend. Not Manfred Lopp, who had a family of his own. Nor Uncle Alfred, whom Evelyn herself had cleared of any suspicion. It wasn't Lothar Kletzsch, who had a crush on the girl but wasn't driven enough for murder. It wasn't Sandro, who was no longer punk, but neither was he a murderer of women. Nor Henrik Vahr, who lived with his girlfriend in Schwedt. Nor was it Andrei Gabulov, who was honestly astonished that the girl had disappeared. In the end, it was a person he had come across only by chance. A young soldier in a foreign country. It was ironic that Adam knew the boy because he had been shot by him. However, this shooting had been a hunting accident, not an intentional act.

Adam suddenly realized that there was a possibility that Immanuel had shot him out of sheer bloodlust. Simply because he had seen him in the forest. Adam could have told Evelyn about the boy. But what was there to tell? There had been no circumstantial evidence then except that he was male. And if he thought about Evelyn's finding the culprit, that was reason enough to slide onto the list of suspects. Because any man who had looked at Anna in a certain way once in his life could be the killer in Evelyn's eyes. Adam's head ached. He stood up and got himself a cup of tea. When he had the hot drink in his hand, he took out one of the letters and stood in the aisle. It was Friedrich Stahl's letter to his son Immanuel, written shortly after the latter had left for the military academy.

Angermünde, November 17, 1987

My dear son!

My heart hurts not to know you at home by my side. Indeed you will say that it was my decision to send you on the great journey. But that, like everything in life, is only the head of the coin. You see the shadow side, the side turned away from the sun, the cold side, I see the light that falls on this decision. For don't we only see what fate intends for us in the light, in the brightest of daylight? I am deeply convinced that you will have integrated quite excellently after the first few days in such a new, almost foreign, environment. You see, now it serves you well, the hours of practice, your old man's insistence on memorizing Russian vocabulary. I think we are of the same opinion about education, my dear son. Haven't I always said that education is never free? I think it often, and it will always pay off in the end. Please see yourself as living proof of this so that learning will be much easier for you. And with learning comes this moment by itself, where you will suddenly understand everything. *Eureka* should be the exclamation of this fulfillment for you.

How are you doing with your teachers? I am sure that you will learn from the best and most experienced military experts produced by the USSR. How I would love to go back to school with these inquisitive boys. Indeed, they are the most capable and brightest in all of socialism. I still remember my own youth in the boarding school, and looking back, it is the most beautiful time of my life. At that time, I was not yet driven by the clouds of adult life. I was able to devote myself completely to my studies and turn the crooked boy I was then into the upright man I am today. That is why it fills me with pride that my son is now following in his father's footsteps. You can be sure of an excellent career, my big boy.

I do not think it impossible that you perceive it as a punishment that I am giving you because of the events in the days before your departure. I can only advise you to put these thoughts out of your mind and banish them to where they belong, namely to the *Orkus*. I have only your best interests at heart, and distractions of the young girl kind are just as much a part of that as the resentment that I have noticed in you time and again and that you have not been able to get a handle on. It is in the nature of things that I have the utmost understanding for your amorous feelings towards this girl, if not acceptance of them. But it is not only the purity of form and appearance that counts but also the purity of heart. And thus, this person was entirely eliminated as a suitable match for my eldest offspring. In this family of hers runs a bloodline of psychological disorder and rebellion. As much as it may fascinate a young person, it is poison for a healthy man, among whom you can and will count yourself. It just goes so far that I had to protect you from yourself.

The *Sturm und Drang* of youth flows out of every Stahl, but this all too often succumbs to the daydreams of a romanticized man, who does not yet know, and after all cannot yet know, what it means to love as a father loves his son. Even if the *filius* may be such a tender plant, with a tendency to immediately confuse any sexual approach with real love. It is a downright foolish attempt to find this love in the opposite sex, as my own experience has taught me most bitterly. We did not always agree about the passing away of your mother. However, it was not and is not your place to judge. The gears of marriage are too opaque, and your own offspring are too biased in their assessment of events. This is just the case with a boy who has always been more devoted to his mother and her caring and warmth of heart than to the reasoning, the pure *ratio* of the father.

The thought of knowing you are in good—no, the best hands fills me with joy. Soon every feeling of rancor will belong to the past, and you will recognize how short-sighted your thoughts and actions have been. Therefore, I am sure to receive a letter from you soon. Your brother sends you his warmest regards and is already looking forward to embracing you as a young officer. I conclude with a quotation from Ovid, whom we hold in such high esteem,

video meliora proboque deteriora sequor
Your father

The Latin verse gave Adam a headache. He translated it and didn't quite know what it meant.

I see the better and I approve of it, but I follow the worse.

Perhaps this meant Immanuel, whom the father apparently believed knew what was best for him but who nevertheless followed the worst. In Friedrich Stahl's eyes, according to everything Adam had read and knew about him, the best thing was to complete military training, and the worst thing was to give in to his own instincts.

Adam had finished his tea and was reading the next letter from the father to his son.

Angermünde, November 28, 1987

My precious son!

I sincerely hope that these lines reach you safely. Your brother and I were very saddened when we realized that you would not be able to join us at Christmas this year. I know that you are well from the director of the Sovorov Military Academy, but I would like to read it from your own pen.

Otherwise, of course, I would like to hear from you by phone. I will keep your Christmas present for you until you have rejoined the family. And do not forget what Vergil said,

fata viam invenient.

Your father

He translated the verse.

Fate always finds a way.

Immanuel had apparently ceased contact with his father. Adam read the undated letter to the father, which the son had not yet sent.

Oh, you fathers!

You think you have the privilege of life. Like kings, you command armies of sons. Our lives, hardly begun and already determined by your hand. You believe in watering the best knowledge with the best conscience, so the sprout will become a strong and vigorous plant that will withstand any storm. But it is not always the most vigorous plant that will withstand the rigors of the weather. Look at the moss that has yet conquered every nook and cranny of the world, how it clings to what is given and yet takes possession of it, making it its subject, so to speak. We want to be the moss that overgrows the dreary concrete worlds with its delicate down fluff.

Oh, you fathers!

You pretend to be concerned about your children. But in reality you only care about what is closest to you, the continuation of your own history with a different but similar face. We are involuntarily thrown into this world and cannot decide how it is, but we can and we must decide how it should be.

Oh, you fathers!

What your fathers and fathers' fathers started with the building of such a proud collective was over the years worn away by envy, jealousy, arrogance, and perversion and ended in the mockery of the masses, the workers and peasants, the simple people.

Oh, you fathers!

I tell you, there is so much more out there for us than the field you have tilled for us. A true revolution of hearts, an upheaval of characters, a society where the fear of the stinking mouths of informants and the defamation of one's neighbor does not reign, but the warm fidelity to its own humanity.

Oh, you fathers!

You do not believe it yet. You are still convinced that you can determine our weal and woe. The thought inspires you that your sons, who are not cut from the same cloth as you are, will get to know the seriousness of life when they are sent to a boarding school, to a military academy. But I throw my resistance, my *no* to all the fathers of this world. This world will not be yours.

Oh, you fathers!

You think we will forget everything. You think we will let you do as you have done until now. You still believe that what you have done could not become a danger to you. You have been able to take refuge in your armchairs and fall asleep peacefully every evening. But do not feel too secure. We will come to you to tear you out of your dreams.

Oh, you fathers!

Did you think you would get away with these crimes until the end of your days? No, we will flay you alive so that you remain only as rotting meat, which hangs sadly on rotten bones. You think you can forge reality to suit you. You think you can blame the years of suffering of your wives on their tender minds. But suppose you listen to yourselves, to the depths of your holey memories. In that case, you know that all the torments will be atoned for and that they have always been atoned for by the generations that have come after you and will come after you like floods that wash away the old and sweep everything away into a deep blue ocean.

Oh, you fathers!

How maladjusted must your minds be that you forget what a child cannot forget when its mother is held captive by its own father like cattle when she is gunned down like a rabid beast? Are you then *in veritas* of the opinion that what you once made into an animal becomes ever again a human creature? How can you stoop to the infantile belief that an animal judges itself? And there now the spawn of your folly lies before us.

Oh, you fathers!

You have not even noticed in your blind self-assumption that that which has been dehumanized, which has been denied all decision-making and consciousness, can no longer decide for itself about its own life and death. You have fallen for your own game and will be judged for it.

And not only in the afterlife, which you have denied the right to exist just like your own wife, but in the here and now.

Oh, you fathers!

We will come for you, and we will take revenge.

Nam impune quae libet facere id est regem esse

We will push you off your shaky thrones. For to us, you are not kings. To us, you are beggars. We will be like moss. We will be the kings of our own world.

Oh, you fathers!

After Adam read the lines, his headache throbbed all the more. This was not a letter. It was a reckoning, a manifesto against all the fathers of this world. And what nonsense it was. He folded up the letter again. He did not understand everything, to say the least. But Adam was struck by the two Stahls' proclivity for vegetable metaphors. With Immanuel, it was the moss, with Friedrich the birch pollen. They probably both believed in a primordial growth that was inherent in things. Adam thought about the Latin verse.

He who does what he pleases with impunity is king.

Immanuel, however, turned the motto upside down, gave it his own sinister logic. The son did not want to let his father get away with it. But what it was exactly that Friedrich Stahl liked and had made himself punishable with, Adam did not know. The hatred of all the sons of this world for their fathers oozed from every line of the letter. He could not explain why Immanuel had chosen this form of address when he wanted to write about his father's transgressions. Immanuel obviously had more in mind than just calling his own father to account, he wanted to change the whole world. It was not a reflection on himself but on the general condition. Immanuel hid behind big words because he himself did not appear in the lines. The questions piled up in Adam's brain. Did Immanuel hate his father because he was a killer just like himself? Could he only get closer to his dead mother by killing? Did he want to avenge his mother so that he could forget his own transgressions? If Adam tried to answer even one of these questions, he had to track down Immanuel. And there was only one place where he could find him. The villa on the lake.

Chapter 4: HARD SLEEPER

December 6, 1987
Moscow
Capital of the Soviet Union
Union of Soviet Socialist Republics

Adam packed up his things. The passengers were already standing all the way down the aisle, waiting for the train to enter Kazansky station. So he sat back down in his seat and looked out the window.

They drove past a bare birch forest and passed Ramenskoye. Then the suburbs of Moscow began. They left behind ducking buildings, factory halls, and high-rise silos. For a long stretch of time, they passed miles of rows of freight trains flanked by sprawling prefabricated housing complexes until the train arrived at the station. People were pushing out of the car. There was cursing and shoving. Militiamen had posted themselves in front of each carriage and were checking the passengers' documents. Were they looking for a man named Aleksey Ilyich Kokorin? Were they looking for him? Adam preferred not to find out and opened the door on the side of the carriage facing away from the platform. He jumped onto the tracks, climbed onto the next platform, and ran to the station's subway stop.

At the Belorussky long-distance train station, he bought a second-class sleeper ticket for the overnight train to Paris via Berlin and strolled through the reception hall. An olive-green sea of soldiers opened up in front of him. Adam squeezed through the uniformed men to the departure platform of the train to Berlin, which had not yet arrived at the station. A diesel locomotive with endless rows of sleeping cars was pulling in and came to a screeching halt on the adjacent track. It was the train destined for the soldiers. A short time later, he was standing in the midst of shoving and smirking Red Army soldiers who had just outgrown school age. It happened what always happened to him when he was among soldiers. He felt carefree and safe. He didn't know exactly what it was that calmed him down and made others afraid. Maybe it was because he knew their unpredictable demeanor was just a facade. After all, they were drilled to be predictable on command. When he was among soldiers, he felt how things fell into place when people were given an education. In that respect, he was no different than Friedrich Stahl. It was just a minor detail for Adam that day in Moscow that this education made them killing machines. A mistake of content, not of form.

Red Army women in long skirts blew their whistles to order the chaos. Clusters of soldiers formed around the entrances. The men crowded into the sleeping cars to secure the best bunks. Soon the stream of soldiers broke off, and emptiness reigned around him again. Adam let his gaze glide along the rows of sleeping cars. Everywhere the same picture. Soldiers pushed their way into the carriages. Three entrances away from him, he saw a soldier who stood a little apart, who did not throw himself into the crowd. He took a step, unconcerned, whenever a few more soldiers were pushed in, making a few more inches of space on the platform for those waiting. Could it be that this was Immanuel? Adam was almost half a day behind him, and yet it was possible that he arrived at the station in Moscow at the same time as him. If it was young Stahl, Adam would have to throw his return plans out the window. Adam took a few steps closer. The suspicion became a certainty. It was unmistakably Immanuel. Adam had to find a way to take that train as well. Time was running against him. He looked around. So far, he had seen only Russian soldiers. Not a single Pole, Czech or Bulgarian. With so little time, his only chance was to reactivate *Leytenant* Popov.

Adam ran to the restrooms and put on his uniform. Only one detail was wrong. The Tokarev was not in the pistol holster. So he took the holster off his belt. No holster was less suspicious than an empty one. Back at the track, the last soldiers boarded the westbound train. Adam pulled the peak of his cap low on his face and stepped into the first car. He did not see Immanuel. The young man must have already boarded. The uniformed women on the platform blew their whistles and the doors closed. On the adjacent track, he saw the night train to Paris arriving via Berlin.

Adam found a free bed in the second compartment. The soldiers greeted him sullenly and paid him no further attention. Immanuel had to be two or three cars further back on the train. Adam asked the soldiers what the final destination of their journey was. They looked at each other, but no one answered. Finally, one responded. But he just said that they were going to hell and everyone laughed. They didn't feel like talking to a Bulgarian officer about their stationing. So Adam stretched out on the hard mattress. The train crept through the Moscow suburbs. A conductor from the state railroad came into their compartment. With a frown, he leafed through the passport, service card, passport, and blank ticket of the soldier of the Bulgarian People's Army and, after an awkward amount of time, gave him back all the documents.

After the check, Adam left the compartment and went down the corridor. As on the outward journey, almost all the beds were occupied by Red Army soldiers. It smelled of sweat and damp army coats. He slowly crept past the compartments, stopping now and then to look out the window. With a bit of luck, he could make out in the reflection who was in the cabin. By the time Adam had roamed the following two cars and still had not spotted Immanuel, his attention waned. He walked past the compartments, already not believing it, but then he finally saw him. Just before his cabin, he stopped and turned to the window side of the car. The German military student was as odd in that compartment as the Bulgarian officer was in his.

The other five soldiers were singing. Adam could also see a vodka bottle that the men were sharing. Immanuel lay unconcerned on his folding bed, reading a book and not noticing him. He also had no reason to be overly vigilant. Immanuel was safe from him in the company of the soldiers. But Immanuel was like chocolate on a platter.

Adam decided to come back later when the singing and drinking had tired the men out. He passed the time playing cards with his compartment mates. The landscape rushed past them incessantly. Then came Minsk, and then again, nothing but flat land for hours. The day went, darkness set in. He had lost most of the games and thus gained no respect but a little of the men's pitying sympathy. Nor had the situation changed when he made his second inspection of Immanuel's compartment. The men were singing and drinking, the boy was reading. He had to exercise patience. Immanuel was trapped.

Late in the evening, they reached Brest. The same procedure as on the outward journey. Getting off the Russian-gauge train, walking across the platform, boarding the already waiting European-gauge train. Adam was the last to get off the train and could not see Immanuel. In doing so, he hid behind the soldiers, who were already pushing their way back into the carriage. Soon Polish border guards came through the train with their Russian colleagues. Again Adam had to show all his documents. Again it took a while until he got them back. Then he went to look for Immanuel again. Adam found the young cadet three cars back. Again he was lying on the bed. Again he was reading. And again, the remaining beds were occupied by Red Army soldiers.

Adam had plenty of time. The train would not reach the German border for another ten hours or so, and sometime during the night, everyone would be asleep. He retreated to his compartment and lay down. With his arms folded behind his head, he looked at the underside of the top folding bed, which had only thin padding. Hard sleeper, as they called them in China. Adam took it upon himself to doze without falling asleep. In the corner of his eye, he had a partial view of the window. The moon was high in the sky. He fixed on the glowing ball, which did not seem to move. The soldiers slept in their beds while the diesel locomotive tugged at the cars with two thousand horsepower, vibrating with tons of weight over the tracks. Every time the wheels rattled over the weld of the rail joint, the wagon jolted with a metallic clack. Over and over again. Clack-clack, clack-clack. Rail joint after rail joint, minute after minute. Clack-clack, clack-clack. His eyelids grew heavy. Clack-clack, clack-clack. His breathing slowed. Clack-clack, clack-clack. It was getting warm. Clack-clack, clack-clack. The other beds were empty. He was alone in the compartment.

Suddenly, a man's face emerged from the darkness. Adam recoiled. Immanuel bent over him and put his hands around his neck. Adam tried to struggle, but he realized he couldn't move. His arms and legs were strapped to the bed. The boy squeezed tighter. He could no longer breathe. Outside, the sun was rising. Immanuel squeezed harder and harder. Adam tore at his restraints. They cut into his skin. Blood came out from under the straps. Immanuel showed him his teeth and laughed loudly. Before his eyes, it went black.

Chapter 5: POLONAISE

December 7, 1987
Train 432
Brest–Berlin
People's Republic of Poland

Adam opened his eyes and grabbed his neck. The memory of the night's dream was still in his bones. Immanuel had not discovered him. Overcome by sleep Adam was not able to surprise him at night. Adam looked at his watch. He had been asleep for almost eight hours.

"Where are we?" he asked into the compartment.

"Poland," said one of the soldiers.

"Is Warsaw coming soon?"

"Long gone. We'll be in Poznań in a minute, *tovarish*."

He had slept through Warsaw and Łódź. From here, it was not far to the German-Polish border. It was high time for an inspection round. Adam stepped out of the cabin. Not ten yards away from him, Immanuel was standing in the aisle. Any element of surprise was gone. The boy's appearance caught him off guard. Immanuel immediately drew the

Tokarev he had taken from him. With quick steps, Immanuel ran down the corridor, keeping his eyes fixed on him. As he did so, he aimed at Adam with an outstretched arm. All of a sudden, two soldiers came out of a cabin between them and filled the aisle. He could see Immanuel hide the gun from the men. Then Adam could no longer see him. When he had a clear view again, Immanuel was gone.

Adam walked toward the soldiers and pushed them out of the aisle into the compartment from which they had come. Then he saw Immanuel again. He had already run into the next carriage. This was not how he had imagined meeting the boy again. Adam had to adjust a plan again. And that much faster than he would have liked to. At least the boy could not escape him so quickly now. Adam slowed his pace as he watched Immanuel enter his compartment. At the end of the car, his eyes lingered on a fire extinguisher and an ax mounted on the wall. He plucked both from their moorings and walked with them to the cabin. In the reflection of the window, he could see that the boy was packing up his things.

Quick as a flash, Adam stood in the compartment doorway, Immanuel pointing his pistol at him. But Adam was faster and sprayed extinguishing foam into the small room. Immanuel pulled the trigger. He missed. But the glass of the train window in Adam's back shattered. Adam held his hand over his nose and mouth as he stormed the compartment, ax raised. He could no longer see Immanuel through the fog. He heard three shots in quick succession and let the ax fly into the haze. Suddenly he felt a suction—the foggy wall of the extinguishing agent was sucked out of the train. Immanuel had kicked the glass out of the window frame and jumped out.

Adam dropped the ax and the fire extinguisher. Soldiers screamed wildly. He stepped to the new opening in the train wall and leaned out. The train was moving slowly. He saw Immanuel getting to his feet at the level of the last car. Then he ran across a snow-covered field. Adam wondered what he should do. Without being fully convinced of the action, he also jumped out into the cold. Even as he jumped, he realized that he had made the wrong decision. Below him was an embankment. Adam landed feet first, fell forward, and slid down the slope. At the bottom of the slope, he stopped. He moved his joints. Nothing seemed to be broken, so he straightened up and looked in the direction from which the train had come. Immanuel just leaped lightly across the tracks to the other side of the rails.

Adam struggled up the embankment. He just saw the end of the train disappear in the distance when he reached the tracks again. Immanuel was already running through the deep snow. The boy must have been half a mile ahead of him. Adam focused on his target. He looked straight ahead and ran as fast as he could across the open field. He felt that he was getting closer. Gradually, but inevitably. In the process, he was jumping through the deep snow rather than running. Immanuel looked more in flow. He virtually glided over the snow cover. But points for style were not awarded.

Adam had closed the distance between himself and the boy by about a quarter of a mile when a cluster of houses came into view. Immanuel had disappeared behind one of the humble houses with a pointed gable roof. Adam passed the town sign of Zbąszynek. Not a person for miles. He stopped and tried to listen to Immanuel's movements, but the only thing he heard was the roar of an engine at his back. It had to be Immanuel. Adam turned and ran toward the car that was pulling out. When he reached it, it had just left the parking space. Immanuel was behind the wheel and stepping on the gas. Adam ran alongside the car. Immanuel looked intently at the road. Adam pounded the glass with his fist. One, two, three times. Then he pushed the shattered laminated glass into the cab and grabbed Immanuel by the collar. Adam pulled at him with all his power, but he couldn't yank him out of his seat. The car was speeding up. Adam could no longer keep up and had to let go of him.

Adam looked around and found a bottle-green Polski Fiat on the side of the road. Easy to borrow without the consent of the owner. The 125p had a smaller engine than the pale orange FSO Polonez Immanuel was steering. But Adam didn't have time to pick the best car. So he smashed the passenger-door window and hot-wired the ignition. The car took ages to get up to speed. He floored the gas pedal. In the distance, he could see the Polonez. Adam was getting closer. But then Immanuel spotted him. As expected, the car was faster than Adam's. Soon, he could no longer see the taillights. Adam was outdistanced. So Adam slowed down again and drove down the ramshackle country road at the speed officially required. The cold was sucked into the interior, causing him to shiver. But unlike Immanuel, he at least enjoyed an intact windshield on the driver's side.

Then Adam got lucky. A few hundred yards ahead of him, he could again see the car, which had been held up by a cattle truck. First, Immanuel overtook the farmer, then Adam did. They sped through Smardzewo, Jeziory, Lubinicko, Świebodzin without him getting even a little closer. They continued through the villages of Wilkowo, Mostki, Gronów, Poźrzadło, Koryta and Torzym. The two cars pushed along the flat fields and sparse woods along the Polish country roads, always at the same distance from each other. The Polonez and the Polski Fiat danced through the space without getting closer to each other, like in a polonaise. In Torzym, the picture changed when a police Lada with blue lights came up behind Immanuel. Adam was able to catch up with the police car. There were only a few inches of space between the three vehicles. Adam stepped on the gas and touched the police car. It was knocked forward. Immanuel slammed on the brakes, Adam kept his foot on the gas. The blue-and-white police car was wedged between them. Then Adam stepped on the gas pedal all the way, and the police Lada shifted to the side. The policeman still tried to steer against the movement. But the Lada became transverse and briefly clawed its wheels into the roadway. Then the car overturned. Adam immediately hit the brakes, Immanuel accelerated. The Lada came to rest on its roof.

Adam pulled into the oncoming lane. He was now close behind Immanuel. They drove bumper to bumper through Pniów, Boczów, and Rzepin. Neither of them could afford to make a driving mistake. A sign announced the Polish-German border three miles away. In Nowe Biskupice, the road went through a sharp bend that pushed the cars to the very edge of the road. Immanuel almost shot into an oncoming car behind the curve, just barely swerving out of the way. Adam also jerked the steering wheel around. The oncoming vehicle touched his mirror and scraped past his flank. Immanuel's Polonez went off the road and crashed into a tree. The engine's coolant hissed steamily from its collapsed hood. Adam stopped and jumped out of the Polski Fiat. He expected to see a bloodied, unconscious traffic victim pressed into the steering wheel by the force of the impact, if not a dead man. Instead, the car was empty, and the passenger door was pushed open. He hadn't seen Immanuel leave the vehicle. But he saw the tracks in the snow. Again, he took up the pursuit.

Behind the houses of the village, the view opened onto fields. He saw Immanuel running in front of him. Seemingly unharmed, he sprinted across the icy furrows. The boy did not give up. What was driving Immanuel Stahl? Was it the knowledge of having a pursuer at his back, or did he still have an assignment that had to be completed as quickly as possible at home?

The young Stahl was running cross-country toward a locality. It was the border town of Słubice. Adam could see a bridge where cars were jammed westward at the border with the GDR. Beneath it, the Oder River had rigidified into a mass of ice. When he spotted the first uniformed men, he walked more slowly. Immanuel was walking toward the border controls, not fifty yards ahead of him. The young man was almost within reach but unassailable under the watchful eyes of the border guards.

Adam looked down at himself. His pants were ripped open. His uniform jacket was wet and soiled. His officer's cap was riding alone on the train to Berlin. He was in a disastrous condition, but at least he had his forged papers with him. He had to make it across this last border. If the KGB was too close on his heels and they caught him here, he would be back in the Soviet Union faster than he could say *do svidaniya*. Border guards monitored the clearance process with Kalashnikovs at the ready.

Adam asked the woman in front of him if she wanted to let him go ahead. She didn't. The process was extremely slow. Exactly six people waited between him and Immanuel to enter the GDR. Immanuel's uniform still looked immaculate, unlike his. The boy greeted the border guards with one hand on his cap and passed effortlessly. The minutes stretched into eternity. Finally, it was Adam's turn, and he spread out his documents in front of the border guard. He spoke Russian to the man, who asked him where he came from and who he was, what he was doing in the GDR, and why his uniform was in such a pitiful state. He answered the questions patiently. After that, the border guard had a lengthy discussion by telephone with his superior. It dragged on and on. Then he was allowed to pass. So, a Bulgarian officer could cross the border into the GDR without a permit to enter. At least on that day. Or it was pure luck. Adam would never find out.

Immanuel had been gone for a long time. Adam had chased him for miles, he had almost had him in his hands, and then he had escaped him after all.

Chapter 6: FAMILY TIES

Adam had less than one hundred miles to cover from the Polish border to the Schorfheide. As he drove through the familiar area, he had the feeling of having been away for years. He pushed through Angermünde. It had snowed here, too. On the side of the road, he saw a bicycle that had apparently been carelessly parked by its owner. Adam recognized the white paint splotch on the front wheel as he passed. It was unmistakably his bike leaning against the stone wall not far from the factory. Had he left it there on November 6 and then not found it when he had needed it so badly? Things would have taken a different course if he had tracked down and killed the man that night Anna had disappeared. He would not have run into Evelyn the following day and would not have learned of her sister's disappearance until much later. Moreover, he would not have run through the woods, been shot, or made the acquaintance of the Stahls. Instead, he would have sat in his cold apartment, drinking hot water and letting the rest of his life come to him. Eternal bliss.

When Adam turned onto the forest road to the Stahl estate, it was already getting dark again. The detour he took to the secret pit had been essential but also time-consuming. Adam felt the reassuring weight of the pistol in his jacket pocket and reached the gate. This was as far as he could go by car. There was no point in trying to break through the iron fence with the low-powered Trabant he had stolen in Frankfurt/Oder. So he got out of the car and took a look inside the guardhouse. Since it was deserted, he put the gun in his waistband, climbed over the hood onto the car's roof and from there swung himself over the fence. In this way, the tiny vehicle performed one last service for him.

Adam ran along the asphalt access road until a fork led to a narrower unpaved path through the woods. By following it he hoped to reach the house undetected. The wind caught the tall fir trees and made them sway with a creaking sound. After a long walk, the forest cleared, and he reached a gravel parking lot. By now, it was pitch dark. Adam made out the outline of a building. He walked closer. It was a wooden hut, at least two stories high. Possibly a carriage house that belonged to the main building. He walked around the house to the back. Under a protective canopy was a car with only the wheels peeking out from under a tarp. He pulled the weather protection up a little. It was a Horch from the thirties. Next to it was a hay wagon with wooden wagon wheels that was certainly even older. On the outside wall, hunting trophies were lined up from the height of his hip to below the roof's ridge. Hundreds of deer had given their lives for this collection.

Adam found the front door and pushed down the handle. It was unlocked. It smelled burnt as he took a step into the dark cabin. Next to the door, he found a switch made of Bakelite. As he turned it, a lightbulb hanging from the ceiling on a long cord began to buzz dutifully. In the sparse light, Adam could make out antique tools on a wooden counter that had acquired a thick layer of patina over the years. In front of them stood large wooden troughs and metal canisters with yellowed paper labels. In this room, unmistakably, the hunted animals were deboned and skinned. Adam went further into the hut. Behind another door was a small room. Here he could barely stand upright. And from here came the burning smell. For here, fish from the lake were smoked. On the wooden floor, he discovered a trapdoor. The hatch was secured with a lock. It was made of iron, was set accurately into the floor, and stood out from the rest of the furnishings in the wooden hut. The metal was spick and span and could not be more than a few weeks or months old. If there was any place he could find Anna, it was under this hatch.

So, Adam lay down on the hatch and listened into the silence. Nothing. He knocked. Again, nothing. Then he drummed on it with his fist. He held his breath. A barely perceptible sound drifted up to him. Or was it just the rush of blood through his head he heard? Adam jumped up and searched for a tool with which he could get the lock open. He found an iron bar in the skinning room, which he used to pry open the hatch. He pulled hard at it and it swung open. Only a little light made it to him. Adam peered into a chamber no larger than a few square meters. He climbed down. There was no one here. Adam found a mattress, canned food, candles, and books. So, he climbed back up. What was it he had discovered there—a secret hiding place or a treacherous dungeon?

He left the hut behind and walked the path that had to take him to the villa. Adam had not found Anna, but he was sure that she had been held there by Immanuel. Perhaps for weeks, until he had finally killed and buried her. Could it be that Friedrich Stahl had already imprisoned his wife in such a dungeon and then killed her? Had he provided the blueprint for his son's deeds? Was Immanuel carrying on the terrible family tradition?

Something off the path caught his eye, where the forest floor was covered with inches of snow. Just a stone's throw away from him, a rectangular black area was amidst the white. It gave the impression that the snow had melted in that spot to reveal the dark earthen ground. Adam left the path and walked toward the site. A mound of sand piled up next to the black area. He walked closer to it. It was a pit. Freshly dug.

Adam stood at the edge and looked in. The hole must have been as deep as he was tall. Beside his feet, he saw a shovel and a pickax. Digging the hole in the ground must have taken great strength and plenty of time.

He jumped in. The pit was even deeper than he had guessed. Sounds came closer from the forest. If it was Immanuel, he was trapped. One shot, and he would be dead.

Already lying in his own grave—one that, to make matters worse, he had also jumped into himself. Hastily, he climbed up and propped his legs against the pit wall. Then he reached the edge of the pit and pulled himself up. Adam saw nothing. Then he heard sounds again. It was a pack of wild boars searching for chestnuts, roots, and beechnuts with their snouts under the snow cover. Relieved, he stood up and returned to the path. Was this pit meant for Anna? And if it was, where was she?

A few hundred yards away, he saw a bright glow of light behind the trees. He felt for the pistol at his back. Everything was in place. Nothing stood in the way of his confronting young Stahl any longer. He walked faster. Now he could see the villa, brightly lit in the forest. At the last tree, he stopped and watched the house. Lights were burning on the ground level, and on the second floor, it was black behind all the windows. Adam drew his pistol, ran across the yard to the house, pressed himself along the wall, and ducked under the windows. The front door was ajar. Carefully, he pushed it open. Music drifted from inside. Cautiously, he pulled the door closed behind him. He recognized the piece of music. It was the first act of *Götterdämmerung* by Richard Wagner. The brass resounded eerily through the spacious rooms. The music had its source in the salon, behind the hall. The strings kicked in. He walked past the hunting trophies. The deer, boars, and bucks hung from their wooden panels with expressionless glass eyes. On a sideboard, he saw the photos of the family again. One showed them all in front of the house. Friedrich Stahl next to his wife, who held an infant in her hands, between them a little boy. Immanuel as a child and

Ephraim in the arms of his mother, later killed by Friedrich Stahl. A fearsome clan.

Adam entered the salon. In the middle of the room, Friedrich Stahl sat bound and gagged on a chair. He was stripped to his underpants, and his head hung down lifelessly. His son Immanuel sat at the table with his head resting in his hands and the Tokarev beside him. The boy took no notice of him. Adam went to the record player and took the needle off the vinyl record. Absolute silence. Adam cocked the hammer of the pistol and pointed it at the boy. Immanuel looked up and reached for the gun. His face was puffy, his eyes red.

Immanuel wiped the tears from his eyes and pointed the muzzle at him. "Oh, it's you again. Hard to get rid of you."

"I read the letters," Adam said.

"Which ones?"

"The ones between you and your father."

"So?"

"I know what you did."

"You have no idea," he said tearfully.

The pistol trembled in his hand. He could barely hold it purposefully. Immanuel stood up and held the gun directly to his father's drooping skull. "If you've read the letters, then you know what my father did."

So Friedrich Stahl was only unconscious after all and not dead yet.

"Here and now, it will stop. My father must face his fate."

Adam continued to keep the pistol pointed at the boy.

"He took her from me. Because he couldn't stand that I was happy with her. Because he thought she was making me soft. He couldn't stand that I didn't want to have a career in the Army."

So Immanuel had been serious when he had said that he had not killed Anna. His father had done it. That was why he had gone back to the GDR as fast as he could. Adam was only the bearer of the sad message.

"Immanuel, he's going to jail for this."

Adam had no idea why he wanted to protect Friedrich Stahl from his son. He should have shot him on the spot. But the pitiful creature on the chair looked as if every bullet was wasted on him.

"No, he has to answer to me for that. Do you really think someone like my father will go to jail? And even if he did, it will not be a just punishment. He killed my mother. He locked her up like an animal. Whenever she didn't do what he wanted, he locked her up in the forest hut. For the smallest things, he punished her. When she wanted to meet with friends in Berlin, he yelled at her. Then, when she laughed, he hit her. First with the flat of his hand, then with his fist. I saw it all when I was three or four years old. That was his idea of humanistic education. Whoever didn't toe the line had to be punished. At some point, he didn't let her out of the house at all. He didn't let anyone in either. He sent the household help away. We were alone in the house. Most of the time, my mother and I were alone. In good times we were allowed to go out, walk by the lake, play hide-and-seek in the woods. In bad times we were locked up in the house. For days when he was working in Berlin and didn't come home until the weekend. Back then, I had to go to my room and was not allowed to come out. And once I did, I saw how he tied her to the bed and had his way with her. This went on for hours. When he was gone again, I had to take care of her. She smiled less and less. At some point, she didn't even want to leave the house anymore. Her nerves were at the end. She cried. She was always crying. Can you imagine what it's like for a little boy to have to comfort his mother every day? When she tried to drown herself in the lake, he locked her away. He didn't even let her decide about her death."

He sobbed and then collected himself again.

"Then one day, she did it. She escaped. That's when he hounded her to death and then gave her the coup de grâce."

He remained silent. Adam didn't know what to say.

Immanuel took a deep breath. "After that, we moved here. A fresh start without our mother. But it didn't stop. Then he also killed the only thing I held dear. It will never stop. The love of my life he took from me. But this time, he won't get away with it. Someone like that must not stay alive."

"Immanuel, if you do that, there will also be blood on your hands. Are you sure you can live with that?"

"Fuck that."

"But you're not alone. Your brother is still little. He'll need you when your father is in jail."

"Man, don't you get it? He's not going to jail. He's a big shot in the Stasi."

Friedrich Stahl slowly regained consciousness. Immanuel stepped up to him. Then he cocked the hammer of the Tokarev and pressed the muzzle against his father's forehead. Friedrich opened his eyes wide, snorted wildly through his gag, and tore at his bonds.

Immanuel yanked the gag down with his free hand. "Why don't you tell him what you did to her?"

"Boy, you've lost your mind. I had nothing to do with Kathrin's death."

The boy hit his forehead with the pistol's pommel with full force. The skin burst open. Blood ran darkly down his face.

"Who is Kathrin?" asked Adam.

But the two paid no attention to him.

Friedrich Stahl looked contemptuously at his eldest son. "That won't do you any good. You are like your mother. You won't dare. Come on, untie me, and we'll settle this like real men. Or do you want me to put you over my knee and make you cry again, the way you've always cried?"

Immanuel lashed out and hit him in the jaw. Friedrich spat blood. It spluttered from his mouth and ran from there down his naked chest.

The man laughed through bloodstained teeth. "What's the worker doing here, anyway?" He gave Adam a quick glance and then looked at Immanuel again.

"He is of the opinion that he has to hold me accountable," Immanuel said.

Friedrich Stahl looked at Adam. "What do you say, worker Hedman? I felt it in my gut that you couldn't help but make trouble. Well, let's get on with it. The best thing to do is to pull the trigger and put an end to the fuss. That's not my son anyway. Wouldn't have been the first time that his bitch of a mother whored around somewhere. He got nothing from me, and you can't teach him anything either. The ingratitude he got from his mother. It doesn't exist in our family. You send the boy to the military academy so that he becomes an upright officer, and this is the thanks you get. Tying his old man to a chair like a thief. Shoot him. Do it before my eyes. I have no feeling for him. My compassion is forfeit. Just as my pity for his mother was eventually exhausted."

Immanuel struck again. There was a cracking sound. The jaw fractured. The man snorted in pain. His eyes darkened.

"Pop him already." He only brought the words over his tongue with great effort.

"Tell him what you did to Mother."

"I set her free. Freed her from herself. And you can be glad that your girlfriend drowned in the lake. You would have made the same mistake I did. Far too soon, you would have gotten involved with a woman—oh, what am I talking about, with a child—whom you would have grown tired of. Who had no decency and no intellect. She was beautiful, but so was your mother. That was all. At some point, the nagging starts, and then it's all over. And the same thing would have happened to you. But I had nothing to do with her death."

Adam put the gun down. He tried to make sense of the story. Kathrin was apparently Immanuel's girlfriend, and she was the girl who had been found dead at the Mündesee. But how did Anna fit into the account? And why his father denied being responsible for the death of his son's girlfriend, when he usually admitted to every outrage, was not clear to Adam.

Friedrich Stahl looked at his son penetratingly. "Send him away. We'll settle this between us. Just the two of us, Immanuel. Send the worker away."

"What have you done to her?" cried Immanuel.

The man did not dignify him with a glance. "Send him away, Immanuel."

The boy pressed the muzzle harder against his father's head. "I should have shot you in the woods the day you shot Mother."

"You'd have to learn to shoot first, though, little boy."

Immanuel punched his father in the face again, who looked at him with bloodshot eyes. "Why don't you strike me dead? Just strike me dead. This will haunt you until the end of your days. You won't sleep through another night in your life. A father killer won't sleep a wink."

"I'm not your son anymore."

"You have always been just your mother's son. I raised a fucking bastard. But I failed. I failed to make a decent human being out of you."

Adam looked at Friedrich Stahl. "What did Immanuel do to Anna?"

"That's beyond your horizon."

Immanuel raised his head. "Answer him!"

"Well, then, my wife's son gets to choose something for a change."

He looked at Adam. "Herr Hedman, dear Frau Sievers was guilty of wanting to leave the Republic. She no longer wanted to be part of our beautiful collective. Can you imagine that?"

Adam grinned. "Not by any stretch of the imagination."

"Did you know about her *Ausreiseantrag*?" he asked referring to the request to leave the country.

Adam remained silent.

"The application was going to be approved. Imagine that. Then she would have been gone real quick. But I made sure that didn't happen."

Adam still couldn't make sense of the sequence of events. "And then you killed Anna because otherwise, she would have been dangerous to you?"

They both looked at him, puzzled. Adam could not explain this reaction.

"Anna is not dead," Immanuel said.

Adam could not process the information. "So not only was the photo of the dead Anna a fake—" he said quietly to himself.

Friedrich Stahl pulled up one corner of his mouth, faking a slight smile on his face. "Oh, the fine gentleman worker figured that out? It should have been convincing enough for a real proletarian."

"I guess I'll have to disappoint you on that one."

"Believe me, the employee who is responsible for this is now only allowed to open letters under steam in the basement of the MfS. But respectfully, who would have thought that a worker and a mental patient could investigate so tenaciously? We were honestly surprised."

Immanuel's facial expression relaxed. "Anna is in the West," he said casually.

There it was, the truth they had never even considered in their investigation. Because it was simply an absurd idea that Anna could have escaped from the GDR on her own. This was not a border merely sealed off with a barbed-wire fence, but in the truest sense of the word an iron curtain. By 1984 the third-generation border fortifications had been installed, making crossing almost impossible.

Getting to the wall unnoticed would have been hard enough for Anna. Because parallel to the border ran an area three miles wide that she had no authorization to access. The access roads were blocked by checkpoints. In addition, there was a signal fence lined with low-voltage electric barbed wire. A silent alarm would have been triggered if she had touched or cut the wire, alerting nearby sentries. In the unlikely event that she had made it to the actual inner wall, border guards with night vision equipment and German shepherd dogs should not have spotted her climbing over. Behind it, an open area at least nine hundred feet deep with spikes, tank traps, and anti-personnel mines was waiting for her. Plus border guards in watchtowers equipped with rotating thousand-watt searchlights and shooting slits.

And in the almost impossible event that she made it across this death strip, the outer wall followed. It was just as high as the inner one. The only difference was that Anna would then have been in the direct field of vision of the border guards if she wanted to cross it. Even for a poor marksman, shooting Anna off the wall would have been no problem.

Anyone who wanted to cross the wall alive had to have a damn good plan, plus be in top physical and mental shape. And, in addition, they had to have excellent helpers.

"Yes, the fucking cunt went over," Friedrich Stahl roared. "And who made it possible for her? My son. Because I taught him everything he needed to know. But a decent socialist does everything to make sure our people stay here, not that they can escape."

"And that's when you guys pretended that Anna killed herself rather than admit that she had escaped? But you didn't have a body. And that's when the problems started," Adam said.

"You can't take a piece out of the game," said Friedrich Stahl. "Then the whole system doesn't work anymore. And above all, the stone can't take itself out of the game."

"What a perverse view of a society of equals. If people like you wouldn't exist, no one would have to leave here. You have only yourselves to blame," Immanuel said in rapture.

Friedrich Stahl laughed contemptuously. "And that's why you have to help a little mouse like Anna Sievers escape?"

"Yes, that's exactly what I had to do."

Adam remembered that he had seen Immanuel sneaking out of the house that hunting weekend. "I saw you the day I was here, outside by the cabin. Was Anna here, too?"

Immanuel nodded.

"The cabin with the trapdoor ...," Adam said to himself.

"Yes, the smoke shack. I hid her there. In the evening, I brought her bread. We left that very night."

The old Stahl interrupted the conversation. "Enough. I can't listen to any more of this drivel."

He took a breath and looked between his son and Adam. "Everything I have done and will do is in the best interest of my family. No whore of this world will stand between us and our destiny."

His son pointed the pistol at his father's forehead and pulled the trigger. The bullet shot through his skull and exited the back of his head. Parts of his skull bone came loose due to the force of the projectile and splattered brain matter, bone fragments, skin, and hair with it against the wall. Immanuel lowered the pistol. Adam leaned against the wall and took a deep breath. Then Immanuel went to the stereo as if in a trance, turned down the volume, and put the needle back on the record. The wind instruments sounded soft. Then the strings came in again.

Adam took a seat on the sofa. Immanuel sat down opposite him in an armchair. Beside him in the back, his father hung dead on the chair. Adam tried to block out the sight and concentrate on Immanuel. The hatred in the young man's eyes had finally vanished. Immanuel told him the whole story. About his love for Kathrin and meeting Anna, who quickly became a close friend. Of the rejected application to leave the country, which was the incentive for the two of them to make a plan to flee the Republic. Of the benefit of the confusion that reigned around the church fire in Angermünde. Immanuel looked tired but relieved.

"What will you do now?" asked Adam.

Immanuel shrugged.

Adam leaned forward. "What about these murders of women in Russia?"

"You thought I had something to do with that? There's a crazy serial killer on the loose. It's been going on for years. But thank you for giving me credit. Now I understand what possessed you to drop by my place. No, I really had nothing to do with that. Did you go to Anna's apartment? I bet you didn't find anything that pointed to me. That's how it is when you have a father in the Stasi. Then how did you find out about me?"

"You're the man with the boy in his eyes, aren't you?"

Immanuel looked puzzled. "What?"

"Anna called you that. After a song by Kate Bush."

The astonishment disappeared from his face. "Oh, that's what she meant. Yes, maybe." He sat back and smiled. "I'm glad Anna made it. I wanted the best for her, and she couldn't have that here."

"And where is Anna now, exactly?"

Immanuel smiled, barely visible. Suddenly, his eyes widened. A gunshot cracked deafeningly through the parlor. Immanuel looked through him and opened his mouth slightly. But he made no sound. Then he tried to raise a hand but failed. Before Adam could wonder what had happened to him, a bloodstain ate through the fibers of Immanuel's shirt at the level of his chest. The bullet hit him right in the heart. The young man's vision glazed over, and then he stared blankly into nothingness.

Adam heard the discharge of a rifle, jumped up, and turned toward the hall. As he did so, he reached into his waistband. But his gun was next to the record player on the sideboard where he had put it. Adam was unarmed and heard a rifle being loaded.

He looked into the face of a child. "I know you," Adam said.

"Yeah, we know each other. You're the worker my brother almost shot dead."

It was Ephraim, Immanuel's younger brother. He wore camouflage clothing that was filthy with mud. There were blood splatters on his jacket. He held a hunting rifle in his hand. A holster was attached to his thigh with a hunting knife in it. Beside him lay three dead rabbits, tied together in a bundle with rope.

"Why Immanuel?"

Ephraim lost his poise for a moment, slumped a little. "Because he murdered Papa."

The family coalitions were clear. Ephraim stood immovably on his father's side. In life as in death.

"How old are you, anyway?" asked Adam.

"Old enough."

"You are just a boy."

Ephraim shrugged. He obviously wanted to appear as if this didn't bother him. Then he chambered a round. Adam put his hands up.

"And what have you to do with all of this?" asked Adam.

"With the silly fight between Immanuel and my father? Nothing. Never understood what the big deal was."

"Your father killed Immanuel's girlfriend like he killed your mother."

"Kathrin?"

Adam nodded. Ephraim grinned.

"What is it?" Adam asked.

"Nothing. It just shows, once again, that my brother can't even put one and one together. Why would my father kill her?"

Adam did not respond to the question.

But Ephraim asked again. "Tell me, why would my father want to kill her?"

Adam shrugged his shoulders.

"You see, you have no idea. How could you? Think about who would get a kick out of seeing her boyfriend suffer.

Here's a hint: it's the brother of the son who has always been favored by his mother."

Adam looked at the dead rabbits at Ephraim's feet. "As I see, you like to kill animals as well."

"The Lord gave it, and I took it away from him again. Sometimes three rabbits, sometimes a horse, sometimes a cow. Or sometimes a silly cow." He grinned again and seemed visibly pleased with his joke.

Here was the man his colleagues in the VEB had been looking for for months and in whose search he had not participated. But it was not a man but a boy, almost still a child, who had caused fear and terror in their region. Adam considered handing Ephraim over to the foreman to crush him with his paws. There would be no mercy, and it would be a short trial. The *Uckermärkers* would sleep more peacefully again because they would no longer have to fear for their cattle and daughters. But first, he had to disarm the boy.

"Come now, enough of the chatter," Ephraim said.

"Where to?"

"Just a little walk."

"To that pit out there?"

"Almost clever of you to get that right away. So far, you haven't been the smartest kid. Even trusted a dreamer like Immanuel to commit such a vicious murder. If he had ever killed anyone, it would have been by accident. For example, during a hunt," he said, laughing once briefly.

"Do you really think you'll get away with killing me?"

"Think so. Besides, you'll be buried nice and deep. They'll have to find you first. That's where my brother's been digging pretty hard."

He paused for a moment. "No one's going to look for you anyway, are they?" he then said.

Probably not, Adam thought and didn't answer.

Immanuel took a few steps aside and let Adam pass toward the front door. When Adam opened it, he saw the forest bathed in blue light. A pack of Volkspolizei patrol cars came across the driveway toward the house and stopped in the front yard. Policemen got out and drew their weapons. Ephraim dropped his rifle.

"Doesn't look good for you now, boy," Adam said.

Ephraim slumped, tears springing to his eyes. "That's him. He killed my father and brother," he cried in a brittle voice.

Adam admired the boy's acting. However, he had not expected this turn of events. The policemen approached them.

Ephraim straightened up again and stood close to Adam. "The death penalty awaits you, boy. Too bad I can't be your executioner anymore," Ephraim whispered.

The boy had apparently missed the fact that the GDR's State Council had announced the abolition of the death penalty on July 17 of that year. One hundred sixty-six people had been sentenced to death up to that point.

The policemen walked up to Adam and handcuffed him. They paid no attention to Ephraim. Out of one of the police cars got another man in civilian clothes. It was the man who had beaten him up in the holding cell and whom he had run into again and again since then. So he was no illusion, not a trick played on Adam's mind. Again the man grinned at him. His teeth looked even sharper than before. His eyes were dark and dull as pieces of coal.

Adam was led away, blue light flashed again between the trees. Shortly after, black limousines stopped in the forecourt. Men in leather coats got out of the cars. The German policemen pointed their guns at them.

One of the men in a leather coat held up his badge with a grin. "Friends, don't worry. You guys put your guns down now, yes? Everything is under control. Just a little family squabble. A dead father and his son, tragic. But please, let the man go," he said with a thick Russian accent.

Immediately they put down their weapons.

"You better get in the house. Take care of the boy and the dead."

They hesitated for a moment but then all ran into the house together.

Only the man with the black eyes remained motionless by the car. How the men knew there were dead people in the mansion was a mystery to Adam.

Two of the Russians walked up to Adam. "Friends, wait a minute."

The men stopped.

"Keys," one of them said, pointing to Adam's handcuffs.

Quickly, one of the policemen ran up to the man and handed him the key. The Russian grinned and thanked him. However, he did not unlock the handcuffs but led Adam away. He put the key in his coat pocket.

"We weren't here. You didn't see us. Do you understand?"

"But ...," a young German said and was immediately grabbed by the arm by another. So he stopped what he wanted to say.

All the Germans nodded. Adam saw them off with a smile. The Russians went on their way. In the end, the men from the KGB were right. It was all just a family quarrel, and they had been caught between the factions. Evelyn and Anna as well as himself.

Adam had to get into the back seat of the Russian limousine. The car drove off. He turned around and could only just see two men escorting the crying Ephraim into the villa.

Soon they reached the gate where the Trabant was still parked. Shortly thereafter, the lakeside estate was just a memory.

Anna was alive. She had a future. He lived for the past, which was only there to make his present existence bearable. It was the last spark that gave him drive. To track down and finally kill the man who had destroyed his life. Even if it would take another seven years—but first he had to escape the KGB. However, what had always been true was still true. Take one step after the next and see that things work themselves out. Ahead of him was only forest.

PRIOR

They were lying in the dunes. Above them, the wind blew gently and drove gray clouds into the land. In front of them spouted the spray of the cold sea. From the Brandenburg forests to the Mecklenburg beach, the drizzle had laid a wet film on the landscape all along the way. Now fog stood in leaden swaths between sky and earth. Gloomy tension had given way to hopeful anticipation. They gazed into the murky darkness and found that the night was perfect. It was theirs. The overland route was done. Now only came the sea. And then freedom.

They had to have one last talk. Just to go through the plan to completion once more. They knelt in the sand. He looked her right in the face. Just as he had always looked her in the face since they had met, full of openness and affection. She trusted him as she had never trusted anyone in her life before. He was the best friend she would ever have. On this side and the other side of the wall. Not even her sister would she trust with her life without a doubt.

He took her hands in his and told her about the man she was about to meet. The one who had made this crossing dozens of times before. Who knew the shoals and tides in these waters like no other. Who acted out of conviction and had never lost any of his passengers. Not to the sea and certainly not to the border troops on their patrol boats.

He stood up and walked down to the beach. One last time he looked through the binoculars. Then he shuffled back to her in the soft sand. He had good news. Everything was as it should be. She shouldered her backpack. Then they both walked over to the rubber dinghy that lay sheltered in a dune depression a short distance away from them and pulled it down the slope to the beach. After carrying it down to the water, they set it down and hugged. One last look, and she got into the boat. He was already standing with his legs in the water. Then he put his hands on the boat. He pushed it so deep into the water that the crests of the waves beat against his chest, and he could no longer find a ground under his feet. He paused, gave the boat one last push, and looked after her. Saw her red hair blowing in the wind one last time until it disappeared in the mist.

She rowed against the waves of the Baltic Sea. Dipped the oars into the water again and again until finally, a mast peeled out of the milky darkness. Then she saw the hull and rail of the sailboat. A few more strokes, and she had reached the rope ladder. She moored the dinghy and climbed up. A hand came out of nowhere to meet her and pulled her up onto the deck. First astonishment, but then relief at the familiar face.

"Ephraim!" she called out.

He threw a blanket over her shoulder. "Take this. You must be cold."

She wrapped herself in the warming cloth and looked around. "Where is the man who owns the boat?"

He pointed to the cabin. She took a few steps toward it, opened the door, and climbed down. Saw first the feet, then the bashed-in skull. A lifeless body stretched out long on the floor. A silent horror. Then a scream that did not carry to the shore, swallowed by the wall of fog and the sea's roar. She turned around, tried to escape, and received a blow on the head.

It wouldn't take much to send an unconscious woman to the afterlife on the high seas. One push over the railing and the sea would swallow her forever. That would be a picturesque death, almost poetic. But Ephraim has no flair for poetry. He loves suffering, the prosaic nature of mechanically invading the senses of his victims.

So he has to begin his preparations. Dragging big brother's unconscious friend onto the deck, stripping her down to her underwear, tying her up by her arms and legs. He is putting on a performance for his lusts. Withdrawing himself again. Waiting from a distance until she regains consciousness. First enjoying the panic that hits her when she realizes she is alone and at the mercy of the elements. Then soaking up her horror as he shows first himself and then the knife he uses to slice her open inch by inch until the guts spill out of her body. Leaning over her, delaying the moments until death, and watching the sparkle in her eyes go out. Then and only then, gaining inner peace so that the body can finally be handed over to the sea, which may then eat it beyond recognition with its saltwater. Handing over to nature a sacrifice from the ruler of life and death.

Special thanks to:

Christophe Bugetti for the illustrations and cover artwork. What a wonderful sight to behold. They say you shouldn't judge a book by its cover, but in this case, I hope you do. If you like the contents a fraction as much as I like the cover, my work has been worthwhile.

My editors Eliza Dee, who teaches me proper English, and Konrad H. Roenne, who keeps pointing out my other shortcomings. Many thanks for that. I couldn't have done it without you.

My friends Kathrin, Nico, Sebastian, and Fred, for all your enriching comments. You guys have helped me a lot.

The helpful people at IBPA, Ilse and Christopher.

My father for taking me on countless trips to his childhood home around Angermünde when I was a little boy. That doom, that gloom.

AUTHOR

Raf Beuy writes thrillers. He is focused on Cold War stories. This is no wonder as he was born in West Berlin when the Wall was looming and Allied soldiers patrolled the streets.

His critical disposition is fed by the state of the world around him and too many chilled beverages.